Praise for *Life Flight*

"This book is an edge-of-your-seat suspense thriller from start to finish. . . . Eason, a seasoned suspense author, has no trouble developing the plot flawlessly over the pages. With great character development and enough excitement to keep readers hooked, this novel is sure to keep patrons talking for months to come."

Library Journal

"*Life Flight* by Lynette Eason is a heart-stopping, breath-stealing masterpiece of romantic suspense! I read it in one gulp and could not put it down. It's the best novel I've read this year. Highly recommended!"

Colleen Coble, *USA Today* bestselling author of *A Stranger's Game* and the Pelican Harbor series

"Ready for a book that is a race from page one to the end? Then you need to read *Life Flight*, the latest from bestselling author Lynette Eason. The pages hurtle us from a life flight that crashes in the North Carolina mountains to a race against time and a serial killer. Laced throughout are enough additional plotlines to keep the characters desperately figuring out how to stay one step ahead. Layer in a blossoming romance, and this book has all the ingredients for a story I could not put down. I highly recommend this for those who love romantic suspense with enough twists to keep the most astute reader guessing."

Cara Putman, award-winning author of *Flight Risk* and *Lethal Intent*

"A life-threatening medical emergency, a helicopter crash, and an escaped serial killer . . . Lynette Eason packs in all the ingredients for a thrilling edge-of-your-seat read! *Life Flight* will grip readers by the throat on the very first page all the way to the shocking ending, leaving them gasping for breath."

Elizabeth Goddard, bestselling author of *Present Danger* and the Uncommon Justice series

"Lynette Eason's latest book, *Life Flight*, grabs you from the opening words and doesn't let go until the final chapter. I'm green-eyed with envy over her ability to craft such a heart-pounding, nail-biting story. I know one day she'll even teach me how to write the sweet romance she so effortlessly weaves into her suspense novels. Another outstanding winner!"

Carrie Stuart-Parks, award-winning, bestselling author of *Relative Silence*

"Once again, Lynette Eason delivers a suspense-filled romance in *Life Flight*. Prepare to stay up all night as this book grips you from page one and won't release you until the satisfying conclusion. The twists and turns had me holding my breath. Highly recommend!"

Robin Caroll, bestselling author of the Darkwater Inn series

"When you pick up Lynette Eason's *Life Flight*, buckle up and brace for a wild ride! The story dips, twists, and spins with danger and deception on every page, all leading to the breath-stealing conclusion."

Lynn H. Blackburn, award-winning author of the Defend and Protect series

CROSSFIRE

CROSSFIRE

LYNETTE EASON

Revell

a division of Baker Publishing Group
Grand Rapids, Michigan

© 2022 by Lynette Eason

Published by Revell
a division of Baker Publishing Group
PO Box 6287, Grand Rapids, MI 49516-6287
www.revellbooks.com

Printed in the United States of America

Library of Congress Cataloging-in-Publication Data
Names: Eason, Lynette, author.
Title: Crossfire / Lynette Eason.
Description: Grand Rapids, MI : Revell, a division of Baker Publishing Group, [2022] | Series: Extreme measures ; 2
Identifiers: LCCN 2021052150 | ISBN 9780800737351 (paperback) | ISBN 9780800741488 (casebound) | ISBN 9781493436217 (ebook)
Classification: LCC PS3605.A79 C76 2022 | DDC 813/.6—dc23
LC record available at https://lccn.loc.gov/2021052150

Some Scripture used in this book, whether quoted or paraphrased by the characters, is taken from The Holy Bible, English Standard Version® (ESV®), copyright © 2001 by Crossway, a publishing ministry of Good News Publishers. Used by permission. All rights reserved. ESV Text Edition: 2016

Some Scripture used in this book, whether quoted or paraphrased by the characters, is taken from THE HOLY BIBLE, NEW INTERNATIONAL VERSION®, NIV® Copyright © 1973, 1978, 1984, 2011 by Biblica, Inc.® Used by permission. All rights reserved worldwide.

Baker Publishing Group publications use paper produced from sustainable forestry practices and post-consumer waste whenever possible.

22 23 24 25 26 27 28   7 6 5 4 3 2 1

Dedicated to those who put their lives
on the line every day for others.
Thank you for your service.

So do not fear, for I am with you;
    do not be dismayed, for I am your God.
I will strengthen you and help you;
    I will uphold you with my righteous right hand.

Isaiah 41:10 NIV

CHAPTER
ONE

MAY
THURSDAY MORNING

FBI Special Agent Julianna Jameson glanced at the alert on her phone. "Hostage situation in progress," she murmured, reading the text aloud.

> Federal judge taken hostage in full courtroom.
> Suspect threatening to kill her and everyone
> else.

The address was a good thirty minutes away from her home.

"Let me guess." Dottie leaned back in her chair and looked up at Julianna through the dark bangs that hung over her striking aquamarine-colored eyes. "You've got to go."

Julianna pushed her half-eaten omelet aside and drained the rest of her orange juice in one swallow. "Yeah, sorry. You good?" Her sister had been living with her since her eighteenth birthday nine months ago—when their mother had no more say in where Dottie had to live. They'd settled into a pretty good routine, but Julianna's occasional sudden departures still took the teen by surprise.

"Sure. We've got all of this end-of-school stuff going on, along with exam reviews, so I'm staying busy." With only four weeks left in her senior year, Dottie was determined to experience it to the fullest.

Julianna grabbed her gear and shoved her weapon into her holster. "I'll text you when I'm done."

"Cool."

She paused and held her sister's eyes. "I'll be fine. I promise."

"I know." Dottie stood, her red sneakers squeaking on the hardwood floors. She snagged her backpack, detached her plethora of keys from the hook on the side, and threaded them through her fingers.

Her own version of brass knuckles—or more likely a sign that she felt stressed. Before Julianna could decide whether to mention it or not, Dottie strode to the door. "I've got to get to school. I'll be looking for your text."

Julianna followed her. "Dottie—"

"It's all good, I promise." She whirled back to face Julianna. An abrupt move that took her by surprise and almost sent her crashing into the girl. "I know you're careful," Dottie said, "but I need you, okay? I can't go back to living with her." She grimaced. "*Not* that that's the only reason I don't want you to die, but—"

"I know. I promise." She squeezed Dottie's shoulder. "I need you too, Dot. You're good for me."

Dottie relaxed a fraction. "Okay, then." Another slight pause. "And I know what I do with the keys. It chills me for some reason. Makes me feel ready to fight back should I come across the enemy."

Even when it was an invisible enemy like anxiety. "Whatever works for you, hon. I'm not judging."

"I know. Thank you."

Julianna followed her sister out the door and climbed into her Bucar, a Bureau-issued late-model Ford sedan, while Dottie cranked her ancient Jeep Wrangler. Julianna still couldn't believe the girl had driven it from California to Charlotte, North Carolina, all by herself. Thoughts of the trouble that could have happened still sent shudders through her. "Nothing happened," she muttered, backing out of the drive. "She's fine. She's safe. She's in a good place." And she'd stay that way as long as Julianna had a say in the matter. For now, she did.

More texts came through, blowing up her phone. She activated the Bluetooth, listened to the messages through the car's speakers, and responded to them individually via voice texting.

She drove as fast as she dared and made it to the courthouse to find local law enforcement on scene along with fire trucks, ambulances, and the FBI mobile command post. SWAT was on standby. Julianna parked, pulled on her vest and windbreaker, and headed for the RV.

When she stepped inside, Supervisory Special Agent Hector Rodriguez looked up. "Glad you could make it." His dark eyes, normally serious, held a new level of intensity. A neatly trimmed black mustache graced his upper lip, and he stroked it with one finger, as he was known to do when stressed or thinking.

"Got here as fast as I could." Julianna slipped on the headset that would allow her to connect with the man holding the judge and a roomful of people hostage. "Do we have eyes?"

"We should any moment now."

"Catch me up."

"This was the Nicholas Manchester trial."

"Ah yes. The guy who hijacked the plane last year and killed six passengers."

"That's the one."

Rodriguez ran his finger over his mustache once more. His collateral duties included supervising SWAT and the field office coordinators for crisis negotiations and the Behavioral Analysis Unit. No doubt, both were on call, ready to conference as they learned more. "Apparently, Nicholas didn't like the guilty verdict. He had a crew in place ready to help him out. Complete with masks and tear gas. SWAT is attempting to get a camera under the door, but so far no luck."

11

"How'd Manchester's crew get the stuff in there?"

"The security footage is still being scanned, but so far, it looks like someone allowed them access to a back door late last night. The perpetrators hid out in the building's mechanical space, and when they got the guilty verdict, they stormed the courtroom. I'm sure we'll be learning more as the investigation continues."

The monitor in front of her flickered and the courtroom scene came to life. Julianna leaned in, processing the visual. She counted. Eleven jurors in the box, seated. Several crying, some with stone-faced fear. Two US Marshals lay on the floor in front of the bench with a woman kneeling next to one of them. Judge Lisa Stevens sat in her chair staring straight ahead. The man behind her held a fistful of Lisa's chin-length blond hair and a gun aimed at her right temple. The room was still smoky, but only in the far left corner. The people who'd been closest to the tear gas had their shirts pulled up over their faces, and several were coughing.

"Who set the tear gas off?" she asked.

"Guy posing as a US Marshal is our best guess. It was a small amount. Enough to cause a distraction, but not enough to reach Manchester and his cohorts. Someone slipped him a weapon. Again, that was probably the fake marshal. When the real marshals went after him, he opened fire. One's wounded but seems to be okay. As for the other one?" He shook his head. "No word if he's still alive. Life Flight out of Asheville is on the way."

Julianna wondered if Penny Carlton would be the pilot. The company Penny flew for covered eighteen counties across the Carolinas and into Tennessee and Georgia. "All right, so first order of business is to get the wounded out of there." Before she could make that happen, she needed Manchester talking. "Anyone in communication with him?"

"No. Not yet. Waiting on you. He's not answering the courtroom phone. We have a couple of the hostages' numbers. Thought you could try them and see if someone would chance answering."

"Okay, let's start dialing."

They dialed three and no one answered. "But the phones are on. They're ringing," she said. "Could be on silent." She rubbed her chin, thinking. "How'd you get the information about the wounded marshals and how everything went down?"

"Manchester sent out a pregnant woman who thought she was going into labor when all the excitement started." He showed her the picture of the woman being helped into the back of an ambulance. "Turns out it was false labor."

Julianna raised a brow. "He sent her out? I would have thought he'd just shoot her."

"Guess there's a conscience in him somewhere."

She frowned. "No, not him." She'd studied the airplane case after it happened. Manchester hadn't surrendered—and he hadn't planned on being taken alive. But one of his own had turned on him and allowed agents into the plane, where Manchester had taken two bullets and then tried to turn the gun on himself before a passenger tackled him. "He sent her out for a reason," she said. "She's not his wife. I remember her being interviewed after it was stated Manchester would survive his wounds. So, this woman . . . is she related to him? His sister? Sister-in-law? Girl-friend? Mistress? Is the baby his? Because she means something to him."

Hector studied her, then consulted his laptop. "Her name is Abigail Freeman, goes by Abby. She was among those in the gallery. I'll get someone to ask her if and how she knows Manchester." He sent a text to one of the agents, then turned back to Julianna. "They're talking to her now."

"Did he send anyone else out?"

"No."

"So, just her."

"Yeah. What are you thinking?"

She closed her eyes and tried to put herself into Manchester's head. "He's not answering the courtroom phone because some-thing happened with the plan. He wasn't supposed to be trapped in there. So now he's planning, concocting escape plans, working them out in his head, then discarding them. He's desperately trying to figure out how to get out of this impossible situation. When he has what he thinks is a workable plan, he'll answer the phone. Maybe. Or, he already has a plan, is implementing it, and doesn't want to talk."

"Like what?"

"No idea, but it's possible Ms. Freeman is a part of the plan. I'd keep an agent with her in the ambulance and at the hospital. Then take her to the field office for a more thorough interview. Get a signed statement from her."

"Already on that."

Of course he was. She drew in a steadying breath. "All right. Let's try this again. While I'm working on getting him on the phone, I need to know everything about him and every single person in that courtroom. You know the drill."

"I've already set that ball rolling. Daria Nevsky is your analyst and will be feeding you all the information she gets."

"Great. She's good."

He snorted. "They're all good."

"Yeah, but she's special. I like her accent. And she likes me." Some of the analysts were just downright rude, but not Daria. Julianna picked up the phone and dialed the courtroom number again.

No answer after four rings. Okay . . .

She tried calling four more times. "This isn't working. I don't want him thinking for too long."

"Keep trying. He'll answer eventually."

"Or he'll just start shooting when he can't come up with a way out." Julianna chewed on her bottom lip and pondered her options. First things first. Get him to answer.

The screen went blank and Hector slammed a hand on his thigh. "They found the camera."

So now she was blind, deaf, *and* mute. Not a good position to be in.

■ ■ ■ ■

AROUND 8:30 AM

Clay Fox's phone buzzed again. He ignored it until he finished typing up the report. As a school resource officer for one of the biggest high schools in the area, he was never caught up on the paperwork. Sixty seconds later, he looked up from his report to glance at his phone.

> **Unknown**
> 911 at courthouse. Hostage situation. Help.
> Don't call this #. Reese

Clay shot to his feet. He didn't recognize the number, but Reese was his baby sister and serving on the jury of the Manchester trial.

Jason Belue, another SRO for the school, looked up from his desk, green eyes clouded with concern and brow furrowed. "What's going on? You okay?"

"I need to leave. Family emergency. I'll explain when I get back." Clay grabbed his lightweight police department–issued windbreaker and headed to the school's office while typing,

> On my way. Where are you? Are you safe?

Probably a dumb question, and while he desperately wanted to hear her say she wasn't one of the hostages, his gut knew differently. Why else would she be using someone else's phone? And why did she have it? Where was her phone? He stepped through Steve Callahan's door without knocking. The principal looked up from his computer. "Clay?"

"Sorry, family emergency. I have to run."

Steve stood. "Of course. Anything I can do?"

Clay almost said *pray*. "No, nothing. I'll fill you in later." He bolted to his cruiser and climbed behind the wheel. He clipped his phone into the holder on the dash where he could see if Reese texted him again. He didn't dare call her like he wanted. *Please—*

He shut down the instinct to pray, then flipped on his lights and sped to the scene. When he arrived at the courthouse, it was organized chaos, but somewhere behind the police barricade and inside the building was his sister. A hostage. His heart pounded a furious beat, but he ignored it and ducked into the fray, his uniform blending with the others.

For a moment, he stopped and let himself process the area. The FBI command post RV was stationed to his right. That's where the negotiator would be. He started toward it when his phone pinged again. His best friend, Vince Covelli.

> What's going on at the courthouse, dude?
> I thought Reese was there.

> She is.

> She okay?

> I'm not sure. Will explain later.

> I'll be praying for her.

> Not sure that will do much good, but fine.

> Do I need to come down there? I have a badge.

Vince had just joined the US Marshals.

> No. I'll update you when I know something.

His phone flashed again. Reese.

> Gotta go. Will touch base later.

He returned to Reese's text.

> 22 hostages. 2 USM wounded, 1 conscious.

1 possibly dead, can't tell. M. threat to k all. Furious. Judge tackled him when tear gas went off. 2 others with guns. Barricaded all 3 doors w chairs & people. Wondering if they can get out via ceiling.

> Stay low. Do NOT let them catch you with the phone. Make sure it's on silent, not vibrate. SILENT.

A thumbs-up emoji flashed at him.

Oh, God, please . . . Honestly, if he thought God would listen, he'd discard his pride and pray. For Reese.

He bolted to the door of the command post and knocked. The door opened and he stared into the hard dark eyes of an older gentleman with a neatly trimmed mustache over tight lips. "What?"

"My sister's in there. She's texting me."

Clay held up the phone and the man stepped back. "Get in here." The man shut the door behind him. "Julianna, take a look at this."

A woman in her early thirties spun in her chair. She had her chestnut hair pulled up in a tight ponytail, and it slapped her in the cheek at her quick move. When her blue eyes locked on his, Clay blinked. She looked familiar. "I'm Clay Fox," he said. "My sister, Reese Fox, is in there."

The woman scowled at the man next to him. "Why's he in here? We don't let family in here. Not even cops with family in trouble."

"Reese texted me," Clay said, refusing to be intimidated or insulted. He knew the protocol. "I know you probably have eyes and ears already in there, but I thought you might like to know what she's saying."

The woman's eyes sharpened and her annoyed look fled. "That would be amazing. Our eyes and ears have been shut off."

He handed her the phone. "She texted in a kind of shorthand, but you can figure it out."

"Yeah." She looked up. "This is Hector Rodriguez. He's the boss around here."

Clay nodded and Rodriguez shook his hand. "Where'd she get the phone?"

"I don't know," Clay said. "I didn't ask her. I didn't want her texting anything that wasn't necessary. For now, all that matters is she has it and is sending information as she can."

A knock on the door interrupted them. Rodriquez opened it and another agent stood there. "Abby Freeman, the pregnant woman, is Manchester's sister. She was the only family in attendance."

"Well, at least now we know," Julianna murmured. "She have anything to do with his being able to pull this off?"

"Doesn't look like it, but we'll do a full investigation."

"Good."

The phone buzzed, drawing Julianna's attention. Clay tensed. "What'd she say?"

"Oh boy."

"What!" Clay shouted the word.

"She said they're talking about killing one of the hostages to let everyone know they're serious."

Clay pressed his palms to his temples. "So, tell them you already know that."

"I would if I could get him to answer the phone." She glanced at Hector and took the headset off.

"Julianna—"

"I have to. It's the only way."

"You can't. You have Dottie to think about now."

"I know. I'm not going to get myself killed. As soon as I can convince him to answer the phone, I'll skedaddle to safety, I promise."

"No—"

"I'm the only negotiator here at the moment, and I need to talk to him. I can't do anything with the silent treatment."

"The other two negotiators will be on-site in less than ten minutes."

"We might not have ten minutes."

Clay's gaze bounced between the two. "You're thinking of going in."

"Not in. But close enough for him to hear me. Hector, I'm going to need that radio to toss in should I get the opportunity. If he refuses to speak in spite of the fact that I'm just outside the door, then he'll at least have to hear my voice before he smashes the thing. And if he does that, then . . ."

"We'll know."

"Yeah."

"Know what?" Clay asked.

Her big blue eyes met his. "That things are way more serious than they'd be if I could get him talking."

His gut twisted.

That kind of next-level serious most likely meant no one was walking away alive.

CHAPTER
TWO

Julianna had been completely truthful with Hector. She had no plans to get herself killed. But she had to figure out a way to get Manchester talking to her while agents covered the ceiling, making sure there was no escape route that way. Someone would be studying the blueprints, placing agents and local officers all around the building.

The phone Clay Fox had handed her buzzed in her pocket. She pulled it out to take a look.

Unknown
Not trying to escape via ceiling. They had tools stashed there. He's talking about demanding a chopper.

What kind of tools and for what?

Just as she started to type the words, another text came in.

Clay? U there?

I'm here.

Julianna didn't identify herself. She didn't dare type anything that would tip off Manchester, should he catch Reese with the phone.

What kind of tools?

Can't tell yet.

Just do what he says and you'll be fine.

?????

Julianna ignored the question marks and typed,

He won't talk to the negotiator. Is he even
considering picking up the phone when it rings?

He'd have to if he was going to ask for a chopper.

He looks at it. Even reached for it one time.
Then picked up receiver and hung up.

Well, that was accurate. She'd thought for a moment she had
him on the line.

Does he have a cell phone?

DK. Two others do.

"DK," Julianna whispered. "Don't know." Probably not, since
the man was on trial. But one of the others working with Manchester could have supplied him with one. Or he could have taken
one off a hostage. Either way, he probably had a cell phone on him,
but there was no way to know the number. Of course, they could
just start calling all the hostages' phones and see if they hit the
jackpot, but that could possibly put someone's life in danger, not
to mention the time it would take to do such a thing.

And time was something she had a feeling they were in short
supply of.

Where is he? Can you give me the location of
all three?

M still standing behind judge, holding gun on
her head. Thing 1 by door at back waving his
gun. Thing 2—

The text pinged, then the phone went silent.

Julianna waited, praying no one had seen the woman texting. She pictured the man who'd brought her the phone. He was about her age. Good looking with gray eyes rimmed with thick lashes that most women only dreamed of. His full lips had been pressed into a hard thin line. His worry was a tangible thing, and she couldn't say she blamed him one bit.

Finally, the three little dots appeared, indicating Reese was back.

Standing on judge's desk trying to find a way to
get to ceiling.

A pause.

They also said they have explosives just in case.
Haven't seen any, but they have bags and stuff
so could be in one of them. Picture coming of
room setup.

The phone sounded again and she had a good look at where everyone in the room was. *Please don't let her get caught.* Julianna let the prayer whisper heavenward and sucked in a breath. "Reese just texted and said they have explosives," she said, her voice carried by the comms in her ear to the command post.

"I'll notify the division's bomb specialist," Hector said, "but you need to back off."

"Just give me a few more minutes, please?"

Instead of turning around and placing distance between her and a possible bomb, she hurried to the entrance of the building, pulled the glass door open, and stepped inside the lobby.

"Jules," Hector said.

"I know. I promise. Just a few minutes, please. SWAT needs to get out, though."

"I'll give the order."

In the next second, the order came over the comms. SWAT had taken up their positions in view of the courtroom door, but started moving as soon as Hector's order came through.

Julianna drew in another steadying breath and walked to the double doors of the courtroom. "Nicholas Manchester! This is Special Agent Julianna Jameson. I'm a negotiator and I need to talk to you!"

Silence.

"Please! We need to find a way to get you what you want, and I can't do that if you won't talk to me."

Silence. Then she thought she heard footsteps heading toward her from the other side of the door. She pulled her weapon, then stepped to the side and waited, while adrenaline pumped through her.

The door cracked and a pair of frightened green eyes peered out at her. "He said to go away and that if I tried to run, he'd kill someone."

The hostage started to shut the door and Julianna shoved the radio at her. "I understand. Give him this, please."

The young woman took it and the door snicked shut. Nicholas had chosen his messenger well. A meek, mild-mannered person. Which indicated he was good at reading people.

Julianna lowered herself to the floor next to the door and leaned back against the wall. She lifted the radio. "Nicholas, please talk to me," she said in a soft tone. Quiet, reassuring. The kind of tone that said "You can trust me."

She released the button and waited.

Nothing.

Come on, Manchester, please. If she could just get him to talk—

"You've got my attention."

Oh, thank you, Lord. "Hi, Nicholas. Is it okay if I call you Nicholas? Or do you prefer Nick?"

A pause. "Nick's fine."

"Thank you for picking up the radio."

"You're still right outside the door, aren't you?"

"Not for long, now that you're willing to chat."

"You think you're going to talk me down?"

"I don't look at it as talking you down. We're just going to have a conversation and, of course, my goal is that no one dies. I'm really hoping that's one of your goals too."

"And if it's not?"

"Then you know as well as I do, we have a problem." She released the button and drew in a steadying breath. So far no one had said anything in her comms. "I need a sitrep."

"You got him talking," Hector said. "Good job. Sitrep is still no eyes or ears. This is on you at the moment."

"Right."

She pressed the button to turn her attention back to Manchester. "Can we use the phone?"

"What's the matter with the walkie-talkies?"

She pressed the button. "Nothing wrong with the walkie-talkies, just worried my finger might get tired. If I call, will you answer?"

"Yeah, sure. Why not?"

She disconnected the radio.

"Call him," she said into the comms, "and patch him through to my line."

"Come on back," Hector said. "If he really has a bomb . . ."

Yeah, that could be bad, but . . . "No, I think I need to stay right here." Julianna didn't claim to have any kind of sixth sense or supernatural power, but she had good instincts and those instincts were telling her to stay put.

Blades beat the air in the distance. Life Flight was almost there. The sooner she could get the marshals out, the better.

Her phone rang and she swiped the screen. "Thank you."

"I doubt you were worried about your finger."

"I wasn't. It's just a preference thing," she said. He laughed. A harsh sound, but she'd take it. "So, I'm just curious, Nick, how do you see this ending?"

"With me and my boys walking out of here."

"And the hostages?"

"That's up to you." He paused. "Just so you know, I do have an explosive that can bring down the whole building. I'm willing to set it off and die before I'll surrender and go back to prison."

Julianna bit her lip and mentally flipped through her responses. She wasn't sure he was telling her the truth, but she had to assume he was. "I see. Well, I would prefer that you not do that. So, before we talk about how to avoid blowing yourself and everyone else up, I know you have a couple of marshals in there who are hurt. We could see them on the camera before you disabled it. Would you be willing to send them out?"

"Why should I?"

"Because it builds some goodwill. If you're willing to work with us, we're a little more likely to work with you."

"What if I just say give me what I want or I start killing people?"

Julianna closed her eyes. "Well, that's certainly an option for you, but what do you think is going to happen if you start shooting? How is that going to help the situation?" She paused. "At least send out the one who's hurt the worst. If he dies . . ." *Please don't let him be dead.*

Manchester fell silent. "I suppose I could use some goodwill," he finally muttered. "I'll send the marshal out. In fact, I'll send both of them out."

"They're still alive?"

"Last I checked. One of them's got a nurse helping him out. His lucky day, I guess. And the fact that I'm letting her."

"Thank you for that. Can they walk out, or would you let some other hostages help them?"

"Trying to get more than the two, huh?"

"You know I've got to try."

He went quiet again. Julianna waited.

"What do I get if I send out a few hostages with them?" he finally asked.

"What do you want?"

"Well, since we might be here a while, food and water would be a good start. Enough for everyone. Hostages will eat it first."

So, he was going to dig in and stay put. Or he was making her think that's what he had planned. "No drugging the food, I promise. We can arrange for that. Breakfast biscuits okay?"

"Whatever." He paused. "Yeah, chicken."

"How many people need to be fed?"

"Two dozen should cover it."

"Hold on while I get that ball rolling." She put her phone on mute and went back to the comms and Hector. "You got that?"

"Got it," he said. "Placing the order now."

Julianna unmuted her phone. "I've arranged it," she told Manchester. "Are you willing to trust me to keep my word on the food and allow the marshals and the others to come out? I appreciate you letting go as many as you will."

"Yeah. I don't need all of these people." He snickered. "I got me a judge."

She drew in a steadying breath again. "Well, like I said, we'll appreciate as many as you want to send out."

"Keep that in mind when it's time for me to ask for something else."

"Absolutely."

"Because you know I'm going to want some transportation at some point. Gotta go for now."

The line went dead.

Julianna frowned. Something wasn't right. Why would he give up his bargaining chips? Why not ask for the car or chopper or whatever right now?

She pulled out Clay's phone. Still nothing more from his sister. She texted Hector.

Eyes? Ears? What's the holdup?

Still working on it.

"Daria, I need information on Manchester," she said over the comms.

"There's not a lot out there," the analyst said. "He's married, two young kids. The sister that was in the courtroom that he sent out. I talked to the wife and she said he hijacked the airplane because the company stole his idea for the new model and didn't give him credit. Probably nothing that you don't already know. Interviews are still going on, of course. You know how long these things can last, but if anything pops up on the radar, I'll let you know ASAP."

"Okay, thanks." She hurried to the glass doors, away from the area. "Hector, hostages coming out," she said. "Have ambulances and chopper on standby."

"10-4."

"Daria, anything else?"

"Favorite color is green. Stand-up guy, according to his coworkers before the whole hijacking thing. They never saw that coming."

They usually didn't.

"Oh wait! I have his psych profile from his workplace. Looks like the perfect employee on paper, but the psychiatrist noted he was extremely intelligent and slightly arrogant."

Clay's phone buzzed and Julianna yanked it from her pocket. "Hold on, Daria."

> They're arguing. M is pacing, but marshals r coming out w/ almost the whole gallery of hostages. M and other 2 have radios now. In communication w/ someone. Jury told to stay put.

Julianna relayed the information to Hector.

The bomb dog and handler stepped up beside her. Thirty seconds later, the doors swung open and two men carrying the marshal reportedly in critical condition stepped through. Another man helped the second marshal, who was able to walk with support.

And the gallery followed—including the woman who'd taken the radio.

"Hands where we can see them," one SWAT member directed. "Nice and easy. Walk past the dog. Then you'll step through the metal detector."

Law enforcement met the exiting group and herded them away from the scene to another spot where they would verify identities and get their statements—including as much information as possible that would help her out.

Because she had a feeling she was going to need all the help she could get.

■ ■ ■ ■

Clay watched the monitor and noted the exit of the hostages. None of whom were his sister. His already tight stomach clenched harder. Had Reese been texting? Had the negotiator—Julianna—answered? Had Reese been caught? He scrubbed a hand down his face and slipped out of the command post. It took everything in him not to push his way through to the courthouse, but he had no time for the trouble that would cause him—and Reese.

The marshals were now en route to the hospital via the Life Flight chopper, but he edged close enough to overhear the conversation between one of the hostages and his interviewer. "He's not crazy," the man was saying. "At least not wild, lunatic crazy. He's in full control. He doesn't raise his voice, he doesn't yell. He speaks and the two helping him act. Immediately. Which is what he expected the rest of us to do."

Clay closed his eyes, not sure whether to be comforted by those facts or not.

"What else?" the agent asked. "Every detail no matter how small you think it might be is important. Like, did he say the names of the others?"

"No. They never called each other by name."

"What are they armed with?"

The questions went on and Clay digested each answer.

"They finally moved the judge to sit with the jurors," the nearest hostage said, "and were talking about getting rid of some of the others in the gallery."

"Get rid of how?"

"Didn't say, but the tone made me nervous. I'm glad he let us go. But he kept the entire jury, plus the judge and the attorneys."

So, he still had quite a few people that could wind up dead. Clay desperately wanted his phone to do a search on the negotiator who held his sister's life in her hands. Giving control over to someone else wasn't something he was used to—and he definitely didn't like it.

Commotion pulled his attention to his left. The bomb squad had arrived.

"Ellen! Ellen!"

Clay swiveled his head toward the shout.

A woman broke through the police barrier and raced toward the courthouse. "My baby's in there and I'm going to get her!"

When she crossed in front of him, he launched himself at her and tackled her with a hard thud. The breath whooshed from her, cutting off her scream. As they hit the ground, he rolled to keep from crushing her but kept a tight grip on her wrist. "Breathe, ma'am. Just breathe."

When she caught her breath, she lashed out at him with her free hand, landing a harmless punch on his vest before he could manage to get her hands under control. Other officers had reached them by this time, and one hauled her to her feet.

She looked at him, tears running down her face. "You shouldn't have stopped me. I have to get to her. I have to save her!"

He held up a hand to stop the officer from cuffing her. "I know you're scared, but you have to trust the agents to do their jobs." He stood, his hip aching from the fall, and glanced at the cop holding her. "Let the paramedics check her out, will you?"

"Yeah. Nice tackle."

Nothing felt nice about stopping the terrified mother.

She sobbed, her uncontrolled cries breaking his heart. The truth was, he wouldn't mind joining her.

The officers led her away toward the ambulance. And for the first time in a little over a year, Clay prayed. *Please, God, if you care about me at all, get Reese and the others out of there.*

CHAPTER
THREE

Clay's phone buzzed and Julianna pulled it out, noting Clay also had a text from someone named Vince. She ignored that one and focused on Reese's.

> They're working on the floor behind judge's desk.

The floor? Why? She bit her lip. What was the point in that? Did they plan to dig their way out?

> He's sending people to bathroom by 2s. Said if anyone tried anything he'd kill others. No 1 has tried anything. Yet. 1 guy looks like he might be ready to cause some troub—

The text was cut off like she'd had to send what she had in a hurry to hide the phone. "Don't get caught, my friend, don't get caught." *Please.* "Hector?" she said into the comms as she walked toward the command post.

"Yeah?"

She passed on Reese's information. "What's under the courthouse?"

"I've got the blueprints right here. Um . . ." The sound of clicking keys came over the line. "Uh . . . nothing."

"No basement?"

"Nope."

She frowned. "Then why would they be messing with the floor?" She stepped inside the command center and settled into her chair. Before she called Manchester back, she tapped a message to Reese.

Are you okay?

No answer.

She looked at Hector. "When was the courthouse built?"

"No idea, but I know it's old. Why?"

"Was it built on top of another historic building or site? Maybe one that *did* have a basement? Sounds like they think something is under the floor. I want to know why they think that." She'd done her research on the city she was going to be living in after her transfer from Quantico, but didn't know the facts about the old courthouse. One thing she *did* know was that those guys were digging for a reason. She was convinced they knew something she didn't. Which meant she needed to figure it out. "Daria, did you get all that?"

"Got it. I'm looking."

"I am too," Hector said.

He clicked his keys on his laptop while Julianna dialed Manchester back. She didn't want to be disconnected for too long. He answered on the first ring. "Where's the food?"

She glanced at the screen tracking the delivery. "Five minutes away."

"We'll talk after we have the food." He hung up.

Julianna sat back, then sent a text to Dottie.

Just checking in with you to let you know all is good on my end.

Thank you!

The return text was fast. Almost as though she already had it written and was just waiting to hear from Julianna.

The minutes ticked past slowly while Hector worked on his computer.

"Okay," Daria said, "got it."

Julianna leaned forward. "What?"

"The original courthouse was built in the late seventeen hundreds but was destroyed in the Revolutionary War. The land sat empty for a hundred years, but in 1860, the courthouse was rebuilt, and these are pictures of the blueprints."

She looked at the images on the screen. "There are tunnels," she whispered.

"Yeah, and look where they run."

"Right under the courtroom on the south side of the building."

"Exactly."

"So, what were they used for?" Julianna asked. "Smuggling during the Revolutionary War?"

"Nope, they're from the gold rush in the 1830s."

"Gold rush? In Charlotte?"

"Yep. It gets overshadowed by the California one, but yeah, gold was discovered here—quite a lot."

"Can people still access the mines?"

"Most of them were flooded with groundwater or filled up, but if they found one that wasn't blocked—and people have found them—then, yeah, it wouldn't be any trouble to get into them, especially if one of the entrances was under the courthouse floor. Which it looks like it might be." She let out a low whistle. "These things are all over the city. There's no way to know which ones are open and which ones aren't, but if the ones under the courthouse are open . . ."

"Yeah. That might explain the need for explosives. They're prepared to blow their way out."

"Maybe."

"Can the public access those records, Daria?"

"Yep. It's free and open to all who go looking."

Julianna drew in a breath. "I think I'm getting a good picture of what's going on." Her phone rang and she glanced at the screen, then Hector. "It's him."

"Play along," Hector said to her, then spoke into his phone. "Daria, I'm going to need any possible exits from those mines closest to the courthouse."

"On it."

"Thanks, Daria." Julianna tapped her screen and checked the delivery status. It was here. She accepted the call. "Someone is coming with your food, Nick. Don't shoot them, okay?"

"Not planning on it. I want to keep goodwill between us because I'm going to have more demands."

More demands. Right. He needed to keep yanking her chain while his cohorts dug. She glanced out the window and saw Clay watching the courthouse, his hands on his hips. Responsibility weighed heavy on her shoulders. He and everyone else was counting on her to get the hostages out safely.

"Will you let any more people go when I bring you the food?"

"No, but if you'll promise me a chopper on the top floor, I'll let six more out."

He had no intention of using the chopper. His demands were now just ways to kill time until they managed to get through the floor. But she'd do it, and hopefully, he was being straight with her about releasing six additional hostages. The more she could get out, the better. She did wish Reese could text her an update on whatever progress they were making digging in the floor. "As you know, I'll have to run that by my supervisor. It may take some time."

"You have an hour. I'll call you back then."

He hung up and she frowned, then looked at Hector. "He's playing this out like when he was in the airplane, making it seem real. Buying his time. Negotiating."

"He learned how it worked when he was negotiating on the plane."

34

"Yeah."

Hector sighed. "When he calls back, tell him you got the chopper approved. I'll have one on standby."

"Copy that." She looked out the window once again to see Clay still standing in the same spot, holding the same position, his gaze locked on the courthouse doors. Julianna stood. "I'll be right back."

"Where you going?"

"To talk to a man who's terrified he's going to lose his sister."

Hector's eyebrow rose. "Why?"

She understood his surprise. Normally, she did her very best to keep family members away from any negotiations, but . . . this felt different. "He entrusted me with his phone—his only communication with the sister who's a hostage. I feel like I owe him . . . something. I don't know."

"Huh."

She took that as approval and slipped out the door just as Hector's phone buzzed. "Hold up," he said.

She paused while he listened. Then he shot her a tight smile. "They found the other end of the tunnel. There are three guys down there digging *toward* Manchester. When they all come out of the tunnel on the other end, we'll nab all six."

"And pray he doesn't hurt the hostages in the meantime."

"No, negotiate and get everyone out that you can."

"Copy that."

She headed to talk to Clay and hopefully reassure him that Reese and the others would be free in another couple of hours.

Please, God, let that be true.

Clay turned when Julianna stepped up beside him. "Shouldn't you be talking to Manchester?"

"I have a few minutes before he calls me back."

"How's Reese?"

"Quiet at the moment." She cleared her throat. "She's a hero in all of this, Clay. Without her we wouldn't know a lot of what we know."

35

"Yeah." He paused. "What do you know?"

"That we're going to get those hostages out of there and they're going to be okay."

"Right." He jerked his chin at the yellow tape. "Media is here, circling like vultures."

"As long as they stay on their side, I don't have a problem with them. They're easy to ignore."

The phone in her pocket buzzed and she glanced at him before pulling it out and tapping the screen.

2 of them are gone. Disappeared down through floor. One left holding a gun on us all.

The little dots blinked at her. More was coming.

Judge just tackled him! Hurry!

Julianna typed,

Bombs???

Took them with them. No one else can see what I can because of my position on floor, but doors no longer barricaded. As soon as judge tackled him, people started moving stuff away from doors, but no one helping judge because of gun and she's bleeding!

So, they were probably going to use the bombs in the tunnels. It would be a risk going in, but . . .

Into her comms, she read the text to Hector.

"Breach! Go!"

At Hector's command, she bolted away from Clay as a swarm of law enforcement descended, aiming themselves at the courthouse. Julianna was closest and hit the doors, beating anyone else by a good five seconds. If the judge was wrestling one of the captors for the weapon, there was no time to waste. She burst through the doors of the courtroom. "FBI! Get out!"

The nearest hostages wasted no time in following her order while she ran toward the two struggling figures on the floor. The judge had both hands wrapped around the man's thick wrist, but he was slowly turning the weapon toward the woman.

On her last step, Julianna pulled back her leg and sent a hard kick to the man's head. He dropped like a rock and she swooped in to grab the weapon less than a second after it hit the wood floor.

Panting, sweat rolling down her temples, she landed a knee into the attacker's back and cuffed him. The SWAT team and others burst into the room like ants on a picnic, directing the remaining hostages out the door.

One SWAT member stopped in front of her and met her eyes. "Nice."

"Thanks."

He grabbed the woozy man and pulled him to his feet while another officer snagged him on the other side. Together, they escorted him from the room, and Julianna passed the weapon to another officer, who bagged it. She then turned her attention to the judge and another young woman kneeling next to her, holding a cloth to the judge's head. "Are you two all right?"

"Yes." Judge Stevens shuddered. "You have good timing. He was stronger than I anticipated. Swiped me with his gun before I could stop him."

"It's just a small cut," the woman with the cloth said. "You'll be fine."

Julianna held out a hand, and the judge clasped it with a grimace and let Julianna help her to her feet. "Ever thought about a career in law enforcement? Or the NFL?"

Judge Stevens gave her a small smirk. "I was a cop before I went to law school." She shrugged. "I needed better pay."

"Sure can't argue that. That was a pretty gutsy move you made, tackling that guy."

"Gutsy or stupid?"

"Since it ended well, let's go with gutsy."

The judge offered a breathy laugh. "Yes, let's." She sniffed and patted her hair back into place. "I don't have time for that kind of nonsense in my courtroom." The cut had already stopped bleeding.

"You ready to get out of here?" Julianna asked her.

"So ready."

She headed for the door, and Julianna's gaze landed on the young woman who'd been helping the judge. Familiar gray eyes locked on hers. They were a perfect match to her brother's. "Reese?"

She nodded. "I recognize your voice from the radio. You're the negotiator."

"I am."

"Thank you."

"No, hon, *thank you.*"

They shared a smile, then Julianna nodded to the door. "Your brother is pretty desperate to see you."

"The feeling is mutual."

■ ■ ■ ■

Clay had never been so tense. His shoulders felt like boulders and the base of his neck was in serious danger of snapping. He drew in a deep breath and forced it out slowly, keeping his eyes locked on the door of the courthouse. Everyone but Reese and the negotiator—Julianna—was out, and maybe one other SWAT member. He knew because he'd counted the hostages as they'd scrambled away from the building.

Where were they?

A breeze blew, and even though it was the beginning of May, there was still a chill in the air. He shoved his hands into his pockets and waited.

Finally, the door opened once more, and he curled his fingers into fists at his side. A SWAT member walked out, then Clay's sister. "Reese!"

"Clay!" She spotted him and raced down the steps toward him.

He broke into a run and caught her up in his arms. "Reese, you scared me to death."

"I guarantee you weren't nearly as scared as I was."

"Okay, you can have that one." When she stepped back, she shuddered and he noticed the blood on her shirt. "You're hurt!"

"No, no. It's not my blood. I . . . It's the marshal's."

A shiver racked her and he slid out of his windbreaker, ignoring the fact that the short-sleeve uniform shirt didn't provide him much warmth. He handed the jacket to Reese and she wrapped it around herself.

Relieved, he hugged his sister again, but she pulled back and turned to Julianna. "Did they catch them?"

"They haven't come through the other side of the tunnel yet, but as soon as they do, agents are there waiting to swoop in and nab them."

"Tunnel?" He and Reese echoed the word at the same time.

"Yeah. From the mighty Charlotte gold rush back in the 1830s."

Reese's eyes went wide. "So that's why they went through the floor." She shook her head. "Someone did a lot of research on that. I hate to say it, but the plan was actually pretty brilliant." She grimaced. "Not that I'm impressed or anything."

"It was brilliant," Julianna muttered. "And they would have gotten away with it if you hadn't decided to be a hero. We're in your debt."

Reese flushed at the praise.

"How'd you get the phone?" Clay asked.

"When the marshal was shot, I didn't even think. I just raced toward him and pressed on his wound. He unhooked the phone—clip and all—and slipped it into the pocket of my cardigan." She pulled the device out and passed it to Julianna. "Do you know if he's still alive? His name is Shane."

"I don't. But he was when they transported him to the hospital."

"Which hospital?"

"Carolinas Medical, I believe."

She nodded. "That's where I work, so I'll find out."

As she swiped a stray hair from her eyes, Clay noted her hand shook. "You have to give your statement, but then I'll take you home, all right?"

"How long will that take?"

"A couple of hours," Julianna answered for him. "They'll walk you through the whole thing step-by-step, so it'll be a pretty long ordeal. And you may have to testify to everything when his trial comes up again, but you can be sure security will be massive."

She gave Julianna a tremulous smile. "Yeah."

Julianna narrowed her eyes. "You should probably consider counseling. It can help reduce the PTSD that may come after this."

"I'll be fine."

"Come on," Clay said. "Let's get this over with. Then I'll take you home. Just give me a few minutes to call the school and let them know what's going on. The other two SROs can handle anything that comes up."

"I'll be fine. I'm actually starving. We didn't have time to eat the biscuits." She laughed. A short hollow sound that spoke more about her mental state than her exterior "togetherness" let on. "I couldn't have eaten it anyway. But now . . . for some reason, I'm ravenous."

"I'll grab you a biscuit from the stash," Julianna said. "That should tide you over while you give your statement."

"Then I'll take you to eat afterward." Clay hugged her to him again, so relieved she was here and in one piece.

"I'd really like that."

"School?" Julianna asked.

"Midtown High School," Clay said. "I'm one of the SROs there."

"My sister is a senior there. Dottie Jameson."

Clay nodded. "I know Dottie well. She's a great young lady with

40

a good head on her shoulders." He glanced at his watch. "Hey, this is going to sound weird, but when school lets out, would you and Dottie like to join us? You have to be hungry too."

Julianna pressed a hand to her stomach. "Now that you mention it . . ." Then sighed. "I have so much paperwork to do, not to mention the debrief. I can do that while Reese is giving her statement. Where did you have in mind and I'll text Dottie to meet us there in"—she glanced at her watch—"two hours?"

"That works. Have you ever been to the Bad Burger Barn?"

Her eyes widened. "That's one of our favorites. We're definitely in. I'll text her now." She pulled her phone out and tapped the screen, then tucked the device back into her pocket. "All right, an agent will be over shortly to take your statement. I'll see you in a bit."

"Sure."

She headed back toward the command post, and Clay pulled Reese to him for another hug.

"Come on, Clay. Enough with the hugs."

"Sorry. I'm just so glad you're okay."

"I know. I am too." She eased away from him. "My car is here and I don't want to leave it. After I'm done telling what little I know, can you follow me home and let me take a shower and change before we meet them?"

"Yeah. If you're sure you can drive. It's not that far, I can always bring you back."

"And I need my phone." She groaned. "Manchester had his goons take it."

"It's evidence," Clay said, "as is mine. We'll get new ones for now. I was ready to upgrade anyway." The agent Julianna mentioned was approaching. "Come on, we'll take care of that after you get cleaned up." He glanced at Julianna, who was in deep discussion with Rodriguez. "I'm pretty sure we'll have time." He'd be surprised if she made it to the restaurant as planned.

"Great."

Clay wrapped his arm around her shoulders and led her away from the ongoing organized chaos to meet the agent. But couldn't resist one last look back at the pretty negotiator. She was strong, smart, and a little intimidating.

And he wanted to get to know her more.

CHAPTER
FOUR

Julianna stepped inside the command post to see Hector tuck his phone into the clip on his belt. He shot her a tight smile. "Manchester and his two goons are all wrapped up. They set one of the explosives off to get through a blocked area, but as soon as they came above ground, agents nabbed them."

"I can't believe the explosive didn't bring the whole tunnel down."

"Manchester chose his help wisely. The guy is an explosives expert. Worked a lot of construction gigs, so he knew what he was doing."

"Well. Good. Glad Manchester is out of commission."

"Of course, the media was right there to get everything on video. Everyone did everything by the book. Manchester is definitely done."

She nodded and glanced at her phone to check the time. She was going to be late to meet Dottie, Clay, and Reese. Surprise, surprise. "I think I've finished everything I can do here and need to get going."

He touched her arm. "That was good work, Julianna. The fact that you figured out what they were doing . . ."

"I had help, Hector. Reese Fox is the hero in this situation. And Daria—as always. Couldn't have done it without her either."

He grunted. "Whatever. You never do like to take credit."

She laughed but squirmed on the inside. "Yeah, well, I take credit when I've earned it."

"No, you don't. Go. Get out of here."

She didn't waste another minute but headed for her Bucar. Within ten minutes, she was walking in the door of the burger joint, noting she was only fifteen minutes late.

Dottie looked up and waved at her from a booth in the corner. "Hey, Jules, over here."

Clay and Reese were already there. Julianna slipped into the seat next to Dottie. "Sorry I'm late."

Dottie rolled her eyes toward Clay and Reese. "She's always late—except when she has to talk someone off the ledge."

"Don't worry about it," Clay said, "we were just catching up with Dottie."

"Officer Fox is the SRO at school. One of them anyway. The only thing that matters is he's the cool one we all like well enough to listen to. Most of us, anyway."

Clay laughed. "Thanks. I think."

Dottie shrugged and Reese waved the waitress over. After they gave their order—Dottie emphasizing no onions, please—Reese pressed her palms to her eyes, then looked up and blinked.

"You okay?" Julianna asked.

"Yes, I think so. I guess it just feels a little surreal to be sitting here getting ready to eat a burger after such intensity. I mean, we were in there for about five hours, right?"

"Five hours and twelve minutes," Julianna said. "It was an incredibly traumatic experience. Are you sure you feel up to this?"

The young woman held up her hands. "What else am I going to do? Go home and replay it over and over in my mind?" She shook her head. "No thanks. I'd rather drown my PTSD in a chocolate shake, burger, and fries. At least it's something . . . normal."

Julianna caught Clay's concerned glance at his sister, then Clay met her gaze. PTSD was a real thing—especially after being held hostage at gunpoint, seeing two men shot, and risking her life to send texts. Julianna started to say something, but Clay gave her a minuscule shake of his head and she snapped her lips shut. Reese was his sister. She'd let him make the calls on the best way to help her.

Then the waitress was standing next to her with a tray full of food. Once they had all taken at least one bite of the juicy fare, with Dottie double checking that they'd left the onions off, Dottie turned to Reese. "What made you want to be a nurse?"

Reese took a sip of water, then folded her hands in front of her. "Well, I haven't been one very long. I just passed the NCLEX and got my first RN position at Carolinas Medical a few months ago. I'm in the ER and work a lot of traumas."

"NCLEX?" Dottie asked with a frown.

"It's the nursing exam you have to pass in order to be licensed. As for why?" Reese shrugged. "I didn't know what else I wanted to do, but I knew I liked to help people and I was good at science and math."

"So, why just a nurse? Why not become a doctor?"

"*Just* a— Dottie." Julianna frowned at her sister. As much as she loved the girl, she sometimes checked her filters at the door.

Dottie's eyes widened. "What?"

"Why ask her that? And make it sound like nursing is *less than*?"

"Because she's good at science and math. Why stop at nursing when you can make bank as a doctor?"

Julianna dropped her face into her palms. "I'm so sorry, Reese," she mumbled around her hands.

But Reese chuckled. Then giggled before releasing a full-on belly laugh that turned into another. A tear leaked from her left eye. She snorted and that sent her into more giggles. She caught her breath and shook her head. "Oh, my," she said on a gasp. "It wasn't that funny, sorry. I must still be a little 'off.' But, I like you, Dottie. I hope we can be friends."

Dottie grinned. "Sure. That would be awesome."

Reese's smile faded and she looked at her brother. "Thank you for suggesting this. I needed to do this rather than go home and brood."

"Why don't you stay with me tonight?"

She grimaced. "I'll think about it."

Clay looked at Julianna, and she found herself captured by the color of his eyes. She'd thought they were gray, but now they looked like a light blue.

What the heck? Since when did she notice men's eyes?

Dottie nudged her. "You okay?"

"What?"

Dottie shot her a half smile, even while her brows dipped inward. "Are you going to answer him?"

Oh, Clay had said something while she'd been mooning over his pretty eyes? Heat crept up into her neck and she cleared her throat. "Sorry, I zoned for a minute. What did you say?"

Clay studied her, amusement turning those eyes to silver. How was that even possible?

"I asked if you have any time off in the near future," he said. "We have a monthlong career program going on at the high school that ties into the end-of-the-year activities and graduation."

"And you want to know if I have time off because . . . ?"

"I'd love for you to be a part of a series we're doing on law enforcement. I have an ATF agent, a detective, a uniformed patrol officer, a K-9 and handler, an SRO"—he tapped his chest—"that one was pretty easy, and a Secret Service buddy. They've all agreed to come a couple of times over the course of the month. The first time you're there, you give an overview of what your agency does, talk about your specialty, and why you chose it. The second time is a wrap-up. It's brief demonstrations by the various agencies to give a behind-the-scenes look at each job. Something the kids can really get into. As of yet, I don't have an FBI agent. A lot of the students looking at a career in law enforcement have asked for someone from the FBI and the CIA to come talk to them. I told them not to hold out hope for the CIA, but if you would be willing . . ." He raised a brow at her.

"Do it," Dottie said, her eyes shining. "That would be so cool!"

Julianna shifted her gaze to her sister, even while the thought of telling anyone why she became a hostage negotiator was enough to send her fleeing. "You think so?" She kept her tone light, hoping it hid her dark thoughts. "I won't put a crimp in your style?"

Dottie wrinkled her nose. "Ew. Don't start with those ancient-sayings stuff. You can come as long as you don't say things that make you sound like you're fifty years old."

"I see. So what should I say instead of crimping your style?"

"Killing the vibe," Dottie and Reese said together. They looked at each other and laughed.

"Got it," Julianna said. "No killing of the vibe." Dottie groaned and shook her head. The teasing lightened Julianna's thoughts, and hiding a grin, she glanced at Clay. "I think I can probably help you out. If you send me some dates and times, I'll forward the request to the media and recruiting coordinators and let them know I'm willing to do it. Pick some that work and I'll pass those on." She gave him her email address and phone number while Dottie and Reese looked on. Then the two girls exchanged a look that sent a pang of worry through Julianna. Even though there was a five-year age difference between the two, it appeared they were going to be tight friends. Julianna wasn't sure if that was a good thing or not. They already looked like they could communicate silently—with their main topic of interest being her and Clay. That had the potential to be all kinds of uncomfortable.

"Perfect," Clay said. "I'll get back to you first thing in the morning."

They finished their burgers, making small talk, while Julianna tried to enjoy the moment of fun. Although, she couldn't help noticing Clay's teasing held an undertone of worry. She didn't blame him. Right now, Reese was doing okay; however, Julianna knew from experience that when darkness fell, the nightmares would come.

She just prayed Reese would let Clay help her through them so she didn't have to suffer them alone.

Like her.

∎   ∎   ∎

The national news played on the television in the background while the patrons at the McCoy Diner enjoyed their food. This was my second week on the job, and while it wasn't what I'd dreamed of in high school, it was a job, and I'd try to take my doctor's advice and be thankful for it. I wiped the table and wondered why people had to be so messy when they ate. Seriously, were they pigs at home too? I read the captions scrolling across the bottom of the screen and my movements slowed.

Hostage situation resolves peacefully.

Camera footage recorded earlier showed men coming from a tunnel in the ground and being greeted with guns in their faces and, a short time later, cuffs on their wrists. I laughed out loud at their shocked expressions. "They were not expecting that," I said to no one in particular.

"That's something, isn't it?" Milo said. He was one of the bar's regulars. He had a wife and two kids at home, but he said he preferred the company of a good drink because it didn't talk back to him or nag him.

I could understand that.

"Yeah," I said, "it's something, all right. Says the bomb squad was there and explosives were found." The words continued to scroll and I kept reading. "Wow. They set off one of the explosives in the tunnel."

"That's crazy. I can't believe the whole thing didn't collapse."

"One of the suspects was a bomb expert. Guess he knew how to work it so that it wouldn't."

Milo shook his head. "This world's gone bonkers. Can't believe some people and the nerve they have." He drained his drink and plopped the glass onto the counter even while his eyes stayed glued to the television. "Glad no one got hurt. That negotiator did a great job. Everyone's saying she's a hero."

"Really." It wasn't a question. "The negotiator. Who was it? Did they say?"

"Julianna Jameson."

"Huh."

"Why? You know her?"

"Nah. Just wondered."

Milo stood and placed a twenty next to his glass. "Can I ask you a question without you thinking I'm rude?"

"Sure."

"How'd you get those scars?"

"An accident." His question wasn't rude. I just didn't want to talk about it.

"Sorry about that."

"Yeah, me too."

"See you later. You're a good addition to this place, kiddo."

"Thanks, Milo. See you tomorrow. Tell the missus hello from me."

He grimaced, but I barely noticed when he slipped out the door. I was too busy soaking in all the information playing out on the screen.

It's time.

"Time?" I swallowed hard and tried to shove the voice away, but it was right. I'd been working toward this moment for a long time.

We're all here for a reason. I think you know yours now.

How will I know it's the right time?

You'll know.

The voice was right. I did know.

Sometimes the law fails. They don't mean to, they just do, and we have to make things right through our own efforts.

Yes, yes, we did.

If she was dead, how would you feel?

I'd asked myself this question over and over. And I'd finally come to the conclusion that I'd feel like justice was served. It would mean she got what was coming to her. Right?

So, how can we make that happen?

Another question that I'd asked myself a lot.

It hadn't been easy to make my brain work through the haze of drugs, but it seemed the more I thought about making her pay, the clearer my thinking became.

So, now, it was time to even things out. Make life a little more fair.

The plan was simple.

First, she'd suffer, *then* she'd die. Or maybe I'd let her live. If death would be merciful, then she'd live.

Maybe.

Stupid girl! You're so stupid. He's dead and it's all your fault!

I gasped. "It's not my fault, it's not. It's hers!"

"What'd you say?" The customer who'd just taken a seat at the bar in front of me frowned.

I shook my head. "Nothing. Sorry. Just talking to myself."

"Well, you know what they say if you answer yourself."

"Yeah, I know what they say." Wonder what he'd say if he knew I answered all the time. They'd probably have me committed— again.

When the station went to a commercial, I served three other customers before I noticed the blood on my hands.

I let out a low yelp and grabbed a clean rag from underneath the counter. I went to the sink and ran the water as hot as I could stand, then scrubbed at the blood, over and over, not understanding why it wouldn't wash away.

"Hey, you okay?"

I looked over my shoulder to see my boss frowning at me. "Yeah. Just trying to get my hands clean." The steam from the hot water swirled around the faucet.

"Looks like you're trying to scorch them. Don't you think you have enough scars? Be careful, will you? I don't need any workplace accidents, okay?"

"Yeah, sorry." I definitely had enough scars on the outside. Too bad the gaping wounds on the inside hadn't healed over.

When I looked back at my hands, the blood was gone. I dropped the rag and turned the water off, feeling nauseous, hands throbbing and flushed a bright pink.

But no blood on the rag or in the sink.

And now I wasn't sure it had ever been there.

You need purpose. I can help you find that. The voice echoed in the back of my mind.

It's your fault he's dead! You did this! Now you need to make it right! The second voice shouted louder.

Purpose is important. If we don't have purpose, we slowly die. Everyone needs to find something that gives them a reason to get out of bed in the morning.

Your fault! Your fault!

Sometimes the voices blended into one and I couldn't figure out which one to listen to. Tears welled and I blinked hard. Crying was for the weak and I couldn't be weak.

Still, despair slammed me, and I whirled, grabbed my jacket from the hook, and bolted out the door. I could hear my boss calling my name, but I ignored him.

I had to get away.

It was time to fulfill my purpose. To find justice for the one who couldn't find it for himself.

CHAPTER
FIVE

Clay stood in the doorway of his guest room, watching his baby sister sleep. Eight years his junior, she'd been an unexpected blessing to his parents. They'd thought Clay was going to be an only child, but God had other plans, according to his mother. Born when his mom was forty-nine years old, Reese had grown up knowing nothing but love and acceptance. And that's what she'd learned to give in return to those in her life.

He'd be the first to admit that she'd probably been spoiled, but her sweet spirit and compassionate nature had kept her from becoming entitled. She was innocent, but today had changed something inside her. He saw it at the restaurant, then later, when she'd hugged him good night and climbed into the bed. He'd asked her to talk to him and she'd shaken her head.

"Later, maybe. Right now, I just need to think. And pray. And sleep."

So, he'd left her alone.

When he was sure she'd fallen asleep, he shut the door with a quiet click and walked into the den to look out of the large bay window that gave him gorgeous views he never tired of.

His home sat on twelve acres in Kings Mountain. That put

him about forty minutes from the high school, but he didn't mind the drive. He had a horse barn with no horses and a cow pasture with no cows.

He hoped that would change one day, but for now, he'd hold on to the dream while he battled his inner demons. He glanced up at the sky. *God, I know we've had our differences, but thank you for sparing Reese today. I . . . I . . . just thank you.* He waited a moment, but when silence was his only answer, he sighed and headed to fix himself a snack.

In the kitchen, he used the remote to turn the television to a national news station. With the sound on low, he moved to the refrigerator to retrieve salad items to go with the leftovers he'd brought home. While he'd enjoyed dinner, he'd been so concerned with Reese's state of mind, he ate less than he usually would have, and now he was hungry and needed a snack. A meal-sized snack.

While he fixed the salad, he decided Reese seemed to be doing okay—and that allowed his thoughts to turn to Julianna Jameson. And his promise to text her some dates. He grabbed his laptop and sat at the table to look up the information, then texted her four dates.

Had she been serious about helping him, or did she just agree because it would have been awkward to say no after Dottie's enthusiastic encouragement?

Guess he'd find out shortly.

He set the computer aside and finished off the food, loaded the dishwasher, then planted himself in the recliner to watch a replay of the news footage. The media was going to milk the story for all it was worth, and one thing he found interesting was that they were doing a whole documentary on the North Carolina gold rush.

He wondered how many people would be fighting to get in those tunnels now. In spite of the documentation stating that all gold had been removed from the tunnels, he had no doubt law enforcement would have their hands full over the next few months keeping gold seekers out of trouble—and out of the tunnels. They'd rope them off, but there were always ways around those barriers.

His phone dinged with a text from Julianna.

I can do next Friday.

> Next Friday is great.

He got a thumbs-up emoji, then three little flashing dots.

How's Reese?

> Sleeping. Seems to be doing okay. No
> nightmares yet.

You're a good brother.

> I try.

It was nice to meet you, Clay. Have a good night.

> You too.

He couldn't help but stare at the phone, wishing to prolong the conversation, but he was at a loss as to what to say. And if experience was anything to go by, he needed to quit while he was ahead. He had a bad habit of awkwardness when it came to women he was interested in.

And he was definitely interested in Julianna Jameson.

Unfortunately, his awkwardness wasn't the only thing keeping him from asking her out. How he wished that was all.

But as long as his past remained part of his present, he'd be alone.

And that looked like it might be for the rest of his life.

■ ■ ■ ■

Later that evening, long after the sun had set, Julianna sat in her home office with her gaze fixed on the desk calendar. Honestly, the red circle around the date was so cliché, she winced every time she saw it. But she couldn't help it. She'd done it every year for the past fourteen years. And in this fifteenth year, she wasn't going to break the habit—the reminder. Not that she needed it, but . . .

Yeah. And it was two weeks away.

It had been fifteen years since her life had gone tragically wrong. Most days, she managed not to think about it, but as the date drew closer and closer, it was all she could do to *not* think about it. Except when she was working. She'd trained herself to let nothing distract her when she was on the job.

Not a date from the past. Not even a handsome SRO. But she wasn't working right now and she had to admit, she was looking forward to seeing Clay again next Friday.

"Hey."

Julianna turned to see Dottie standing in the doorway. "Hey."

"You okay?"

"Yeah." She forced a smile. "Just sending Clay a text confirming I'll be there next Friday." A week would give her time to figure out what she wanted to say. And how much.

Her sister raised a brow. "Cool. That's really good of you to agree to do it. I know you're busy."

"I am, but I can make the time. I don't mind."

Dottie looked at the floor.

"What is it?" Julianna asked.

"I just . . ."

"If you don't want me to come, let me know. It's not too late for me to back out."

"No, it's not that, it's . . ."

Julianna rose and walked over to her sister to clasp the teen's biceps. "Tell me. What is it?"

"Maybe I shouldn't have been so enthusiastic about you coming. And not because I don't want you there. It's just . . ."

"What?"

"Not everyone has respect for what you do." Dottie finally lifted her head to meet Julianna's gaze. "Some of the kids might be ugly to you."

Julianna's heart squeezed. "Aw, kiddo, don't worry about that. I have a pretty thick skin."

"I know, but you're so kind and try to help everyone no matter who they are, that the thought of someone being mean to you just because you're in law enforcement . . . hurts."

Dottie stepped closer and Julianna pulled her into a tight hug. "Look," she said, "I know you worry about me. And that's perfectly natural. If our roles were reversed, I'd do the same." She shrugged. "But I chose my profession to do good. Unfortunately, others—and I do mean a very small percentage—don't have the same motivation, and they give the rest of us a bad name. All I can do is be the best agent I know how to be, save as many lives as I can save, and pray about the rest."

"God again, huh?"

Julianna laughed and stepped back. "Yes. And one day, you're going to love him as much as I do."

Dottie grimaced. "I doubt it. I can't see this good God that you talk about. He stuck me in a lousy home with lousy parents and then took you away from me when you wound up in that lousy juvenile detention center."

"Dottie, you weren't even old enough to remember that!"

"I don't have to remember it. Facts are facts."

"And Mom meant well. Honestly, I think she just didn't know what to do with me. Or you."

"Who are you kidding? She didn't even *want* me. Whose mother names them after a character in *The Wizard of Oz*?"

Julianna gasped. "Why in the world would you think that?"

"She told me. She was mad at me one day and yelled that I was an ungrateful so-and-so and needed to change my attitude. That she should have named me Toto instead, because I acted more like a dog than a—" Tears welled and Julianna grabbed her hand.

"Oh, Dottie, that's a horrible thing for her to say." Fury blazed a path from her brain to her heart, and she bit her tongue on the next words that wanted to escape. "And anyway, that's totally not true about where your name came—"

Dottie cut her off with another hug. "Don't worry about it. As long as you're okay, I'm okay." She paused. "Are you okay?"

"Yes, why?"

Dottie glanced at the desk calendar. "I noticed that the other day. You still think about it."

"Of course."

"And you're dreaming about it more, aren't you?"

"Yes. Why?"

"I hear you at night sometimes." Dottie bit her lip. "You cry out. I don't know whether to come in or leave you alone."

Grief and guilt tugged at Julianna. "I'm sorry. I didn't realize." She exhaled. "Yes, as the date gets closer, the nightmares intensify. It's like this every year, so I know the pattern."

"What is your dream about? You keep telling me to talk to you about what's going on inside me, that keeping it bottled up isn't good. Well, if it's not good for me, then it's not good for you. Tell me. Please."

There were a lot of things she hadn't told Dottie. Mostly because she didn't like revisiting that time in her life. But Dottie was right. And Julianna couldn't expect the girl to open up to her if she wasn't willing to reciprocate.

"Jules? Please?"

"There was a school shooting when I was eighteen." Julianna kept her voice low and let the memories come at her. "I lost one of my best friends and I was helpless to do anything about it." She pressed her eyes with her thumb and forefinger, then dropped her hand. "It eats at me. But don't worry. As soon as the date is past, the nightmares will fade once more."

Dottie's eyes had widened at her words. "School shooting?"

"Yeah. It's a long story and I'll tell you about it one day. Later. If I talk about it too much, the dreams will just get worse."

"Then don't talk about it now, but I do want to hear the story."

"Thanks."

"Okay, then." Dottie looked at her watch. "I came to tell you that I'm going to see Trey. I'm meeting him and a couple of other friends at the Bad Burger Barn." Trey Garrison, a young man in Dottie's class who Julianna hadn't made up her mind about yet. He was polite and yet guarded at the same time, and she couldn't decide if that was just his personality or if he was hiding something. Probably the former and she needed to stop being so suspicious. "We just came from there."

"Hours ago, Jules. Look at the clock."

She did. "Wow. Time flies." She waved a hand. "But that's a lot of grease for one day, don't you think?"

"Eh." Dottie shrugged. "Let me enjoy it while I can. I need to take advantage of my fabulous metabolism before age catches up with me." She winked, and Julianna forced a laugh like she was supposed to. "And then we're going to do some studying at the café across the street. They have great coffee and strong Wi-Fi, so I'll be late."

"Okay, be careful."

"Always." Dottie smirked, then was out the door, leaving Julianna alone.

She let the smile slide from her face and walked back to the desk calendar with the big red circle. She knew she'd never have a year where she wouldn't think about that day from her senior year of high school, but she thought the pain would have dimmed a bit by now. And it had, for the most part. But each year around this time, it returned. This year, it was so much worse. So many memories, so many dreams. She closed her eyes.

"Put the gun down, Dennis. Please, don't do this."

"You're mine. If I can't have you, no one will."

It didn't take a genius to know that the memories were stronger because of her involvement in Dottie's senior year. Fifteen years may have passed, but each anniversary brought that day back in vivid high-definition color. Every sight, smell, even the taste of her fear and agony at the final gunshot—

Her phone buzzed and she opened her eyes to glance at the screen. Grace Billingsley.

> Hey, friend, let me know when you have some
> time for lunch. We need to catch up. I know
> "the day" is fast approaching and I wanted to let
> you know I was thinking of you . . .

Grace, a behavioral analyst, also worked for the Bureau. She was in the Columbia, South Carolina, office and was the BAU coordinator. It would be a little over an hour's drive for Grace, but she promised she didn't mind.

> Lunch on Sunday a week from now? Penny and
> Raina said they'd work around your schedule and
> Penny would fly her and Raina in the new bird.

Penny Carlton, soon to be Penny Satterfield six months from now, had built her own helicopter from a kit she'd ordered, and looked for any excuse to fly. Julianna hadn't seen Grace, Penny, or Raina in several months, and the need to be in their presence was intense. They were friends from another life, but friends she made every effort to see as often as possible.

> Next Sunday is fine. Subject to change.

> Same here. Our usual?

The Wood Fired Grille in Rock Hill. Her stomach rumbled in anticipation.

> See you there next Sunday for lunch.

Julianna walked back to the desk and let her gaze fall on the circled date once more. Then covered it with a stack of papers and left the room. If she was going to speak to a group of high schoolers, she'd better be prepared.

For anything.

CHAPTER
SIX

Felicity Banks raked her hair into a ponytail and hurried into the kitchen. She was going to be late yet again—and she couldn't afford to lose this job. The tight knot in her stomach had loosened only a fraction during the year after her husband's unexpected death, and she wondered if she'd ever laugh again with the carefree joy she used to know.

It seemed doubtful, but she believed God had a plan. And as long as she believed that, she'd live with expectation, in addition to the grief and agonizing hole in her tattered heart.

A cartoon played on the television in the den and six-year-old Tommy clutched the remote. His little legs swung, thumping against the couch every so often. While Felicity fixed breakfast for him, she turned on the small television on her kitchen counter. A national news station was running the story of the hostage rescue and capture of Nicholas Manchester yet again. It had been a week and they were still talking about it.

But her husband's death had garnered a mere blip on the radar. *Please, Lord, I don't want to be angry. I know you have a plan.*

Felicity set the cereal bowl on the counter and poured the milk over the nuggets. Through the kitchen window, she noticed a moving truck in the drive next door. She must be getting new neighbors. Maybe they would have children Tommy's age. He'd love to have someone to play with on the weekends without having to get in the car and drive somewhere.

"Tommy? Cereal's ready."

He glanced at her, set the remote on the sofa, and trudged to the kitchen table. She placed the bowl in front of him and handed him a spoon. "Here you go, little man."

"I want a hamburger."

"I know. I do too." She paused, thought about the money in her purse and bank account, then shoved aside the depressing reality. "How about we get one for dinner tonight? I'll bring it home from work."

He looked up, his eyes wide. "Really?"

"Really."

He jumped down and ran to throw his arms around her waist. "Thanks, Mom. You're the best."

Her throat clogged and resentment started to build. She cut it off. "Eat your breakfast. We're going to have to move a little faster this morning."

"You say that every morning."

She laughed. "Yeah, I guess I do."

"It's very repetitious."

"And you're a walking dictionary. Come on, Webster, eat."

He giggled and shoveled the food into his mouth. Then spotted the truck next door. "Hey, you think they'll have some kids to play with?"

"I don't know. Let's give them a chance to get moved in and then we'll ask."

"Cool!"

When he was finished, he hopped up and grabbed his backpack. She tugged him to her and pressed her cheek to his, with her lips inches from his left ear. She felt him smile. "For I know the plans I have for you . . . ," she whispered.

"Declares the Lord," Tommy whispered back.

"Plans to prosper you and not to harm you," she said a little louder.

"Plans to give you hope and a future!" Tommy's shout rang with joy and Felicity's heart lightened. She eyed the picture on the refrigerator, touched her fingers to her lips, and caressed her husband's likeness. "I miss you, honey."

Tommy mimicked her actions. "I miss you, Daddy."

Before emotions could overwhelm her once again, she kissed her child's forehead, handed him his lunch, and they walked out the door.

■ ■ ■ ■

Clay had arrived at the school early, in spite of a slow drive through a pouring rain. The miserable weather couldn't dampen the strange anticipation quickening his squeaky footsteps in the tile hallway, and he aimed himself toward the office he shared with the other two SROs. His phone buzzed with a text from Julianna.

I've enjoyed our chats this week. I'm on the way.

They'd talked every day since the courthouse incident, either via text chat or an actual phone call. The conversations had been mostly the "getting to know you" kind—and hadn't been nearly enough for Clay. He wanted more; he just hadn't figured out how to do that without revealing too much of himself.

Which really wasn't fair to Julianna. He should back off and keep her at arm's length while his heart—and hers—was still in one piece.

But for some reason, he just . . . couldn't.

But he should.

"Hey, Officer Clay, wait up, man!"

He turned to find Andre Wilson chasing him, one hand holding onto the waistband of his pants to keep them from falling down. The teen's dreadlocks gleamed with a fresh application of oil. "You're here early."

"Heard you had a fed coming to campus."

"You been talking to Dottie?"

"Yeah, she's a little worried someone's going to dis her sis."

Disrespect Julianna. "I'm not too worried about it, but if you've got some inside info, I'll take it."

"Naw, man, as far as I know, it's all good. I'd tell you if it wasn't."

Clay wasn't sure why the kid had taken a liking to him, but he wasn't going to look a gift horse in the mouth. "How's your mom doing?"

Andre's eyes darkened. "She's drinking again. Pops got another DUI three nights ago." The teen scowled. "Kinda rough around my house right now."

"Dude, I'm sorry. Marcus okay?" Andre's younger brother was at the middle school and in and out of trouble on a regular basis. Clay tried to help when he could, but the thirteen-year-old was one angry little guy.

"Yeah. For now."

"You need a power bar to get through the day?"

"I don't wanna take your food, old man. You might need a sugar boost later." But the kid licked his lips and his gaze darted in the direction of Clay's office.

Clay motioned Andre to follow him. "I have enough to share." He read between the lines. Andre hadn't had breakfast that morning, and if he had to make a wager, he'd bet Marcus hadn't either. He'd make a call to the middle school and make sure Marcus got breakfast.

Clay led the way to his office and opened the top drawer of his desk. He handed the kid two bars. "You know, you just have to ask if you need something."

Andre pocketed the food, then pulled on the waist of his pants. "Got a spare belt so I don't get yelled at for having saggy pants?"

Clay pulled open the second drawer and retrieved a belt. "What happened to the last one I gave you?"

"Pops took it and—" His eyes slid from Clay's.

"And what?"

"He took it." Andre's fingers tightened around the brand-new piece of leather. "Thanks."

"He hit you with it, Andre?"

"Naw, man. He just took it. Probably trying to sell it." He paused. "You're a good dude, Officer Clay."

"So are you, Andre, so don't forget it, okay?"

Andre quirked a smile at him. "Right."

Andre wove the belt through the loops on his pants and buckled it on the last hole just as a knock on the door turned them both. Clay's heart pounded a fraction faster when his eyes landed on Julianna Jameson. A visitor badge hung on the shoulder of her blue polo shirt with the FBI seal on it. Her khaki cargo pants, boots, and weapon on her hip completed the outfit. She looked calm, professional, and as pretty as he remembered. Not to mention slightly damp from the rain.

She'd come.

Not that he'd thought she wouldn't, but—

"Hey," she said, "sorry to interrupt, but the front office sent me here." She swiped a raindrop from her cheek. "Sorry to get water everywhere."

"They make umbrellas, lady," Andre said.

Julianna smiled at him. "I don't carry them," she said. "I like having my hands free."

In case she needed to respond to . . . whatever. He got it.

"It'll dry," Clay said.

She shot him a small smile. "True. I'm just popping in to let you know I've arrived. I'm a little early, so I thought I'd hang out in the library until you're ready for me if that's all right."

"Or you can just stay here," Clay said, then turned to Andre. "And don't be rude. Her name's not lady."

Andre's gaze bounced between the two of them. "*She's* the fed?"

He let out a low, admiring whistle and Clay nudged him. "Stop it. Use your manners."

Andre laughed. "Nice to meet you, Mrs. FBI."

"That's Ms. FBI, but you can call me Julianna. And thanks. Nice to meet you too . . . ?"

"Andre."

"Andre," she repeated. "Will you be in the assembly?"

"Me?" Andre pointed to himself, then laughed. "I'm not cop material."

"Well, I'm not a cop," she said with a smile. "Like you pointed out, I'm a fed. But who says you can't be one or the other?"

"My pops would shoot me if I joined the po-po. And I mean that literally."

Clay winced, but Julianna's gaze never wavered. "I think you'd make a good one. You should think about it."

The kid hesitated, clicked his tongue, and waved a hand in dismissal. "You don't even know me. What makes you say that?"

Julianna narrowed her gaze at the boy. "Hmm . . . well, you're friends with Clay, you make direct eye contact with those you're talking to, you carry yourself with confidence, you have calluses on your hands, which means you're not afraid of hard work. You're in good physical shape, although it looks like you've lost a few pounds recently due to the baggy jeans—or maybe you just like them baggy, but probably not, since you were putting on a belt when I knocked. A belt you may have gotten from Officer Clay because you didn't have one. And"—she tilted her head—"my guess is . . . basketball?"

"Yes." The poor kid looked completely spooked at Julianna's on-point profile. Even Clay was impressed.

"And," she said, "it's a gut feeling that you'd make a good cop—or fed. Just so you know, my gut's usually never wrong."

Andre backed toward the door. "Um . . . huh. Well, maybe. Thanks."

He disappeared around the doorjamb and Clay started to speak, only to stop when Andre reappeared.

"They teach you how to do that in fed school?" he asked. "That ninja mind-reading thing?"

"Yes." She laughed. "Some of it. And there's no mind reading, I promise. It's just being super observant."

The teen nodded. "Okay. I'ma come to hear what you got to say. And not just cuz you're pretty."

Julianna fist-bumped him. "I'm honored."

Andre gave her the once-over, his look curious and nonoffensive, just one that said she'd gotten him thinking and earned his respect. Then he shook his head and left.

She turned to Clay, her expression one of bemusement. She met his gaze. "What just happened?"

"That was just Andre. Thanks for encouraging him. He needs it."

"Yeah," she said, her voice low but her expression thoughtful.

"And that was a pretty impressive reading on him."

She waved a hand. "It's second nature at this point."

He laughed. "Do I even want to ask what your first impressions of me were?" The mysterious smile that curved her lips narrowed his eyes. "Spill it," he said.

She laughed. "Maybe later."

"You can't do that to me. I'm dying here. Tell me."

"Seriously?"

"Why not?"

"Okay. Well, you're former Army. I'm guessing Ranger?"

He gaped. "Yeah. But . . . how?"

"I got a glimpse of the tattoo on your forearm when you gave your coat to Reese at the scene."

"Oh." Duh. "Anything else?"

"You're confident in your position here and you like to be in control, but you're not power hungry or arrogant." He raised a brow and she smiled. "In fact, I'd say you're probably very humble. You're a protector. You expect a lot of yourself and others but are forgiving when they mess up. You're not so easy on yourself." He caught his breath and stared. "And . . . you're a guy who can keep his cool in the face of danger."

For a moment, he couldn't speak. As much as she'd told him, he had a feeling she hadn't told him *everything*. Unsure what to say, he chose to go neutral and focus on the part about being able to keep his cool. "I had good training." He ran a hand over his head and wished he'd gotten that haircut he'd thought about three days ago. What had he done or said to reveal so much of himself to her? "I have to make a phone call to the middle school. Can you give me a minute?"

"Sure." She paused, then laughed, an endearingly awkward sound that almost made him smile. "I'm sorry," she said. "I probably said too much."

"It's fine. A little unnerving that you got all of that from spending just a few hours with me in person."

"We've talked a lot over the last week, Clay. Words are my thing, remember? Reading between the lines, hearing what the other person is really saying."

"True. That's true." Now, he was trying to remember what all he'd said in his effort to keep the conversations light and fun. They'd talked about the weather, their idea of the perfect vacation, their favorite restaurants, and hobbies. They both liked the shooting range, swimming in the ocean, and hiking. She preferred fall and winter, he loved summer. And more. Light, surface-level conversations. Nothing deep. Nothing too revealing. But she'd managed to get more than he realized.

It was good to know she could do that. At least he had forewarning of the need to be vigilant about keeping his walls intact. So, why was he getting to know her if he was just going to push her away?

Because . . . maybe he wouldn't? "I'm just going to make my call, then I'll take you to the auditorium."

"Sure."

He gestured for her to have a seat in one of the empty chairs at the round table in the center of the room, then snagged the handset of the landline phone off his desk and pressed the speed-dial button.

■ ■ ■ ■

Julianna didn't normally eavesdrop on other people's conversations unless it was related to her job—or she found the conversation interesting. This one told her a lot about the man asking someone on the other end to make sure a kid had something to eat before he was required to put in a full day of learning. While Clay made arrangements, she mentally kicked herself. Seriously, when would she learn to keep her mouth shut about her observations? She'd definitely creeped him out and that was the last thing she wanted.

When he hung up, he turned and she smiled at him. "I didn't mean to get so personal in the observation. I'm sorry. One day I'll learn."

"Learn what?"

"To keep my mouth shut."

"Hey, I asked. I'm glad you were honest. It gives me more insight into who you are—and exactly what I'm revealing to others."

"Hmm . . . well, I'm probably more observant than most people."

"No doubt."

She studied him for a moment. "You really do like your job, don't you?"

"I do."

"And you're good at it."

"I am. As you said, I'm confident in it."

No false modesty, but not a hint of ego either. Just the facts, ma'am.

"At least this one," he murmured.

"Sorry?"

He shook his head. "Nothing. Just thinking out loud."

"How long have you been an SRO here?"

"Almost a year."

"What made you want to work with kids?"

He shot her a smile. "Is this an interrogation, Special Agent Jameson?"

"No, not at all." She laughed. "We talked about a lot of stuff this past week, but neither one of us got very personal. I guess I'm curious to know more about you, not your job or Reese. I think I know more about Reese than I do you." And to be fair, he probably knew more about Dottie than her.

"You mean I'm not an open book?" he asked.

"Not hardly."

"Yo, Officer Clay, catch."

Julianna turned to see a small package fly in her direction. She ducked, but Clay snagged the object in midair. "Thanks, Curly."

Curly? The kid's hair was straight as a stick and hung down to the tip of his nose.

"Mama said to tell you she's got your cupcakes ready," Curly said.

"I'll get them later today, thanks."

"Hey, you hear about that dude who tried to break out of the courthouse and the feds caught him coming up out of the tunnels that used to be gold mines?"

"That's old news, my friend. Where have you been?"

"I been busy." He tried to look offended and failed. Then laughed. "That was wicked cool. Who knew there were gold mines around here?"

"I'm pretty sure they cover that in one of your history classes."

Curly laughed. "Guess I should have paid more attention. Bye."

And then he was gone.

Clay shook his head and laughed. "Curly's mother keeps me stocked with cupcakes." He held up the wrapped treat. "Curly usually delivers a couple a week."

"But you ordered more?"

"Reese's birthday. We're getting together at my parents' tomorrow night to celebrate." He glanced at the clock. "All right, we've got about twenty minutes before the bell rings for the assembly. Want me to show you the way?"

"Sure."

"You've got quite a few who are interested in your profession."

"That's good to hear." He led the way to the auditorium and she raised a brow. "You think I'm going to need this many seats?"

He laughed. "No, you won't, but it was the only free area at this time. You don't have to stand on the big stage. You can hang out here at the front and it'll be a little more personable."

"That sounds perfect. Thanks."

"Okay, one more thing." He handed her the microphone. "Because of all the anti-law-enforcement issues lately, in order to avoid any kind of chaos, we have the kids sign an agreement to follow before they're allowed in. If anyone breaks the rules, they'll be ushered out immediately, no questions asked. You just keep doing your thing."

"Got it." Sounded like he had everything under control.

While Julianna reviewed her notes, Clay took care of a few minor details. A short time later, the doors opened and the kids filtered in, most chatting and laughing. A few others looking at their phones. A pang hit her. Had she ever been that carefree in high school? Maybe. Before.

By the time the bell rang, most of the students were settled in their seats, their curious eyes on her.

Clay stepped to the front and welcomed them. "I'm not going to go over the rules again. You're big boys and girls and you signed a paper stating you'd follow them. If you didn't read what you signed, that's on you."

A few teens snickered. Dottie slipped into a seat in the back and Julianna smiled.

"I want to introduce to you someone who's become a friend

in a very short period of time," Clay said. "Some of you may have seen the news about the hostage situation at the courthouse last week. Special Agent Julianna Jameson was the negotiator for that incident." Murmurs rippled through the room. "Thanks to her—and the actions of a few other people—my sister is alive." Silence fell, their attention captured. "Now, I'd like to introduce Special Agent Jameson. She's going to tell you a little bit about how she got involved in law enforcement, exactly what she does, and how you can pursue the same career if that's something you think you might be interested in. During the last fifteen minutes, she'll answer questions."

He nodded to Julianna and she stepped forward, lifting the mic to her lips. "Good morning, everyone. I'm honored you came to hear what I have to say." If she had to guess, she would estimate there were about seventy-five kids in the place. "So, let me start by giving you a bit of my bio. I'm thirty-three years old. I'm kinda young to be a hostage negotiator, but my path was slightly different than most agents. I was a local police officer in Burbank, California. During my four years as a beat cop, I was trained by the FBI as a negotiator before I even joined the Bureau. So you might say I had a bit of a head start. Anyway, there was one hostage situation that sealed my career. I managed to talk down the suspect, and he surrendered the hostages, then walked out and gave himself up as well. The negotiator who trained me was impressed and recommended I apply to the Bureau. I did so and, at the age of twenty-eight, was assigned to the Charlotte Division. Because of my background, my SAC—Special Agent in Charge—selected me to attend CNU—Crisis Negotiation Unit—Coordinator training, and three years later, I found myself stepping into the role of coordinator when the current one in Charlotte retired. And here I've been ever since."

While Clay's gaze roamed the room, keeping an eye on the students, she could tell he was listening intently. He'd learn a lot about her today, but just the surface facts. Not the part of her she kept locked away in a little box in the recesses of her mind. The part that she didn't like to even acknowledge existed. She focused on the students and noted most were paying attention. Some had probably agreed to come just to get out of class, but that was all right.

Andre sat on the front row to her left. Slouched down, arms crossed, body language shouting disinterest, but his gaze never left her. A group of girls Julianna would peg as those belonging to the popular clique sat behind Andre. They had *the look* she remembered from her own high school days. The popular girls who everyone either despised or worshiped, depending where one fell in the social structure of the school. It was so cliché, but clichés were made for a reason. The girl on the end with her flawless makeup caught Julianna's attention. Her gaze tracked Julianna's every move, but it was the look in her eyes that sparked her internal alarms.

Hate. Scorn. Derision. A mixture of all and more. Julianna let the look roll off. She was used to it. Okay, maybe not used to it, but it wasn't something new. She cleared her throat, realizing her pause had slipped into the awkward phase.

"I was told some of you were interested in a career in law enforcement and I have to say that can be a pretty unpopular choice these days." A grumble greeted her.

"That's cuz the po-po don't always make good choices." The statement came from a young man on the end seat to her far right.

Clay started toward him and she held up her hand. "I'd like to address that statement if that's all right."

He nodded but hovered.

"What's your name?" she asked.

"Gage."

"Well, Gage, I'd say there's some truth to that. But here's the thing. Most people who choose to go into law enforcement don't do so with the idea that they're going to make wrong choices. Most people—the agents and cops that I know—chose the profession because they want to put away the bad guys. They want to make their cities, their country, safer places for their loved ones." She shrugged. "I'm not saying things don't go sideways or that officers and agents don't get jaded, but that's why we need people who believe in justice and are willing to fight for what's right—even when that means sometimes we have to fight those we work with. And again, I want to reiterate, that's a super small percentage."

The teen rolled his eyes, but kept his mouth shut. Julianna turned back to the others. "So, let me give you a rundown of what my day can look like." She gave a summary of the situation with Manchester and then said, "And then other days are like this. Where I get to share about a job I love with people I hope to work with in the future."

Andre raised his hand. "What made you want to be an agent? What made you want to work so hard to be a negotiator?"

She swallowed and the question echoed in her mind. "When I was fifteen, I stole a car and landed in juvie. From that point on, I had choices to make."

CHAPTER
SEVEN

Clay blinked, unsure at first that he'd heard right. Julianna had been a juvenile delinquent? And had turned her life around to become a fed? He almost smiled. That meant there was hope for every kid in this room. Interesting.

What was also interesting was the group of girls sitting behind Andre. Clay never would have pegged them to be interested in anything Julianna might say. And they might not be. They may have just wanted to get out of class. However, as Julianna spoke, they kept their focus on her, never once looking at their phones or each other. Especially Mary Ann. That girl was pure trouble, even though she always kept her shenanigans from crossing the line. Clay moved so he could keep an eye on her and frowned. He really didn't like the look on her face, but nothing he could do about that except hope she didn't act on whatever was going on in her head.

Julianna kept the students engaged up until the end, her words encouraging and relevant, then she held up a stack of business cards. "I'm going to leave these with Officer Clay. If any of you want to talk further, please get one from him and email me or call me. Just know that depending on my circumstances, it may take me a little while to get back to you."

"Like don't call and expect you to answer questions when you're trying to talk down a dude holding a gun on someone, huh?" Andre asked with a smirk.

Julianna laughed. "Yeah, that's probably not the best time." The bell rang and the students clapped. She seemed surprised at the acknowledgment, but gave a slight bow from the waist. "Thanks for coming to see me. Y'all have a great rest of your day."

The students filed out. Many stopped to tell her thanks before hurrying off to their respective classes.

Clay walked over to Julianna and took the cards from her. "That went well. You did a great job."

"Thank you. I hope that was what you were looking for."

"It was. This will just whet their appetite for more. I feel like we'll have a good turnout for the big finale."

"When is it? I'll have to clear that with my higher-ups."

"I haven't nailed the date down yet but should know that in a couple of days."

She nodded. "The sooner I know, the faster I can get it approved."

"I'll take care of that ASAP and get back to you." He rubbed his chin. "I was supposed to have it nailed down three weeks ago, but the date got bumped because the school decided we needed an end-of-the-year pep rally."

"Ah. Priorities."

"Exactly." He sighed. "I'll press for them to get the date on the calendar and hope it works for you."

Her phone buzzed and she unclipped it to glance at the screen. "I've got to go to work."

He frowned. "Where's the situation?"

"A bank." She shot him a tight smile and headed for the exit. "I'm sure it'll be on the news."

"Thank you, Julianna. I appreciate your help in all of this."

"Sure thing." She turned and bolted.

For some odd reason, Clay wanted to go after her, to tell her not to put herself in danger. But she was professional and had taken care of herself without him for a long time. "Be safe," he whispered.

He pulled his phone out to text her those very words. Then added,

Let me know when it's over? Please?

He got a thumbs-up and his heart rate picked up slightly. He ordered it to settle down. She was an interesting woman, and he liked her. A lot. But that didn't mean he needed that feeling to grow. Memories poured over him and he shook his head. Yeah, he didn't need to allow himself to hope he could pursue a romantic relationship with anyone.

Because no one knew better than he just how little he had to offer someone.

■ ■ ■ ■

Julianna called Hector, then pulled out of the school parking lot. His text had included instructions to call him ASAP, and he answered on the first ring. "Where are you?"

"Fifteen minutes away."

"The hostage taker asked for you."

She blinked. "Okay. Why?"

"Said he saw you on the news and heard how you'd figured out the whole situation with Manchester. Wanted to know if you were smart enough to figure him out."

Julianna hadn't watched the news footage. "They mentioned my name on the news?"

"Yes, you didn't watch the footage?"

"No." She grimaced. Great.

"This guy didn't actually say your name, just described you as the smart negotiator Manchester talked to."

She frowned. "Tell him I'm almost there and I look forward to speaking with him." She hung up and drove.

Twelve minutes later, she pulled into the parking lot of the bank and scanned the scene. It looked much like all the others she'd been called to, with the command post set up and the taped-off area holding back spectators. She stepped inside to find Hector there along with two members of the SWAT team.

Hector looked up. "That didn't take you as long as I thought. I told him twenty minutes."

"I drove fast. Fill me in."

"Got a call about forty minutes ago from inside the bank. One of the hostages called 911 and hung up. By the time officers arrived on the scene, he'd let a mother and her child go."

"Okay, that's a plus. I want to talk to the mother."

"Patty's been talking to her and passing on information via comms. She said as soon as the hostage taker stepped into the bank, he set off a smoke bomb and killed the guard."

"Oh no."

"Yeah." One dead meant the killer might not mind adding to the body count.

"All right. Tell me about him. What have you already talked to him about?"

"Only spoke with him long enough for him to tell me he's only talking to you. And his voice was a little robotic, like he was using technology to alter it."

"Good to know. As long as he's talking to me, I don't care what he sounds like." Her phone buzzed and she glanced at the screen. A text from Dottie.

Clay said you got called to a situation. Be safe.

She texted back,

Always.

She slipped the phone back onto her belt clip and dialed the number Hector had for the hostage taker.

He answered before the first ring ended. "Hello?"

"Hello, this is Julianna Jameson with the FBI. You asked to speak with me?"

"You're the one who talked to Manchester?"

The voice vibrated a fraction, a slight robotic pitch mixed with the man's tension to create the odd sound Hector mentioned.

"I am. Do you mind telling me who I'm speaking with?" she asked.

"Just call me Angel."

Julianna didn't bother to ask for a last name. "All right, Angel, can you tell me what we need to do to end this peacefully without anyone else getting hurt?"

"I've killed one person. That should tell you I'm serious, and if I don't get what I want, things are going to go from bad to worse."

"I know. I have no doubt you're serious and I want you to know I'm listening. What is it I can do for you? What do you want?"

A pause.

"Angel?"

A sigh slipped through the line. "No one's ever asked me what I wanted before."

Julianna blinked and frowned. She glanced at Hector, who frowned right back at her. Not the response she was expecting. Most bank hostage takers wanted a path to freedom. And money. "Well, Angel, I'm asking now. I'd love to hear what you want."

"I want . . . justice."

She exchanged another look with Hector. "Okay. Justice for who? Or what?"

"That's not important right now."

"So what is important for you right now? You have our attention and we're waiting to hear what it will take to get those people out of there alive."

"I let the mother and child go."

"I know. And we're very thankful for that."

A pause.

"Angel?"

"I'll call you back." The line clicked off.

Julianna sat back, her thoughts racing. She glanced at Hector. "I'm going to need some backup on this one."

Hector gave a slow nod. "Why do I get the feeling this isn't your average bank robber."

"Because I have the same feeling?" She pressed her lips together, thinking. "Can we pull Grace in on this? I want her perspective."

"I'll get her on the line." He motioned for one of the other negotiators to do so.

"In the meantime," Julianna said, "I need to know as many details as possible."

"We're pulling security footage. Video feed's been disabled."

"He ordered someone in the bank to do it," she said.

"No doubt. We're working on getting eyes and ears in there."

"Still? This feels a bit like the incident at the courthouse."

"Well, we know it's not the same person." He paused, listened to something in his comms, and nodded to the screen on his right. "Thanks, Daria." He turned to her. "Security footage from the bank coming our way. This is outside the bank just before everything went down."

The footage flickered to life. Someone approached the front door, holding an umbrella, and Julianna squinted as if that would help her see the face. "Rats. I can't tell anything about the person entering."

"I know."

Static blipped across the screen and then she could see inside the bank. Only . . . she couldn't. "Smoke?"

"Yeah."

"Again, a little reminiscent of the courthouse incident?"

He nodded. "He seems to know a lot about that. The hostages gave some in-depth details to the media."

Julianna scowled. "The media is going to be the death of us one day. So, this guy did his research and put his own twist on it to make it work here?"

"That's what it looks like."

"There." Julianna pointed. "Some of the smoke is clearing a little."

"And there's our guy with the gun."

"Where are the hostages?"

"Don't see them."

She leaned in. "He was fast," she said, her voice low. "He got them out of sight of the cameras. That's not good."

"How many?"

"Five still in there."

"So, he let the mother and child go," she murmured, keeping her gaze fixed on the monitor, as though staring at it would bring it to life and allow her to see inside. "Manchester did the same thing."

"Yeah, but that was because the woman was related to him."

"I don't think that matters to this person. What else did the mother say?"

"She described the people in there pretty well and said the guy had one hostage zip-tie two tellers and told them to sit behind the teller counter, then he had her zip-tie the three customers and move them into one of the offices."

"Well, that's different. Manchester kept his hostages all in one place." They were all in the courtroom. She replayed what she knew in her head and gasped. "Then again, depending on how you look at it, one might say that he divided his up too, even though they were all in the same room."

"What do you mean?"

"There were three entrances into that courtroom. He kept those doors barricaded with hostages by dividing them into little groups."

"Right." Hector gave a slow nod. "I guess that's one way to look at it."

Julianna pressed her lips with the tip of her finger and studied the monitor. "I'm thinking this guy, Angel, is reenacting that situation. He's just using a bank to do it."

Hector frowned. "But why?"

"Because he wants . . . justice." She paused. "But what's his version of justice? That's the question, isn't it?"

The phone rang and Julianna snatched it. "Angel?"

"N-no." A sob and a harsh inhale and exhale. "This is Zena," the woman whispered. "I'm one of the hostages."

"Are you all right, Zena?"

"I—I'm the last one alive. I think. Please get me out of here before he comes back." Another choked-off cry escaped her, and Julianna's heart picked up speed.

She straightened. "What do you mean? Where is he?"

"I don't know. He moved us into a vacant office. I got loose and freed the others, then I snuck into a side office, the first one in, next to the front door. I heard two muffled pops earlier—like the one that killed the security guard—then nothing. I think he's gone . . . I think he's been gone for a while but I don't know if he'll be back. I think he shot the other two customers. I don't know why he didn't come looking for me or maybe he is and he just hasn't found me yet." A sob choked her.

"Okay, hold on, Zena." Julianna hated to leave the crying woman hanging, but she couldn't ask Hector to send in a team without more information. "How would he have gotten out?" Julianna asked Hector.

"He couldn't," he said.

She thought for a moment, then tapped her comms. "Where's Grace?"

"I'm right here," the woman said in her ear.

"You've been briefed?"

"I have."

Julianna pinched the bridge of her nose. "What do you think? Could this be some kind of trap? An attempt to get law enforcement inside and then set off a bomb or something? To get justice for a loved one who was treated wrong by the police or something?" She shook her head. "I'm grasping at straws here but need to get back to the phone." She unmuted the device. "Zena, I'm

still here, okay? Can you see the suspect anywhere? Hear anything?"

"No," came the tight whisper. "I've been blindfolded for the
most part. I only got it off after I got my hands loose and went to
find the phone." The last word came out on a squeak, followed
by a sob.

So, she wouldn't have been able to see if there'd been any kind
of explosive. "Zena, we're working very hard to get you out of
there. Just trust me, okay?"

"Hurry, please!"

Julianna went back to her comms. "Grace?"

"I'll admit," Grace said, "the statement about wanting justice
kind of worries me. If he's got a beef with law enforcement . . ."

"Yeah."

Hector stood to pace in the small area. "Keep talking to him,"
he told Julianna. "I'm going to talk to the SWAT team commander
and get his perspective. He's not going to want to send his team
in there only to get blown up."

Julianna hesitated. "I guess I could go in there and find out."
It wasn't her job, but . . .

"No," Hector said, "not this time. You stay put. SWAT's going
to handle this."

Julianna settled back into her chair and eyed the monitor just
as it flickered to life.

CHAPTER
EIGHT

Clay pushed back from his desk and stood, stretching his lower back, while his thoughts went to Julianna Jameson. His mind had been doing that on a regular basis since she'd hurried out the door.

He flipped on the television to the local news station, and sure enough, the media had gotten wind of the situation and were camped out as close as they could get without crossing the police perimeter. But they had good zoom lenses and they were focused on the front doors of the bank.

And the SWAT team approaching. *Shut it off. Shut it off.* If the hostage taker was watching . . .

As though he'd been speaking into the comms, the cameras from that angle shut down, but the station switched to the news chopper overhead. The view wasn't as good, but his imagination and experience could fill in the blanks.

A knock on the door snagged his attention, and he turned to find Dottie at the entrance, backpack on her shoulder, keys in her hand and threaded through her fingers.

"Hey, what's up?"

"Any word?" Her tight expression belied the casual question.

He hesitated, then nodded to the screen. "She'll be in the command post all safe and sound."

"Sometimes she gets out."

Yes, sometimes she apparently did, if the situation at the courthouse was any indication. "The cameras haven't picked her up, so I think she's still inside."

Dottie's shoulders relaxed a fraction, and Clay pulled a chair from the conference table and slid it next to his in front of the monitor. "What's your next class?"

"AP Chemistry."

He winced. "What's your grade in there?"

"I have a hundred and three average."

Okay, that was impressive. "Then you can sit for a bit. I'll write you a pass."

He didn't have to ask twice. She let her backpack drop to the floor and planted herself in the chair, gaze locked on the screen. "Thanks."

The SWAT team was ten yards from the front door of the bank and holding still. One lone officer dressed in K-9 gear approached and the officer indicated the door. The dog sniffed and three seconds later—probably on the signal from the K-9 officer—two SWAT members broke away from the others and slammed the door with the battering ram. The glass shattered and they filed inside one after another. He felt sure they'd managed to breach the bank from the back too, trapping those on the inside between them.

The screen went blank, the plug pulled on the media once again.

"Whoa," Dottie said, her voice low, almost a whisper.

"Yeah."

"Isn't that kind of dangerous?"

"Sure."

She shuddered. "I see what Julianna means when she says she has the safe job."

He smiled. "Looks like it's all over. Why don't you go on back to class?"

"Yeah. Okay. Thanks for letting me stay."

"Hey, Lamebrain, you're late for class."

Dottie hissed in a breath between clenched teeth and stiffened. Clay frowned and looked up to see Mary Ann McKinney standing in the doorway, an ugly smirk on her pretty face.

"What's this about?" he asked.

"It's not enough to be teacher's pet?" Mary Ann asked, ignoring Clay well enough that he might have been invisible. "You have to be *everyone's* pet?" She scoffed. "Hanging out with 'the sorry'? Like that's going to earn you popularity points."

Clay sighed. Some of the students referred to the SRO as "the sorry."

"I'm not looking for popularity points, Mary Ann," Dottie said, her voice low. "That's your domain." She looked at Clay. "Could I have that note now?"

"Of course." He scribbled an excuse and handed it to Dottie, turning away from Mary Ann. He could ignore with the best of them. "Julianna's professional, Dottie. Trust. her."

Dottie nodded, her expression thoughtful. "I'm learning to." She turned to leave the office, attempting to slip past Mary Ann, but the girl stepped in front of her.

"I hear you aced the last calculus test. I'm assuming you had a copy of it beforehand because that's the only way you'd get any of the answers right."

"Mary Ann!" Clay stepped forward. "That's enough."

"How's the new apartment?" Dottie asked. "Heard your parents kicked you out and you had to get a job waiting tables. Hope that doesn't cut into your study time too much."

Mary Ann's face drained of color and her mouth worked, but nothing came out. Dottie brushed past Mary Ann without touching her. In the time it took Mary Ann to recover, Dottie had disappeared around the corner. The girl clenched her fist and spun on her heel to leave.

"Hey, Mary Ann," Clay said, "hold up a minute, will you?"

She paired a groan with a dramatic sigh and turned. "What?"

"Just a friendly warning. Calling people names is a form of

bullying. You don't want to get in trouble with that this close to the end of the year, do you? Not with you being up for valedictorian and all, right?"

"And what about her? What *she* said doesn't matter, right?"

"She didn't call you names."

"Of course you would take her side."

"There aren't any sides here."

"Whatever."

"If you need help, Mary Ann, I'm here. All you have to do is ask for it."

She snorted. "As if." She spun on her heel again and flounced off.

He let her go with a mental note to keep an eye on her. Then let Dottie's parting phrase play in his mind once more. *"I'm learning to."*

He had a feeling the words held a deeper meaning than a simple response to his encouragement.

■ ■ ■ ■

"What do you mean, he's not there?" Julianna planted her hands on her hips and glared at the SWAT commander. They stood just outside the command post. "We had the place surrounded. I was just on the phone with him."

"I don't know what to tell you, but he's not in there. We searched every square inch, including the ceiling."

"I want to talk to the two hostages."

Hector nodded. "You think you'll recognize his voice when he was using the voice distorter?"

"They're both women," the commander said.

"Doesn't matter," Julianna said. "I want to hear them talk." She glanced at Hector. "Is the recording being analyzed?"

"As we speak." Sometimes it was possible to reverse the effect of the distorter to reveal the person's true voice.

She nodded. "Good. I'm going to head over to the ambulance and have a listen."

She walked over, thinking through everything. Once the dog had cleared the door for any type of explosive—and going on Zena's reassurance that the hostage taker was indeed somewhere else in the building and away from the doors—they'd breached.

Only to find the three dead and the two remaining hostages—including Zena—in different locations. The second was still blindfolded, zip-tied, and terrified.

They now sat in the back of different ambulances being questioned separately, and while it wasn't her job to investigate, Julianna couldn't wait to compare their stories.

". . . zip-tied me, blindfolded me, and pushed me behind the counter." The one closest to her had short dark hair, red-rimmed eyes, and blotching skin. She was in her midforties, ten pounds overweight, and very pretty. The woman sniffed. "I just came to get some cash to give to my daughter for a field trip and—" A shudder rippled through her. "Then there was all this smoke and he shot the guard and people were screaming and—"

"What time was this?" Julianna asked. This was not the person she'd talked to on the phone.

The agent questioning the woman turned, spotted her badge around her neck, and waited.

"Um . . . a little after eleven, I think."

"No wonder he wasn't there," Julianna murmured. "He left before we even got here."

"But you were talking to him," Hector said, stepping up beside her.

"So, he forwarded the number to a cell phone."

"A burner."

Julianna shook her head in frustration. "He came in, killed three people, then walked out before we even knew what was happening." She'd talk to the other hostage, but had no doubt she wasn't involved.

"And when we called the bank number, he answered on his cell and asked for you. Why?"

"I have no idea."

And people had died. Julianna left the investigation to the agents and headed to her Bucar. Her blood pumped while her emotions clamored for release. She'd held it together this long, she could make it home.

But she couldn't.

Five minutes away from her house, she pulled to the side of the road and dropped her forehead to the wheel while her throat grew tighter and her eyes burned hotter. She'd failed. People had *died*.

She gasped, then wheezed in a breath and let the sobs erupt. She lost track of time, but finally managed to gain control, grab a napkin from the glove box, and clean herself up.

That wasn't supposed to happen. She *saved* people, she didn't let them die. The fact that the hostages were dead before she arrived was the only thing that saved her sanity. There was nothing she could have said, nothing she could have done to change the outcome for them. Because she didn't even know about them until it was too late.

But the hostage taker had asked for Julianna. He'd made it personal. And now Julianna had to figure out why and how this person was related to the Manchester courtroom incident. If he was. She swiped her cheeks and frowned. The date on the dash display caught her eye. Images from her senior year of high school stalked into her memory . . .

"Put the gun down, Dennis. Please don't do this."

"You're mine. If I can't have you, no one will."

Julianna had reached a hand toward her ex in supplication. They'd been talking for hours with him, saying the same thing over and over. Several times, she thought he was going to put the weapon down.

"Mine forever, Julianna. Forever."

There'd been a blur of motion and the crack of gunfire filled her ears.

"Kane!" The high-pitched shriek turned into a keening wail. "No!" She rushed toward the shooter—

Stop! The mental order pulled her from the memory. Julianna cranked the car, aiming toward home. *You can't do anything about the past, so focus on the present.* What was the connection between the Manchester courtroom incident and the bank? A connection with two different hostage takers? Well, obviously Julianna was the connection. Right? But why ask for her? Again, was the bank hostage taker a Manchester fan? Or just a copycat? Or was this more personal in regard to his desire for justice?

She simply didn't know.

"But no one died in the courtroom incident," she muttered, "so not a copycat." Or was the bank hostage taker, Angel, angry *because* no one had died and decided to rectify the situation?

Julianna honestly had no idea.

When she pulled into the drive, Dottie's Jeep was there along with a car she didn't recognize. Great. Had she forgotten something? Try as she might, she couldn't remember Dottie telling her she'd planned to have someone over.

Putting on her "everything's fine" mask, Julianna climbed out of her sedan. When she walked into the house, she found Dottie and Reese at the kitchen table, psychology books open in front of them. "AP Psych, huh?"

Dottie rolled her eyes. "This exam is going to kill me."

"Surely not."

"Well, not literally, of course. I was whining to Reese about it, and she said she'd help me."

Reese lifted her hand in a wave. "Hi, Julianna."

"Hi. Thanks for offering to help."

The woman smiled. "I had the time. AP psych was one of my favorite classes. Granted, it had a lot to do with the cute professor, but I really did like the topic and aced the exam."

Julianna laughed. "Then I can't think of a more perfect tutor." Some of the stress of the day slid from her shoulders. "I hear you have a party in the works."

"You've been talking to Clay, huh?"

"A little bit."

"I hear you're invited." A slight smile curved her full lips.

Heat crept into Julianna's neck and she cleared her throat. "I'm looking forward to it."

"Jules doesn't socialize much," Dottie said with a smirk. "Let's hope she remembers how."

"Haha. You're cute."

Dottie grinned, then frowned. "Hey, you have some explaining to do."

And here it came. "About?"

"I want to hear the story about your grand theft auto days."

Yep. There it was. "It's a long story. I'll tell you after you ace your exams."

"Right." Her sister frowned as though wondering if she really would.

"I will, I promise."

"Okay."

Grateful for the reprieve, Julianna backed toward the kitchen door. "I'll leave you two alone, then." The doorbell rang and Julianna paused. "More study buddies?"

"No," Reese said, "that's probably Clay."

Her heart did *not* just skip a beat at the thought of seeing Clay Fox again. "Okay. And he's here because . . . ?"

"We asked him to bring pizza," Dottie said, hopping to her feet. She brushed past Julianna, heading to the front door.

Reese nodded. "And chocolate."

"Study necessities," Dottie called over her shoulder.

Julianna drew in a steadying breath. She was exhausted, but for some reason, the fact that Clay was now entering her home with pizza—and chocolate—sent her adrenaline surging. She headed for the coffeepot for a necessary caffeine fix.

He stepped into the kitchen and she turned. "Hey there."

"Hi."

He set the pizza on the table between the girls, and Dottie

lifted the cardboard lid to pull out a meat lover's slice. The cheese was still hot and slid over the sides, making Julianna's mouth water.

"I hope I'm not intruding," Clay said.

Julianna raised a brow. "You brought pizza."

"And chocolate." He set another bag on the table.

"Okay," Julianna said, "as for whether it's an intrusion, that depends."

"Jules!" Dottie looked mortified.

"On what?" Clay asked, amusement glinting in his gray gaze.

She eyed Dottie's slice. "What the toppings are. And your toppings look just right. I'm in."

"What are the appropriate toppings?" Clay asked.

"Meat without any nasty veggie stuff to ruin a good pizza."

"You don't like veggie pizza?"

She scowled at him and Dottie laughed. "She hates vegetables of all kinds. It's a wonder she hasn't developed some kind of nutrition deficit."

It was true. Julianna's abhorrence of most vegetables was legendary, and everyone who knew her took every opportunity to tease her about it. "I take a multivitamin each day," she said, "and between that and the food I do eat, somehow I've managed to avoid any nutrient deficiencies." She snagged a piece of the pizza and took a bite, savoring the explosion of flavors. She looked at Clay. "You can stay."

He laughed. "Thanks." Clay claimed a chair while Dottie put her pizza down long enough to grab four bottles of water from the refrigerator.

When they were all seated around the table, Julianna bowed her head and offered up a silent prayer of thanks for the food—for the families who'd lost loved ones today, and for the safety of her team.

When she looked up, the other three were staring at her. "Oops, should I have said that out loud?"

"Nope," Dottie said.

Clay shook his head, and Reese wrinkled her nose. "I'll consider mine blessed as well, thanks," she said.

Julianna's phone buzzed with a text from Hector.

> Voice analysis got nothing. Said if there was a
> voice changer used, it was a good one.

"Great," she muttered.

"Problem?" Clay asked.

She shook her head. "Just work passing on information. It's all good."

"Come on," Dottie said, "forget about work. We have pizza. With meat on it."

"No vegetables," Reese pointed out.

Julianna laughed and glanced at the man across from her to find him studying her. She held his gaze and he offered her a slight smile, but the crease between his brows said he was thinking about something. Something that involved her.

The fact that she wanted to know what it was surprised her. She'd stayed away from romantic entanglements for years for more reasons than one—the main one being she simply didn't believe anyone could handle all the baggage she came with. Which was why she'd had no trouble rebuffing interest from men who wanted to take her out. With her ability to talk through just about any situation, she'd been able to make them believe her rejection was a positive thing. She'd also managed to keep them on the friendship level.

So why did she have a feeling Clay could change all of that?

CHAPTER
NINE

Dropping in on the ladies could have been incredibly awkward, but they'd made him feel right at home. That could have been partly because of the pizza, but even if he'd arrived empty-handed, he had a feeling the end result would have been the same.

Now, he was happily stuffed and raging with curiosity about the woman loading the dishwasher. She worked with efficiency—her movements purposeful and graceful.

His phone buzzed with a text from his buddy, Vince.

We're getting together to watch the Braves play
at my place in about an hour. You in?

Let me get back to you on that.

What you got going on?

Hanging out with Reese and a few other people.

Like?

Some new friends.

What's her name?

LOL!

"Okay, we're out of here," Dottie announced from the kitchen doorway. She had a backpack slung over one shoulder.

Julianna shut the dishwasher and looked up. "Where are you going?"

"To Reese's. She asked me if I wanted to stay the night and help her get ready for her party."

"Oh, cool. Enjoy."

"Thanks."

Dottie and Reese headed for the door and Clay stood. "Hey, Dottie, could I talk to you about something real quick?"

Julianna looked up.

Dottie met his gaze and frowned. "Sure. I need to grab something from the den. Why don't we talk in there?"

Because she wanted privacy or because she really needed something? He followed her into the den and she spun. "You want to ask me about Mary Ann, don't you?"

"Yeah." Man, the girl had some mad observation skills. "Have I been that obvious?"

"Just to me. Don't worry about Mary Ann. I can handle her."

"I have a feeling what I saw in my office was mild compared to what she's capable of. What else is she doing or saying?"

"She's all mouth, Officer Clay. She's just jealous because I'm giving her a run for the valedictorian spot." She shrugged. "You know. I'm the new girl. I'm not supposed to challenge the queen bee."

Mary Ann McKinney definitely thought of herself as the queen. "I need to know if she's bullying you."

Dottie sighed. "Technically, you could probably call it that, but like I said, I can handle her. I know how to put her in her place."

"You shouldn't have to."

"I shouldn't have to do a lot of things, but life is what it is." She patted him on the shoulder. "Leave Mary Ann to me, okay?"

Reese appeared in the doorway. "Everything okay?"

"Everything's fine," Dottie said. "I'm ready when you are."

The girls left and Julianna stepped into the room. Clay tried not to fidget. Should he leave too, or do what he wanted, which was stay and talk to Julianna? He cleared his throat. "I guess I should go. You probably have stuff you need to do."

"You're welcome to stay awhile if you're not pressed for time."

"I'm not." His words zipped from his lips before he could at least slow them down. "I mean, I just have to go home and do some laundry. Talking to you sounds a lot more fun."

"Glad to know I rank above the laundry."

He groaned. "I didn't mean it like that."

"I know." She laughed. "Come on. Would you like something other than water? I have tea, coffee, and soda. Dottie thinks no one consumes enough water, so she doesn't offer other options when she's in charge of drinks."

"I'd love some coffee if it's not too much trouble."

When the coffee was finished, they carried their steaming cups into the den, and he took a seat on the couch while she settled into the recliner with a low groan.

"Long day?" he asked.

"You could say that."

"I heard about the dead hostages at the bank. I'm sorry."

She shuddered and he kicked himself for mentioning it.

"I'm sorry too," she said. "They were dead before we got there." She eyed him. "What was that all about with Dottie? Or shouldn't I ask?"

"Just some school stuff. Nothing major." He cleared his throat. "I do have a question for you."

She sipped her coffee. "Sure."

"Why'd you steal a car when you were fifteen?"

She laughed, a quick choked sound that faded as quickly as she'd released it. "Ah, yes. That's a story."

"Tell me." He kept his voice low.

"Why?"

"Because I'm curious."

"Hmm." She studied him and he held his breath, wondering

if she'd talk or send him home. "Okay," she finally said. "Why not?" She rubbed her eyes. "Dottie asked, but I managed to put off the explanation."

"She'll circle back to it."

"Yeah. She will." She drew in a deep breath and let it out slowly. "Okay, maybe telling it to you will make telling it to Dottie easier. So, my parents divorced when I was eleven. My dad now lives in Germany with his new wife. Mom did her research, found a man with money, and remarried shortly before my fourteenth birthday and had Dottie a year later. I'm pretty sure Mom and Jon were seeing each other before my parents' divorce was final."

"Ouch. Do you get along with your stepfather?"

She lifted a shoulder and tilted her head. "Eh. We tolerated each other back then. Now? I have no idea where he is or what he's doing. He left Mom when Dottie was five. She's actually my half sister."

"But y'all have the same last name."

"Dottie had it legally changed to Jameson last summer."

"Wow. Okay."

"Anyway, Dottie was a precious little girl with big blue eyes and a laugh that could always make me smile no matter how angsty I was feeling. I loved her deeply." She shot him a quick smile. "Still do."

"That's obvious."

"About three months before the car-theft 'incident'"—she wiggled air quotes around the word—"my stepfather's dad came to live with us. In addition to recovering from a mild stroke, he also suffered from emphysema." She pulled in a deep breath and her eyes flickered with something he couldn't identify. "Let's just say that he was not a nice person. He was never physically abusive, but he could tear you down with just a few words. I pretty much hated him, and he felt the same about me. Add to my fury that Mom would allow him to live there, and the house was a ticking bomb."

Clay frowned. "Why let him live there? Did she have a choice?"

"Oh, sure. She ran the house. My stepfather was spineless, and my mother used that to her advantage any chance she got—which was all the time. She also knew my stepfather would inherit big-time from his dad, and so she did her best to suck up to the man before he died."

"Ah."

"Yeah." Julianna pressed a palm to her forehead.

"Headache?"

"Memories of that time in my life always go straight to my head."

He frowned. "Then never mind. You don't have to tell me."

"No, it's okay. Like I said, telling you is good practice for when I have to tell Dottie."

"I can't believe you haven't told her already."

She gave him a wry smile. "Well, after the program this morning, she knows I stole a car at the age of fifteen, but she doesn't know the details. And she doesn't remember her grandfather." Her eyes turned dark and shadowy before they slid from his. "He died." She shuddered. "I killed him."

■　■　■　■

At Clay's flinch, she held up a hand. "Not in a way that would get me arrested, but with my . . . words."

His gaze sharpened. "What do you mean?"

Why was she sharing such personal details? Had today's incident at the bank affected her more than she'd thought? Loosened her tongue more than usual? Or was she just tired of carrying the burden of her past alone?

All of the above, probably.

"I said a lot of things I shouldn't have said."

That moment in time was so clear.

Her step-grandfather had been particularly nasty and she let him have it. "I wish you'd never come here. You've ruined everything! You're a horrible, nasty old man, and I wish you'd just go ahead and die so we could have some peace around here."

97

"Juli!" *Her mother's horrified voice spun her around.* "Shut up!"

But Julianna was on a roll. "And you're not much better." *She jabbed a finger at her mom.* "You let him get away with his nasty accusations and emotional abuse. The question is, How could you? What kind of mother does that?"

"Get out! Get out and don't come back until you can keep a civil tongue in your head."

"So, I left," she said. "I ran out of the house to get myself under control. I hated that I'd lost it with him. He was an old, dying man and I'd stooped to his level, let him get to me. Same with my mother. After a few hours, I got myself together, worked out my apology in my head, and headed home to eat crow."

"How'd that taste?"

"I didn't get a chance to find out. When I walked back in the door, my mother greeted me with the news that he was dead. He had a massive heart attack about five minutes after I left."

His eyes widened slightly. "So that's what you meant about your words killing him."

"Yeah."

"You know that's not possible, right?"

She gave him a small smile. "In my head, I do. Of course."

"But you still blame yourself?"

"Yes. And no." She picked at nonexistent lint on her shirt. "I'll always wonder if he would have died that night if I had just bitten my tongue. I can't get past the fact that my words may have caused his blood pressure and heart rate to spike, leading to a heart attack." Her jaw tightened for a moment, then she let out a low breath. "He didn't deserve that from me. Oh, he was a rotten old man with a wicked tongue, but looking back, he was hurting too, and by allowing my temper to get the best of me, I wonder if I hastened his death."

"Okay, can I say something that may come across as kind of snarky, but I don't mean it that way?"

She huffed a short laugh. "Sure."

"Isn't that giving yourself a lot of power? The power over when a man lives or dies?"

"People do it every day, Clay. Just because I didn't use a gun or a knife to kill him, it's very possible my words did. And don't get me wrong, I'm not saying it caught God by surprise. I'm saying the man's death could have been a consequence of a choice I made." She swallowed against the tightness in her throat. "Could God have stopped it? Sure. But he didn't. I feel like I'm at least partially responsible for his death, and I'll admit that it eats at me sometimes. As awful as he was, his life still meant something. All life is precious. From the unborn child to the person with dementia who doesn't realize they're in this world. Their lives are still important."

Clay was still, staring at the floor. "Yeah," he finally said, "I agree with that. And I see what you mean."

"I do believe that God is in control, but we're not robots. We make choices. Sometimes those choices affect other people, in good ways and not-so-good ways. I just try to make better choices now."

"I used to believe God was in control, but I've been having a hard time with that lately."

"Why?"

"Being overseas, you see a lot of stuff you can't unsee. It stays with you, plays with your head. You have to know what I mean."

"I do. But I still believe God's in control. People have free will. We make choices and those choices have consequences. And, unfortunately, sometimes those consequences change other people's lives forever."

"No kidding."

"Doesn't mean God's not paying attention or doesn't care. He's there to get us through whatever we have to face. We have the choice to believe him or not."

"It's that simple for you?"

She nodded. "It didn't used to be, but"—a shrug—"it's easier now. Some days more than others. Some days I try to snatch the control back, but usually wind up not wanting the responsibility and toss it back to God."

He cleared his throat. "How does stealing the car fit in the picture?"

She pressed fingers to her burning eyes. Then she lowered her hand and met Clay's gaze. "I could tell my stepfather was boiling about something. He was usually so meek and mild that I could almost forget he existed, but three days later, after the funeral, when we got home he exploded." The memories flashed and Julianna let them play out. "He said it was my fault his father was dead, that I was an ungrateful so-and-so, to get out of his house, and he never wanted to see me again."

Clay reached over and took her hand. "Wow."

"I can look back on that moment now and realize it was his pain talking, but the truth is, I was reeling with guilt. I hated myself and the fact that I allowed my temper to rule. I grabbed his keys and ran to his car. I took off with no destination in mind, and forty-five minutes later, I was in cuffs in the back of a cruiser. He pressed charges and I went to juvie."

"Whoa, that's harsh."

"Best thing that ever happened to me," she said.

"Um . . . sorry?"

Julianna laughed. "That's where I met a wonderful woman who counseled me on anger management and introduced me to God. I also met three of my best friends in that place." She smiled. "I know it's crazy, but I'd go through it all again if I had to. I'd never trade the friendships I have with Penny, Grace, and Raina."

"They must be pretty amazing."

"They are."

Julianna just realized Clay still held her hand. She eased away from his grip. "Sorry. You probably didn't plan on a heavy conversation when you asked a simple question of why I stole a car." She stood. "How much do I owe you for the pizza?"

He rose to face her. "Is that my hint to go?"

"Maybe." She crossed her arms. "Sorry, I don't ever share that much and I guess I'm just feeling a little vulnerable at the moment. It's got me antsy."

"Would it help ease the awkwardness if I told you that an innocent man is dead because of me?"

She gasped and stilled. "I'm sorry, what?"

He grimaced. "That was kind of abrupt, wasn't it?"

"You think?"

"I guess I was trying to make you feel better by saying I understand how you feel, but maybe I don't. They're two totally different situations. Never mind. Forget it."

She planted her hands on her hips. "Forget it? Really? I don't think so. You can't just drop that bomb and then walk away."

He huffed a short laugh. "Well, I should probably ask you out and at least buy you dinner before unloading my baggage."

"I just unloaded mine. It's your turn. Proper etiquette and all that. If you think you have to buy me dinner first, I won't pay you for the pizza. Talk." Just as he opened his mouth to respond, his phone buzzed.

He grabbed it like a drowning swimmer would clutch for a life jacket and glanced at the screen. "It's my mom. Probably calling about Reese's party tomorrow, so I should take this. You and I'll catch up later, okay?"

She almost laughed at the sheer relief on his features, but instead, lasered him with a look. "Yes. We will. You can only postpone unpacking baggage for so long before it starts to rot."

"Um, right."

He practically flew out the door, and Julianna bit her lip on a smile. Then let her shoulders sag and the adrenaline crash. She glanced at the clock. Six forty-five. She usually didn't go to bed until around ten—and that was when she wasn't working.

But tonight?

A seven o'clock bedtime was her new goal in life.

CHAPTER
TEN

FRIDAY EVENING

Felicity was tired. It had been a long day on her feet and all she wanted to do was go home, get Tommy in bed, and enjoy a long hot soak in the tub. But the joy on Tommy's face at the moment lifted her spirits and infused a bit of energy into her weary bones.

Ketchup dripped from his chin, and she swiped it with a napkin before it had a chance to hit his shirt. "I'm glad to see you're enjoying that burger."

He chewed and rolled his eyes in bliss. "It's the best thing I've had in *years*."

Felicity laughed, and as always, the laughter was tinged with a hint of sadness. Wyatt would have laughed too, caught her eye, and winked. But he wasn't here and never would be again. She cleared her throat and jabbed the fork at her salad. "Tell me about your day," she said, pasting a smile on her face for her exuberant son. No way would she allow her sorrow to taint his joy.

"Well, Gerald and Bailey got into a fight today over the crayons. It was so *ridiculous*. And Mrs. Young said . . ."

Felicity listened and processed with one part of her brain while the other part sorted through other nagging thoughts. Like maybe she should use what was left of her husband's life insurance money to make their lives a little easier. The payout after Wyatt's death had been enough to take care of their debt and the house, and if she continued to be very careful, by the time Tommy finished high school, he'd have a nice balance for his first year of college. Maybe she was crazy to hold on to that money so tightly, but as long as she could keep the roof over their heads and the car on the road—and the occasional hamburger in Tommy's stomach—she would leave the money alone.

"Mom?"

She blinked. "What?"

"Are you okay?"

The frown on his little face sent a dart of shame through her. She'd thought she'd been listening, but obviously not. "Sorry, hon, I'm just tired, I think. It's been a very long day."

"But we're still going to Nate's house, right?"

Bible study. She'd completely forgotten about it. "Oh, honey, I'm—" The crushed look on his face had her biting her tongue and forcing another smile. "Yes, of course we'll go." She glanced at her watch, all thoughts of having a few minutes of relaxing solitude bursting like the bubbles she'd planned to soak in. It started at seven. They'd be late, but no one would care.

Fifteen minutes later, she and Tommy stepped inside the home belonging to Brian and Lucy Garrison. Their six-year-old son, Nate, came barreling into the foyer, grabbed Tommy by the hand, and the two boys raced up the stairs, heading for Nate's room.

Tommy's little-boy giggle reached her just before the door slammed, and Felicity smiled. Coming was a good thing. They both needed this. Yes, she was tired, but her tired was more than physical. A spiritual rejuvenation was always welcome.

Once she was seated in the den with the other ladies, Lucy opened her Bible. "Let's go to Ephesians 4:32."

Felicity complied, finding the passage easily. It was a verse she didn't need to look up because she prayed it every day, but she read along with Lucy, hoping the words would penetrate the wall around her heart. "Be kind to one another, tenderhearted, forgiving one another, as God in Christ forgave you."

Help me forgive, Lord.

■ ■ ■ ■

Dottie had as much enthusiasm to study as she would if she were going to get a root canal. Not that she'd ever actually had one, but it sounded horrid. She honestly didn't think she'd make it to Reese's house without a shot of caffeine. She activated the Bluetooth on her phone and gave the voice command to call Reese's number. "Hey," she said when Reese answered, "I need coffee. Like a specialty one. Can you pull through that coffee shop at the corner of Bridges?"

"Sure. You just want to study there for a while?"

"Yeah. I might need a refill."

The drive-thru line was wrapped around the building. Good choice to go in. Dottie found a parking spot for her Jeep, grabbed her backpack, and climbed out.

Reese joined her at the door. "This place is super busy."

"You mind waiting?"

"No." Reese shrugged. "This is normal. Normal is good for me right now."

"Yeah. What's normal anyway?"

"Normal is hanging out with a new friend at a yummy coffee shop and not thinking about hostage situations or wondering if someone is going to shoot me."

"Right. Normal has a lot going for it."

Reese laughed, and Dottie was glad it didn't sound forced.

They walked inside and ordered. The crowd left few table options, but she finally spotted one near the corner next to the bathrooms. People would come and go past their table, but Dottie had long ago learned to tune out minor annoyances. She grabbed the chair and placed her backpack on the floor next to it. Her keys clanked against the metal leg of the chair and Dottie smiled. She hadn't taken them off to thread through her fingers since . . . okay, since that afternoon, when she'd been so worried about her sister.

Reese plopped into the chair opposite her, and they got to work, stopping only to get their drinks. For the next hour, they studied, with Reese quizzing her and Dottie answering.

Reese finally set aside the flash cards Dottie had made and shook her head. "You don't need me. You've got this."

"I think I've got this because of your help."

A woman stopped near their table and knelt down next to Dottie's chair. Her long dark hair fell over her shoulders, and she looked up with a smile, her eyes friendly behind her stylish glasses. Her fingers worked a shoelace. "Sorry. Didn't want to trip."

"No problem."

"Well, well, what's this?"

Mary Ann's taunting voice came from behind Dottie. Her nemesis walked over, spotted the study cards, glanced at Reese, then back at Dottie. "You have a tutor?" She laughed. "If you need a tutor, you don't deserve to be valedictorian. Give it up, *Dorothy*. Go back to Oz where you belong."

Dottie stood so fast, her chair slid back and tipped over. Mary Ann's eyes flared with fear for a nanosecond, but it was enough to calm Dottie's surge of rage. She picked up the chair, noting the woman had stopped tying her shoes and was looking on with interest. She ignored her and focused on Mary Ann. "Why don't you taunt me about wondering how it feels to know that my own parents don't want me?" She mock gasped. "Oh wait, you can't because you know how it feels too. Crawl back in your hole, McKinney. I'm not lowering myself to your standards and you're not going to get the best of me."

Mary Ann bared her teeth in a feral smile and let her gaze take note of the attention they were getting. "I'll see you in school." She finished the sentence with an unflattering name and flounced off to the bathroom.

Dottie gathered her things. "Do you mind if we finish this at your place?" She slung her backpack over her shoulder.

"I think that might be a good idea." Reese followed Dottie out to the parking lot. "Just follow me. I only live about three minutes from here."

"Great. I'll be right behind you." She grabbed her keys from the hook on her backpack, then tossed the bag into the passenger seat. She threaded the keys through her fingers. Drawing them in and out, weaving them while she waited for Reese. Then realized what she was doing and sighed. She shoved the key into the ignition and twisted it. "Don't let her get to you," she whispered. She'd dealt with a bully of a mother all her life. If she could handle her mother, she could handle Mary Ann McKinney. The girl was just insecure, hurting, and angry. Much like she had been once upon a time. Before moving in with Jules.

But that didn't mean she had to take the girl's words without fighting back. She'd said she wasn't stooping to Mary Ann's level, but she had. More than once now. Next time, she'd try to be kind and see if that changed the girl's attitude toward her. Mary Ann was smart, she worked hard, and Dottie would freely admit she deserved the valedictorian title.

But so did Dottie, and she wouldn't give it up without a fight.

She followed Reese out of the parking lot and looked forward to the rest of a peaceful evening. She was very tired of drama—and studying—and was ready to chill.

"Go away, Mary Ann," she muttered. "Get out of my head."

When they pulled into Reese's parking lot, Dottie was already feeling better. She texted Julianna.

> Just left the coffee shop. I'm at Reese's house. Talk to you in the morning. Get some rest. Love you.

Reese climbed out. "Want some ice cream?"

"You said the magic words."

Five minutes later, they sat at Reese's table. Dottie lifted her bowl in a "cheers" motion. "To my new friend."

Reese mimicked her. "To friends."

"And peaceful, boring evenings binge-watching . . . something."

"Amen!" She paused and frowned.

"What?" Dottie asked.

"If I can find the remote."

Dottie snickered. Then laughed. And dug into her ice cream.

■ ■ ■ ■

Clay had been right. His mother had wanted to talk about Reese's party and make sure he'd have the cupcakes. "I'll have them, Mom, I promise. I'm headed there now to pick them up." It was the only food item she'd allowed to be purchased, and that was because they were Reese's favorite.

He could have picked them up tomorrow, but now would work better. He'd stopped by the school to finish up some paperwork and now headed to the bake shop, replaying the evening with Julianna in his head. Every time he talked to her, the more time he spent with her, the more he liked her. And the more he wanted to know about her.

And the more he had to steel his heart against falling for her.

So stay away from her, moron.

Easier said than done. He *liked* her.

Which was exactly why he should drop off her radar. Unfortunately, that would be impossible now that he'd asked her to plan a demo for the high school. He'd have to be actively involved in that.

Oh, and she'd be at Reese's birthday party, so there was that. Right. Staying away from her wasn't happening in the near future. But they could be friends. Men and women did it all the time. Became friends and stayed friends.

Too bad his heart didn't agree with that argument when it came to Julianna.

Thirty minutes later, after answering all of Curly's mother's questions about her son's behavior in school, he had the cupcakes in his car and was headed home.

Reese lived in a small townhouse about five minutes away from Clay's home. He'd tried to convince her to buy the house next to his when it had gone up for sale three months ago and she'd laughed at him. "Come on, Clay, it's a nice house for a family, but much too big for me."

Not even his promises of helping her keep the yard mowed could sway her. She had a two-bedroom, two-bath place that she insisted suited her just fine. He had to agree, albeit a bit grudgingly.

The short row of townhomes had been built at the edge of a larger neighborhood. The back of Reese's home faced the wooded area that surrounded the community, while the front overlooked one of the sprawling backyards of the nearest house.

He drove by her home often, playing the big brother card, stating it was his responsibility to make sure she was safe. The fact that it was on his route to his own home made checking on her that much easier.

Tonight, when he rolled past, Dottie's Jeep was parked in the second spot of the unit. He smiled, glad his sister had company. She'd stayed with him for three nights after the courthouse incident but finally insisted on going home. He had no idea how she was sleeping, but her appearance didn't seem to suggest she wasn't.

He wheeled his Ford Escape toward his house while his mind went to Julianna Jameson yet again. The woman intrigued him like no one he'd ever met. Not even the woman who'd broken his heart after the—

Well, *after*.

But what in the world had he been thinking, blurting out that he'd killed someone? An *innocent* someone? He hadn't uttered those words since he'd quit seeing his therapist six months ago. And Julianna's keen observation skills should send him running in the opposite direction. The last thing he needed—or wanted—was someone who analyzed him.

And yet—

Why was it he always had an "and yet" when it came to talking himself out of pursuing something more than friendship with Julianna?

His phone buzzed and he hit the button on the dash to activate the Bluetooth. "Yeah, Reese's-cup, what is it?"

"Clay, I think someone's trying to get in my house."

Clay hit the brake, checked the mirror, and spun the wheel into a one-eighty turn. "I'm on the way. Call 911." He flipped on the blue lights and pressed the gas.

"Dottie's doing that now. I called you."

"Which door?"

"The back French doors off the patio."

"You have your weapon?"

"Yes, of course, but I really don't want to shoot anyone."

Her words sent his blood running cold. "I know you don't, but if he gets in the house, you pull the trigger, you hear me? Aim for center mass. Three pops."

"I will." The slight quiver in her voice caused his hands to clench tighter around the wheel.

"Where are you now?"

"Watching the French doors from the kitchen. I'm on the floor, peering around the cabinet. Dottie's watching the back door and on the phone with 911."

"I'm two minutes away. Can you see him?"

"No. Why is this happening, Clay? First the courthouse and now this?" His sister was used to dealing with emergency situations and staying calm in the face of things that would cause other people to panic, but the edge of hysteria in her words sent his protective instincts into high gear.

"I don't know, Reese. Just keep your head together and stay calm. You can panic when it's over."

Her rapid breaths came through the line. "I know. I'm okay. He's still outside. No need to panic unless he gets in, right?"

"Exactly. One minute away."

"He's at the front door now." Dottie's loud whisper carried to Clay's ear.

"Aim the gun at the door," he told Reese. "Pull the trigger if he comes through." Visions of another shooting flickered through his mind.

"Clay, I don't think I can."

"You won't have to. I'm almost there."

But the truth was, he didn't know if he'd be able to pull the trigger either.

CHAPTER
ELEVEN

Julianna was ready to turn out the light and close her eyes—about two and a half hours later than she'd planned—when her phone vibrated on the nightstand. She grabbed it and answered. "What's up, Max?" Special Agent Max Richardson was often at the scenes Julianna worked. He was a nice man and fabulous agent. If Max was working this case, his partner, Lydia Hughes, probably was too.

"Hey, I hope I didn't wake you?" he said.

"I wish you'd had the chance to do so, but no, I'm not asleep yet."

"Sorry. I just wanted to touch base with you real quick. We're working with local authorities on the investigation of the murders of the hostages at the bank. And how the killer managed to get in and get out before law enforcement even arrived on scene."

"Okay."

"Would you be willing to meet in the morning to go over your paperwork and . . . I have something I need to show you."

"What is it?"

"The hostage taker left something behind. A poem. A bad poem, but it might have a message you can decipher."

"Read it to me?" She didn't want to wait until morning to know what it said.

"Yeah, okay. Hold on. I figured you might want to hear it." He cleared his throat.

"Tick tock, the time has come,
Tick tock, the hands have spun,
No more screams, no more tears,
No more passing of the years.
Blood stains your hands, death haunts your soul,
Your empty words, a vast black hole."

When he fell silent, she let the words echo through her mind, trying to decipher their meaning—and put a face to the author.

"Jules? You still there?"

"Yeah, just thinking. Can you take a picture of it and text it to me?"

"Sure. Doing it now."

Five seconds later, her phone pinged and she ignored the text for the moment. "Are you saying you believe the poem is directed at me?"

"Kinda sounds like it," Max said. "And I'd only say that because the bank hostage taker asked to talk to you specifically during the incident."

He had a point. "And he talks about 'empty words,'" she murmured. "Could this have anything at all to do with the Manchester incident?"

"I don't know. Lydia and I have been going over the similarities—and there are several—but it's definitely a different person at the bank. Manchester and his five cohorts are sitting in prison awaiting their trial date. Of course, it could be someone else connected to him, but it's not looking likely. The bank appears to be a completely separate incident with similar attributes. He cleaned out the drawers before he left, so he's got plenty of cash."

"So, he goes in, kills the guard, points the weapon at another hostage, and tells anyone if they move, they're dead."

"According to the two hostages who survived, at that point, everyone freezes," Max said, playing along with her building the scene.

"He gets one hostage to tie up the rest and separate them out of view of the main area. He threatens them, of course, telling them that if anyone tries anything, he'll shoot them—"

"Or one of their coworkers."

"Yeah, but lets the mother and child go, like Manchester did." She paused. "Why didn't one of the tellers behind the counter press the button?"

"I asked. Zena said everyone was too terrified to move once he yelled for hands up. Said if anyone pressed the button and the cops showed up, he'd kill every person in there."

She nodded. "All right. With the guard on the floor, I'd say they had good reason to obey."

"Agreed," Max said. "Then, according to one of the hostages, the guy disappears behind the counter and cleans out the drawers before going to each group to tell them he's watching them. He kills one person in one group, two in the other . . ."

"But not Zena, because she managed to get away and he didn't have time to find her—"

"Because we were on the way."

"So, he slipped out of the bank's back door."

"Which has a camera."

Julianna raised a brow. "And it shows . . . ?"

"The top of an umbrella. The same umbrella used by one of the customers we saw entering just before everything went down."

"So, which customer did the umbrella belong to?"

"Still working on that one. Assuming the two who survived were being truthful, they said it wasn't theirs. Still asking family members of the deceased. Two said they had no idea. One said no."

"I think it belonged to him," Julianna said. "He used it to disguise his entrance and exit."

"Yeah, that occurred to me too."

"He deliberately picked a rainy day so he could use the umbrella to hide from the cameras without arousing any suspicion."

"Smart." She heard the resentment behind the word. Dumb criminals were always a favorite. Smart ones just made their jobs harder.

"One question I have is, did he deliberately sit outside the bank watching and waiting for a mother and child to go in, or did that just happen?"

"I'm betting it was deliberate."

"Yeah. I mean, mothers take their children to banks all the time, but most use the drive-thru because they don't want to expend the effort in getting their child out of the car seat, et cetera, but maybe this guy just lucked out."

"Maybe. We won't know until we can ask him."

Which would hopefully be soon. "That all sounds great in theory, but . . . why me? And the note?"

"Well, keeping the note out of the equation for the moment, and speculating that the bank hostage taker has a bit of Manchester hero worship—maybe he admired the guy, the fact that he took a plane hostage, killed six people, and so on. He decided to have his own little hostage situation and made sure to get the same hostage negotiator that Manchester had. Because that's cool, right?"

"Right," she muttered. "Because having the same negotiator as a notorious hijacker was status raising?"

"Who knows?" Max said. "But now I'm thinking that theory doesn't hold much water, because of the note."

"Yeah, that makes it kind of personal." She paused. "So, I've managed to make someone angry, and he's decided it would be a good idea to hold people hostage, ask for me specifically to be his negotiator, and then leave a really bad poem behind." She shook her head. "That's just stupid." In her eyes anyway. It sure must make sense to him. "Maybe he thought getting one over on me would raise his status somehow?"

"Whatever the case, it's definitely weird. We're looking at Manchester's sister as a possible suspect, but honestly, I don't think she has anything to do with it. I think she was there to support him, but I don't think she'd kill for him."

But they'd clear her and move on. She rubbed a hand over her eyes. "I'll be in around eight. Will that work for you?"

"That works. We'll go over the incidents with a fine-tooth comb and see if anything else pops out at us."

"Perfect. Good night, Max."

"Sleep well."

If only. "Thanks. See you in the morning." She hung up and flopped back onto the pillow to stare at the ceiling. *God, please let me sleep. Keep the nightmares away. I need to be rested for tomorrow.*

■ ■ ■ ■

Clay wheeled into her drive and pulled his weapon for the first time in a year. "I'm here, Reese."

"I think he's gone," she said, "but he might be close by."

"Stay put until we give the all clear."

Two cruisers pulled to a stop behind him. He'd had Dottie describe his vehicle to the dispatcher so they wouldn't confuse him with the intruder. He was even more glad to see the officers were Paul Fallon and Gayle Standish.

"The other officers are here too," Clay said into the phone. "We're going to check the outside. Just stay where you are until I give you the all clear, understand?"

"Yes."

Clay let the officers know Reese was armed and that she and Dottie would be staying in the house until told otherwise.

"Okay, Reese, where did you last see him?"

"He was trying to come in the front door," Reese said, "then

115

he started going around the house, trying all of the windows. He had on all black, even a ski mask. I only got a glimpse of him, but he was super creepy." She gave a shuddering sigh. "I thought he might just go ahead and break a window, but we heard the sirens and he disappeared."

"All right. Stay alert and stay on the line." Clay joined Paul and Gayle. "Thanks for getting here so fast. I think your sirens scared him off."

"We'll take a look around anyway," Gayle said. She headed for the back of the townhome and Clay aimed himself at the front. Paul walked down the sidewalk, weapon in his hand. The front porch light was on, illuminating the wood planks and the two white rockers he'd bought for Reese when she'd moved in.

The door to the townhome next door opened, and Reese's neighbor, Bob Owens, stepped outside. "Clay? That you?"

"Yes, sir."

The sixty-year-old peered at him over wire-rimmed glasses. He'd finger-combed his salt-and-pepper hair, and pieces of it stuck up around the crown of his head.

"What's going on? The blue lights and sirens woke me up."

"Someone tried to get into Reese's place, but he's gone now. Go on back to bed."

"Tried to get in? Like breaking and entering?"

"Exactly like that."

"Well, how about that? We haven't had that kind of trouble around here. Ever, I don't think." His fierce frown said he didn't like that trouble had arrived basically on his doorstep.

"I know. That's one reason I was glad Reese lived here."

"All right, well, I never noticed anyone out here. Woulda slept through it all anyway most likely." He shook his head. "That girl needs an alarm system."

"We can agree on that." He'd offered to have a friend put one in for her when she'd bought the place, but Reese had refused, saying she felt safe enough in the area. He should have insisted.

"Let me know if you need anything from me."

The dirt on Reese's steps captured his attention. "Hold on, Mr. Owens."

"Sure, what's up?"

"I'm pretty familiar with the dirt around here since I helped Reese change all the shrubbery and plant some flowers."

"Yeah, during the middle of the heat wave. Never knew a body could sweat like you did."

Clay almost smiled, but his focus was on the dirt. "You work with the soil a lot. You recognize that kind?" He pulled the Maglite from his belt and aimed it at the steps.

Mr. Owens walked over and squinted. "Nope. That almost looks more like clay or something. I don't think I've seen that around here."

"It's dry too," he murmured, more to himself than Mr. Owens. "Thank you, that's what I thought."

"I'm going back to bed. You tell Reese to call me if she needs me. I'm happy to look out for her. You know that."

"I know. I appreciate it."

Mr. Owens returned to his home and shut the door. The lights went on in the home on the other side of his, and while the curtains fluttered, no one stepped outside.

Gayle returned from the back of the house, and Paul walked their way, his steps sure on the concrete sidewalk.

"Find anything?" Clay asked Gayle.

She held up an evidence bag. "Plastic wrap from a pack of crackers. Might be nothing more than flyaway trash from someone's can, but the location was kind of interesting. It was discarded in a nice spot to watch the unit."

He nodded. "You'll take it to the lab?"

"I can. Not sure the priority level it'll receive, but at least they'll have it."

"Thanks." Clay knew the priority level. Pretty much nonexistent, but at least it would be there should this turn into the start of a string of attempted home invasions. "Can you take a sample of that dirt?" He pointed to it, and she pulled another bag from her pocket to do as he requested. "The lab can tell us what region it's from, at least."

"Yeah."

"You think you two could ride through here a little more often to make sure this guy doesn't come back?"

"Absolutely," Paul said.

Clay spoke into the phone. "Reese, put the gun away. Y'all can come out now. It's clear."

They must have been hovering by the front door because it opened almost immediately. Reese ran to him and hugged him. He clasped her to him and wrapped an arm around Dottie's shoulders. "You okay, Dottie?"

She nodded.

He explained what they found, then looked at his sister. "You ready for me to help you get that alarm system installed?"

She grimaced. "Yeah. I think I am."

"I'm not sure it's you that has anything to worry about," Dottie said.

Clay frowned. "What?"

She nodded to her Jeep, and he followed her gaze to see a piece of paper fluttering under the windshield wiper. "That wasn't there when I went inside."

Clay frowned. "A note?"

"I guess. I just noticed it."

"I need another evidence bag."

Gayle handed him one.

Using a gloved hand, he snagged the corner of the paper and pulled it from under the wiper. Once it was safely in the bag, he sealed and labeled it.

Then read aloud,

> "Tick tock, the time is nigh,
> D-day is coming, I won't lie.

The hands still spin, ticking off the cost
Of minutes and hours, days and years lost."

"That's really bad poetry," Dottie said, her voice low. "Why leave it on my Jeep?"

His gaze met hers. "I don't know." He handed the evidence bag off to Gayle. "Thanks."

Dottie swallowed and drew in a shallow breath. "I think we need to show this to Julianna."

"I agree. Why don't you try to call her on the way?"

"Already dialing."

■ ■ ■ ■

I stood there watching her sleep. *Julianna Jameson.* I rolled her name around in my head while I let the rage finally bubble toward the surface. It was all her fault I'd lost the only person who'd ever loved me. How easy it would be to simply kill her now. But what would I do after that? If she died tonight, it would all be over and I'd miss the pleasure of watching her confusion as she scrambled to figure out who could possibly be the one taunting her.

If she died tonight, I wouldn't have the satisfaction of watching her suffer.

And she *had* to suffer. It was only fair.

An eye for an eye.

My fingers still curled around the weapon I wasn't supposed to have. Psychiatric patients couldn't be trusted with guns. At least, that's what *they* said.

What did they know?

I'd been very responsible with the gun I had. I'd only killed those who'd been destined to die for the purpose. Those who took me one step closer to the fulfillment of the mission.

Or got in the way of it.

The curtains were open, allowing soft moonlight to illuminate the room. I turned and studied the picture she had on the nightstand. The one next to her gun. I left her firearm alone as I only needed one to fulfill the mission. Instead, I aimed my attention at the photo. Julianna and her sister, Dottie, stood arm in arm in front of a Christmas tree. Julianna had a huge smile on her face and her eyes glistened with what looked like tears.

Her blatant affection for the teen was obvious, and while I'd tried to work with that tonight, I'd failed.

But I wouldn't fail again.

How will I know when it's time?

You'll know.

And now wasn't it.

I eyed the gun one more time, glanced at the sleeping woman on the bed, then turned on silent feet and headed out the bedroom door. No doubt, Dottie would be coming home soon, after the scare at her friend's house. I'd take care of her when she got here, then sit back and watch Julianna deal with the fallout. I slipped out the door and bumped into the small table in the hallway, knocking it against the wall with a soft thud.

I froze, then turned to see Julianna roll over, then still.

Once more I hesitated. Gripped the weapon.

Kill her now and be done with it!

Why did the voices conflict? Which one should I listen to?

I took a step back toward the bedroom.

CHAPTER
TWELVE

Julianna lay still, listening, in tune with the vibe in her home, aware of the disturbance in the air. She must have dozed off, because the next thing she knew, she was awakened by something. A sound? A feeling?

It didn't matter. Someone was in her house.

Had Dottie come home? She glanced at the clock. Ten minutes past eleven. She'd slept for thirty minutes at the most. Julianna sat up and grabbed her weapon from the nightstand, then her phone. Two calls from Dottie and three texts. They'd come in four minutes ago, and Julianna had been sleeping so hard she hadn't heard the phone buzz. The last text read,

On the way home.

Julianna relaxed a fraction. Then frowned.

Why would Dottie turn the light off in the hall? They always left it on. "So, maybe the light bulb burned out?" she muttered.

Are you home?

Julianna sent the text to Dottie, then waited, ears tuned to any noise that shouldn't be there.

Dottie finally responded.

Not yet. On the way. FYI, not texting and driving. At a light. But had a really weird experience we need to talk about.

Weird experience? What could be more weird than her previous texts stating someone had tried to break into Reese's home, but they were safe, just a little shook up, and Clay and Reese were following Dottie home?

Almost there.

Julianna tucked the phone into the pocket of her sleep pants and gripped her weapon. She closed her eyes and tuned all her senses to the air around her, wondering if she was imagining things.

And there it was. The sound of someone in the hall. The feeling of someone watching her.

Definitely not her imagination.

"I'm an FBI agent," she said, her voice sounding loud in the dark room. "I have my weapon. Why are you in my house?" She dialed 911 and turned the volume all the way down.

Silence, then receding footsteps heading toward the front door.

Julianna slid from her bed, aimed her gun at the doorway, then hurried after the intruder. She paused at the door. There may have only been one set of footsteps, but that didn't mean there was just one person. With only a short hesitation, she buttonholed around the doorjamb and dropped into a crouch.

Nothing.

She squinted into the darkness, broken only by a sliver of moonlight coming from the window at the top of the stairs. She ignored the rush of adrenaline and her pounding heart. Why was her house so stinking dark? Every light had been turned off.

Or had someone found her breaker box in the garage?

She crept down the hallway, cautious yet in a hurry at the same time.

A car door slammed, then the front door opened. "Julianna!"

"Dottie! Get back in your car and lock the door!" She hurried to the front door, nerves on high alert for the intruder who'd been headed this way only seconds before.

"What?"

She herded the girl back onto the porch. "Just get back in your car."

Another car rolled to a stop behind Dottie's Jeep, and she recognized Clay's vehicle.

He exited, weapon in hand. "What is it? What's wrong?"

"Someone was in my house and he just came out this door. At least, I thought he did." She glanced at Dottie. "Did you see anyone when you pulled up?"

"No. No one."

Reese had the passenger door open and was hovering as though unsure whether to climb out or get back in.

"Reese, get in the Jeep with Dottie and lock the doors. Lay on the horn if you see anyone who shouldn't be nearby."

Reese and Dottie hurried to comply, with Dottie grumbling something about "this is getting old." Once Julianna was sure the girls were as safe as they were going to be for the moment, she nodded to Clay. "If Dottie didn't see the guy when she arrived, he may still be inside somewhere." She lifted the phone to her ear. "Are you still there?"

"This is 911 dispatch. What's your emergency?"

Julianna rattled off her credentials. "How far out are officers?"

"Four minutes."

"Good. Let them know they have officers on scene and two women locked in a vehicle." She described herself and Clay, and Dottie's Jeep, then she looked at Clay. "Will you help me clear the house?"

"Lead the way."

"First, the layout. Entry into the foyer. Dining room is to the right, my office is to the left. Straight through the door, there's a half bath off the hall. The dining room, kitchen, and den are L-shaped. Master is off the den. The other two bedrooms are upstairs."

"Got it."

Julianna headed back into her home with Clay on her heels. She could only pray he was as good at his job as he seemed to be. She went right into the dining room. "Clear!"

"Office is clear." Pause. "Half bath is clear." Pause. "Master is clear."

In the kitchen, she checked the walk-in pantry, then moved into the den. "All clear."

"Heading upstairs," he said.

She rounded the corner and fell into step behind him.

It didn't take long to clear the upstairs, and she lowered her weapon to her side.

Clay did the same. "Are you sure he didn't head outside?"

"He must have because he's not in here. Unless . . ."

Clay raised a brow. "Unless?"

She nodded to the attic and Clay lifted his weapon once more. "Could he have gotten up there?"

"I honestly don't see how, but I wouldn't have thought someone could get into my locked house, either." Which brought up another question for examination later. She pulled the attic stairs down, and insulation filtered to the floor. She shook her head and replaced the stairs.

Clay nodded. "Well, he didn't go up that way. You had a clean floor before you opened that."

"Exactly." She pressed a hand to her head. "He's gone."

"Then how?"

She hurried down the steps to the French doors in the kitchen that led to her deck. They were shut up tight just like she'd left them. Julianna spun on her right foot and bolted to the door that led to her garage. The dead bolt was unlocked. "Wow. I fell for it."

"What?"

"Whoever it was made sure to sound like he was going for the front door, then doubled back and went out this one. My garage door is down, but I have another door that leads to the back- yard." In lieu of gloves, she grabbed a paper towel and opened the door far enough to slip through. She hit the light and the fluorescent bulbs illuminated the area. "There." The single door that led out the back stood open. She slammed a fist against the wall. "Gah!"

"Don't beat yourself up too bad," Clay said.

"Right." Easier said than done. She turned. "I guess we should go check on Reese and Dottie."

"No one laid on the horn, so that's a good sign."

She opened the garage door. It whirred up, and she and Clay walked out to find the girls still in the car and two police cars on the scene. Clay showed his ID and the two men took their hands off their weapons. The taller one hooked his hands into his belt loops. "I'm Jim Lancaster. This is my partner, Tom Bridges."

"Thanks for getting here so fast. I'm Officer Clay Fox and this is Special Agent Julianna Jameson."

Dottie caught Julianna's eye and pushed open the door. "Did you catch him?"

"No."

Reese climbed out of the Jeep, too, and shut the door.

"The ladies said you two are law enforcement and you cleared the house," Officer Lancaster said.

"Yes, he's gone. He slipped into the garage and out the door that connects to the yard."

Lancaster looked at Clay. "We'll take a look around out here and through the neighborhood if you two have got these ladies covered?"

"We've got them," Julianna said.

"Was it the same person who was at my house?" Reese asked. "Did they leave a poem here too?"

125

Julianna's brow rose. "A poem?

"That was the weird experience I was hurrying home to tell you about," Dottie said. "Someone left a note on my Jeep. I sent you a picture of it."

Julianna pulled out her phone. "I saw you texted while I was sleeping, but I didn't get a chance to respond. I was too focused on the person in my house." She pulled up Dottie's texts, then found the picture.

> Tick tock, the time is nigh,
> D-day is coming, I won't lie.
> The hands still spin, ticking off the cost
> Of minutes and hours, days and years lost.

With each word she read, the breath leeched from her lungs. "Oh my—oh no . . ."

"What?"

She snapped her gaze up. "Where's the original?"

Clay frowned. "The officers that responded to Reese's house took it as evidence."

Julianna pressed her fingers to her bleary eyes. "Okay, good. That's good." She walked away from the three of them for a moment, pondering the enormity of the situation. Dottie and Reese had just been linked to the escaped hostage taker. The same hostage taker who had requested Julianna as the negotiator for the incident. Everything was personal. Right down to this latest poem. The agents investigating the hostage murders would be able to get it from the local police lab.

"What is it?" Clay asked, stepping up beside her, his voice low.

She shook her head and eyed Reese and Dottie, who were having their own private discussion. "I think they're in danger and we need to keep a very close eye on them."

"They're in danger?" he asked. "Or you are?"

■ ■ ■ ■

126

"Maybe both. Either way . . ."

He nodded. "Right."

"Let's go back inside and lock up. I need to make a phone call, then we can have a little slumber party."

"What about evidence and the crime scene unit on the way?"

"We won't bother anything, but it's safer inside than being exposed out here."

She had a point.

They ushered their siblings inside, and Clay noted Julianna's calm handling of . . . everything. Her chill attitude helped put Reese and Dottie at ease, and soon the ladies were chatting and laughing like nothing had happened, but Clay sensed the turmoil beneath Julianna's low-key exterior.

The officers went through the rooms one at a time, collecting prints from the knobs, stray hair fibers, and more. By the time they left, Clay's shoulders were knotted, and he was working on a plan to keep everyone safe.

"Let's watch a movie," Dottie said. She looked at Reese. "That okay?"

"Sure."

Julianna caught his eye. "I'll get the popcorn ready."

"Oh, great idea, Jules," Dottie said. She aimed the remote at the streaming device. "We'll wait on you."

He joined her in the kitchen. "You're really worried, aren't you?"

"Yes." She pulled out two bags of popcorn and put one in the microwave.

"Unfortunately, I think you should be. I am too. I'm guessing that note meant something to you?"

"It did."

"But you're not going to tell me what?"

"I can't. Not at the moment. That information hasn't been released to the public, and I'm going to have to get Dottie to erase it off her phone—and forget about it."

"Good luck with that."

She scoffed. "Right."

"That note scared you."

"It scares me that it was left on Dottie's Jeep. I think until after I make my call, we should all stick close."

"Reese is off tomorrow. I'll convince her to stay here. I'll even talk to her about canceling her birthday party."

"No, don't do that. She may not be in any danger. It could just be my and Dottie's presence that puts anyone else in danger."

"Okay, I won't say anything to her just yet." He paused, absently noting the fragrance of buttered popcorn coming from the microwave. "But if we don't cancel it, there will be a large police presence there."

"That should work nicely."

"Yeah." He glanced around. "You don't have an alarm system, do you?"

"Um, no."

He shook his head. "What is it with you people? Reese doesn't either, but you should know better."

Julianna laughed, but the mirth faded as fast as it appeared. "I just haven't gotten around to it."

"How long have you lived here?"

"About two years." She patted his hand. "Not everyone has an alarm system. Most people are fine if they lock their doors—at least in this neighborhood. I do that and keep my weapon close by when I sleep. Having someone break in like this isn't the norm."

"It is when you're a target," he muttered. "And when locked doors don't keep the intruders out, you have to do something more."

That stopped her and she nodded. "You're right. I'll take extra precautions from here on out. At least until we catch whoever is doing this."

"Good." He supposed it would have to do.

She grabbed the bag from the microwave and handed it to him.

"There's a bowl on the counter behind you. If you don't mind dumping this one in there, I'm going to check on something."

"What?" Clay opened the bag and steam escaped.

"Dottie found her note . . . poem . . . whatever you want to call it . . . on her Jeep, right?"

"Yeah."

"The intruder ran out through my garage. I'm just wondering—"

"If he left something on your car?"

She nodded.

Clay set the popcorn bag to the side. "Then let's go look."

He followed her into the double garage. Her car was parked in the space nearest them.

She looked at him. "Guess I need another evidence bag."

CHAPTER
THIRTEEN

Saturday morning, Julianna woke from a restless sleep. Tossing and turning wasn't exactly her favorite way to spend the night, but on the flip side, sometimes it was productive, as it allowed her brain time to work on problems.

Unfortunately, this was not one of those times. The *note*—she refused to insult poets everywhere by referring to it as a poem—she'd found on her car played through her mind. She'd never had trouble memorizing as a kid, and even now, after a number of read-throughs, the words were permanently etched in her brain.

> Tick tock, they say time flies,
> Tick tock, I'll hear your cries.
> Death can be swift, death can be slow,
> Which way do you think you'll go?
> Only time will tell, it's out of your control,
> I'll see you suffer, for all you stole.
> Then I'll watch you die—
> After I claim your soul.

She ducked her head under the pillow, but when that did nothing but make her feel like she couldn't breathe, she tossed off the covers and rolled out of bed. The lab had the *notes*, and until they examined them and got back to her about them—assuming they found anything—she'd just have to keep putting one foot in front of the other and go about her business.

Of course, part of that business would be going over every case she'd ever worked to see who might be holding a deep enough grudge they'd be willing to kill over it.

In the bathroom, she showered and readied herself for the day, her mind clicking over cases from her past. For the most part, she could remember each one. She went through them, discarding the ones that raised no questions. But there were two that she needed to study a little more.

She had the eight o'clock appointment with Hector, Max, and Lydia. Hopefully, that would generate some more ideas as to who the hostage taker and author of the threatening words could be.

When she stepped out of her room, she headed for the stairs and walked up them, the wood chilly on her bare feet. She peeked in Dottie's room and emotion knotted her throat. Dottie slept in the double bed while Reese snoozed in the daybed against the wall.

Julianna drew in a silent, steadying breath, took a step back, and shut the door with a soft snick. She leaned her head against the wood. "Please, God," she whispered, "please help me keep them safe. Give me wisdom to figure out who's behind this."

She made her way back downstairs to the kitchen to find Clay at the table and two cups of coffee in front of him. He looked up when she entered and slid one of the mugs across the table. She sank into the seat opposite him and gripped the ceramic mug, lifted it to her lips, and took a sip. "Thank you." She looked at him. "It wasn't weird spending the night here?"

"Extremely weird, but at least I was able to sleep some, knowing everyone was safe and I'd wake up if something happened to make anyone . . . unsafe."

"Yeah." She sighed. "I'll admit it was nice knowing you were here for backup if I needed it."

He nodded. "That couch of yours is amazing. I'm ready to toss mine in the dumpster now."

She laughed. "I'll admit I've had my fair share of naps on it and that it's almost more comfortable than my bed." She grabbed a bagel. "Are you okay with staying here until I get back from my meeting? I have no idea how long I'll be."

"I'll stay until the ladies wake up and then text you the plan."

"But you'll keep a close eye on Dottie?"

"Of course."

She nodded and told herself it would be fine. "I'm worried, Clay." She grimaced at the contrast between her thoughts and words.

A shadow darkened his eyes for a brief moment. "I know. I am too. I promise I won't let them out of my sight."

She held his gaze a moment longer. "Thank you." She stood. "I'll be in touch."

"Be safe."

"That's the plan." She grabbed her keys from the foyer table and bolted out the door to her vehicle.

It was a twenty-minute drive to her office, and by the time she made it through the traffic, she only had a few minutes to spare. She parked and hurried inside to the conference room, where she found Hector, Max, and Lydia already seated at the table.

"Hey," Julianna said, "sorry to be so last minute."

"No problem," Hector said, "we just sat down thirty seconds ago." He passed a folder to each of them, then opened the one in front of him. "I had the poem left on Dottie's Jeep delivered to keep all the evidence together." He looked at Julianna. "Any thoughts?"

"Oh, I have thoughts," Julianna muttered. So many thoughts.

"Then let's hear them."

"Okay, let's back up to Manchester. He had no issue killing six people on the airplane he hijacked. And he had no problem shooting two federal marshals in the courthouse."

"Right." Hector nodded.

"So, we know he's serious. He'd planned that escape for months. Had people on the inside and outside helping him. And we stopped him. Could this person be someone who's angry we prevented Manchester's escape? Like his sister or someone else?"

Max shook his head. "We've talked to Manchester's sister and the rest of his family. We're also doing a massive investigation into all of them, but it's looking more and more like they're not involved. We've arrested the courthouse janitor and one of the security guards, who posed as a fake marshal. They helped make it all happen. Manchester even said he made sure to keep his family out of it, as he didn't want it coming back to them."

"What a stand-up dude," Lydia said with a roll of her eyes.

"He has no compunction about killing others, but when it comes to his family, they're everything to him." Max leaned forward. "Get this. He found out about the tunnels from some old history textbook in the prison library. Then he started researching even more and asked Dietrich Simms, an explosives expert friend of Manchester's who came to visit on a regular basis—and before you ask, no, he didn't have a record of any kind—to bring him more books on the topic of the Charlotte gold rush. The books were examined, of course, but as they were just books, they were allowed to be passed on to Manchester. Once Manchester realized the courthouse and the tunnels were in the same vicinity, with the help of his outside buddies, they finally figured out one of the tunnels ran right under that courtroom. What are the odds?"

"Not even Einstein could do that kind of math," Julianna said. "What about the others who helped him?"

"One of the other guys was a contracted security guard. He was also a cousin to the janitor. The two of them snuck in all of the equipment needed and hid it in the ceiling. Then the two working with Manchester stowed away in the electrical closet and, well, you know what happened after that."

Julianna nodded. "So, if the hostage taker isn't ticked that

Manchester failed in his escape attempt, then maybe the person is a *fan* of Manchester's. Could it be possible he wants to reenact the whole thing from the courthouse and 'do it right'?"

"You mean show Manchester what he should have done?" Hector asked.

"Something like that." She shrugged. "It's a shot in the dark. Here's another scenario. The hostage taker admires Manchester and the plane hijacking. Then follows the incident at the courthouse. When it fails, he attributes the failure to me and decides to get back at me by re-creating the incident at the bank, making sure I'm the negotiator at the scene. Only he doesn't want to get caught like Manchester—and the only way not to be caught is not to be there—"

"So, he kills the hostages before we even arrive," Hector said.

"Making sure he has time to escape."

"In the form of a customer using an umbrella. All of the security footage is leading in that direction. While we can't see the person's face, it's really the only explanation, because no one goes in or comes out after that—at least not until after we got the call from one of the hostages."

"Zena," Julianna said, her voice low.

"Yeah," Hector said.

"How's she doing?"

"She gave us all the information she could. Because the suspect blindfolded and separated them, she could only tell us what she heard."

"And that he shot the two other people she left behind in the room," Julianna said.

"Yes, and that. She said she thought she was next and has no idea why she was spared. All of the hostages' hands were tested for gunpowder residue and were clean." Hector shook his head. "None of them were the shooter."

"So for some reason, she and one other hostage were allowed to live," Lydia said. "And, of course, the mother and child he released."

"Well, when you think about it, not all of Manchester's hostages from the plane died," Julianna said. "So, this other suspect leaving a few alive makes sense—in a weird copycat kind of way."

Lydia raised a brow. "Good point."

"And *none* of them died at the courthouse," Hector said. "Even the marshal who was critically wounded is expected to make a full recovery."

"So, basically what this is looking like," Max said, "is that this all comes back to the hostage taker being a fan of Manchester, and Julianna is the connection."

Hector nodded. "She was Manchester's negotiator, so the bank hostage taker wanted her too."

"That's the assumption we're working with for now," Max said. "Although, I will say these poems kind of throw a monkey wrench into things. Like why send the poems to Julianna? Why put one on her sister's Jeep? What's the message?"

"I think the message is pretty clear," Julianna said. "I may not know the exact meaning behind the words, but I really feel like this is some kind of revenge thing going on. These are threats. Dying fast or slow? Which way will I go?" She tapped a finger to the picture. "And this last line? 'I'll watch you die—after I claim your soul.'" She suppressed a shudder. "Can't get much more clear than that."

"Are you sure the message was meant for you?" Lydia asked.

Julianna stopped and stared at the agent, and the others looked at her as well. "Who else would they be for?"

"Dottie lives with you, right?"

"Yes."

"And someone tried to break into the home where she was staying, so"—Lydia spread her hands—"they had to be following her, right? I mean, it's just a thought."

For a moment, Julianna let her mind play over everything, then shook her head. "No, I don't think so. I think this person is targeting me for whatever reason. It could be that he was following

Dottie because he wanted to send a message through her—and we definitely need to make sure she's safe—but I think I'm his main target." She tapped the table. "It talks about tears and years and all that I stole. It's me he's after."

"All right," Hector said, clasping his hands in front of him and leaning forward, "then who is it?"

Julianna pressed her fingers to her temples to massage gently. "I've been thinking about it, and I've come up with two names who might be possibilities. Evelyn Seymour and Christopher Makin."

"Who are they?" Max asked.

"Evelyn was the wife of Jason Seymour. I talked him into letting their nine-year-old daughter go, but then he turned the gun on me, and a sniper shot him."

Hector nodded. "I remember that."

"And Christopher Makin was the sniper who shot him," Julianna said. "I confronted Makin and let him know I thought he was wrong, not realizing anyone was listening. He was furious with me and said some things that could be considered threatening, but I didn't take them personally. He was angry, we had words, then we went our separate ways."

Lydia gaped. "You *yelled* at someone? I can't picture it."

Julianna shook her head. "I didn't yell. We had words. I was in complete control at all times." To be otherwise wasn't an option. "But Makin didn't like me questioning his decision. I didn't think Seymour was going to shoot me. Makin disagreed and took the shot. I still think it was just a tragic loss of life that didn't have to happen."

"And he requested a transfer so he didn't have to work with you anymore," Hector said. "That's what he told me anyway."

"Right. The thing is, I apologized for confronting him where another person could hear. I admitted that I'd been careless in that regard, and that I was sorry about the way I'd handled the aftermath. Not that I'd changed my stance on the fact that I didn't think he should have taken the shot. He told me to forget it, he'd said some things too. And that was it. The next thing I knew, he was reassigned, and I worked to move past the incident."

"But what if Makin didn't?" Lydia asked.

"Yeah." Max shifted and rubbed a hand over his face. "Why is Seymour's wife on your radar?"

"When he was holding the gun to her head, I promised him that all would be well if he just let them go. And then he wound up dead." She paused. "Maybe Evelyn thinks I lied on purpose or gave Makin some kind of signal to shoot." She glanced at Hector. "Which I didn't, of course."

Max scribbled on the paper in front of him. "We'll look into the incident."

Julianna rubbed her eyes. "I've never lost a hostage," she said, almost under her breath. "Ever. So it can't be someone who's angry with me for one of their loved ones being killed in a hostage situation."

"Could it be this person is angry that the courtroom hostage situation ended before people died?" Lydia asked. "I know it sounds stupid, but that doesn't mean it's not a possibility."

"Even stupid has to be considered," Hector said. "All right, Max and Lydia will run down these leads. Julianna, you keep yourself safe." He studied her. "And keep an eye on Dottie."

"Of course."

"I can arrange for the tech guys to install the alarm—"

"It's not nec—"

"I think it is. I also think it might be time to think about some security for you and Dottie."

"Hector . . ." She sighed when he narrowed his eyes. "All right. Security for Dottie for sure. I'm not convinced I need it yet." She paused. "And, honestly, I don't want this person scared off. I want to catch them."

"I know, but it's not worth sacrificing your life."

No, it wasn't. "I agree. Keep an eye on Dottie and I'll watch my back."

He obviously didn't like it, but he nodded.

Julianna walked out of the meeting feeling restless and annoyed—she was missing something. And if it didn't come to her soon, there could be serious repercussions.

■ ■ ■ ■

When Julianna had walked in the door half an hour ago, Clay could tell she was preoccupied, but she'd greeted him with a smile. "Everything okay here?"

"Yeah. Reese and Dottie just wanted to chill, so that's what we've been doing. I'm really enjoying basketball on your big screen."

"I got that for movies, not sports."

He laughed. "You don't like sports?"

"Meh. I can take them or leave them."

He gasped, letting his horror show. "But, but, but . . . *everyone* loves sports."

"I hate to break it to you, my friend, but no, not *every*one. And I don't *dislike* sports, I just don't watch them very often because I don't see what all the hype is. Grown men and women yelling at the television?" She rolled her eyes. "That's pathetic."

"You realize you just threw out a challenge, don't you?"

She wrinkled her nose at him, then frowned. "Why are there balled-up socks on the floor in front of the screen?"

Was she serious? "Because when the ref makes a bad call, you can't throw shoes. You might damage the screen." How did she not know this stuff? "It's actually very therapeutic."

"I'm . . ." She shook her head. "I don't even know what to say. Where did the socks come from?"

"Um . . . I might have asked Reese to ask Dottie if she could find some."

Julianna laughed. A real laugh without strain or stress, and Clay couldn't remember the last time he heard something so sweet and . . . attractive. Her dimples flashed and he couldn't help but stare. When she sobered, their eyes met and stilled.

Before the pause could get too awkward, Clay cleared his throat. "I can see you have a real gap in your education. We'll have to fix that." A knock on the door interrupted her response and Clay lifted a brow. "You expecting company?"

"No." He rested his hand on his weapon and she shook her head. "It's okay. I doubt whoever was in my home last night is going to knock. Besides, someone is watching the house."

He raised a brow, but noted she still checked the window before opening the door.

"Grace?"

The joy in her voice relieved the tension in his shoulders and he dropped his hand.

"Grace!"

While Clay stood to the side trying not to intrude, Julianna pulled her friend into an embrace, which Grace returned with fervor. Grace's light brown eyes met his and he offered a small wave. She grinned at him and waved back.

"And me," a voice said behind Grace.

"Penny!" Julianna transferred her hug to the red-haired woman with multiple bags in her arms. "What are you guys doing here? Come in."

The two women stepped inside and Julianna waved to Clay. "Ladies," Julianna said, "meet Clay Fox. He's the SRO at Dottie's school. His sister, Reese, is the one who helped catch Nicholas Manchester—or at least stopped him from escaping the courthouse. And"—she shot him a smile—"he's become a friend."

"Nice to meet you," Clay said, his heart beating a little faster at the look she gave him when she called him friend.

"Clay," Julianna continued, "this is Grace Billingsley, Special Agent and Behavioral Analyst for the FBI. She works out of the Columbia field office, but we see each other as much as possible. And the redhead is Penny Carlton-almost-Satterfield. She's the Life Flight pilot who came to the courthouse and airlifted the two marshals to the hospital."

"That was you." Clay nodded. "Nice job."

"Thank you." Penny, with several brown bags clutched in her arms, headed for the kitchen and the rest of them followed. "We brought lunch, but we can talk before we eat. It'll keep." She dropped the bags on the counter, then whirled and headed for the living area. Again, everyone followed her.

Grace lowered herself onto the couch and helped herself to a handful of M&Ms from the dish on the end table. Penny did the same and curled her legs under her. "Grace said you needed company," she said to Julianna.

"Grace did, huh?" Julianna narrowed her eyes. "She say why?"

"Of course not. And I didn't ask."

"You just hopped in your chopper and decided to go pick her up, then come see me? I thought we were getting together tomorrow for lunch." Not that she would have been able to keep that date, the way her life was going at the moment.

Penny shrugged. "It was the fastest way to get her here, and we didn't want to wait until tomorrow, since Raina backed out on us."

"You have a chopper?" Clay asked. The more they talked, the more fascinated he became.

"Penny finished building her own helicopter a few weeks ago," Julianna said.

"Holt made me," Penny said with a smirk.

Grace laughed. "Holt encouraged you." She looked at Julianna. "I had the weekend off and so did Grace. Raina's working, unfortunately, but she insisted that not keep us from coming to see you today since she couldn't make tomorrow after all."

"Raina Price works with Penny at Life Flight," Julianna explained for Clay. "She's the critical care transport paramedic."

Life Flight, the medical company based in Asheville at Mercy Mission Hospital. Julianna studied him and he wondered if his face was conveying his bemusement. "We've been friends for a very long time," she said. "We met in juvie."

He raised a brow. "When you stole the car?"

"Yep."

"What were the rest of you in for, if you don't mind me asking?"

"Truancy," Penny and Grace said together.

"We didn't like school," Grace said, "so we decided to skip it."

Penny shared a wry smile with Julianna. "Too many times for the law to like."

"And yet you all turned into amazing people and have incredible careers," he said. "Be careful, you might become the poster children for why skipping school is great for your future."

Julianna laughed. "Not hardly. It wasn't the skipping school part that was good, it was the person we met in the facility. The psychiatrist, Mrs. Gibbs, was a wonderful Christian woman who dedicated her life to saving the lost by introducing them to God."

"And we were definitely lost," Grace murmured.

Penny clasped her hands in front of her. "But she found us and we found each other—and God. It was a win-win situation for all of us."

"We know that's not the case for most kids who wind up in juvie," Grace said, "but we decided to take the win and be glad, grateful—and proud—that we beat the odds."

"Good for you," Clay said.

"Julianna?" Dottie's voice stopped the conversation, but as soon as Dottie stepped into the room and noticed the visitors, she let out a low squeal. "Oh, hey!" She ran to Grace and hugged her, then transferred her affections to Penny. "I'm so glad to see you two. What are you doing here?"

"We heard there was some funny business going on," Grace said, "and thought we'd pop in to make sure you guys were okay."

Dottie scowled. "We're okay. For now." She looked at Julianna. "But I think we need to change the locks."

"What do you mean?"

She held up her keys. "I was looking at them when I got up and noticed something came off on my hands. It was small, but

I think it's clay." She glanced at Clay and gave him a tight smile. "And I don't mean him."

"You mean like the kind of clay someone would use to make an impression of your key?"

"Yes."

Julianna frowned. "You're always messing with your keys."

"I realize that."

"Follow me, will you?" She walked into the kitchen. Dottie followed as requested. So did Clay, Grace, and Penny. Reese had yet to make an appearance, and that was probably a good thing. "When was the first time you noticed the residue?"

"Just now."

Julianna grabbed a paper bag from the bottom shelf of the pantry and held it out toward Dottie. "Drop the keys in here."

"What?" Dottie's eyes widened. "No, I need my keys."

"And we need to know what's on them. Come on, kiddo, drop them, please. I'll get them back to you as soon as possible."

With a heavy sigh, Dottie did so. Julianna closed the bag, taped it up, and labeled it with a Sharpie. "Well, it's not a true evidence bag, but it'll do. I'll get this to the lab. In the meantime, you can use the spare key for the Jeep."

"Fine." Dottie's jaw was tight and she hadn't taken her eyes from the bag.

"As soon as we get the locks changed, we'll make sure you have that key as well."

"Right."

"In the meantime, use the garage door app on your phone to come in and out of the house."

Dottie's jaw tightened further. "I got it, Jules."

Julianna caught Dottie's hand in a light grasp. "What is it, hon?"

"Nothing."

"Something. Tell me." She kept her voice low and concerned without a hint of accusation in her tone. "Please."

Penny took Grace's arm. "We'll just let you guys chat for a minute while we wait in the living area."

Once they were gone, Clay backed toward the door. "I'll give you some privacy."

Dottie bit her lip and tears filled her eyes. "You can stay. You've been here since the start and probably need to know this too." Her gaze swung back to Julianna. "I don't know when someone could have gotten an impression of my keys, but he did and he managed to get into the house. If something had happened to you—"

Julianna squeezed Dottie's fingers.

Her sister drew in a sharp breath. "I'm just feeling guilty, that's all."

"There's nothing for you to feel guilty about," Julianna said. "You had no way of knowing what someone else was planning."

"But they came after my keys to get to you, right?"

"Yeah, that's what it looks like."

"They thought I'd be an easy target."

Julianna lifted a hand, palm up. Then dropped it. "Possibly. Or it could have simply been a moment of opportunity."

"Yeah, an opportunity that person created." She bit her lip and narrowed her eyes. "It had to have happened at school."

"Really? Why do you say that?"

"Because the only time I don't 'mess with my keys,' as you put it, is when I'm in school. At least most of the time. Sometimes I do. Like when I'm nervous right before a test. Or if someone says something to me that's mean or . . ." She threw her hands up. "Argh! I don't know."

"Wait a minute. Back up. Who's saying mean things to you?"

Clay held his tongue when Dottie's gaze whipped to his. He tightened his lips, hoping she'd take the hint and tell Julianna about Mary Ann.

She grimaced and focused her attention back on Julianna. "No one important. Seriously, we're in high school. Mean people are everywhere. It's not a big deal and nothing to worry about. What *is* important is that, for some reason, weaving the keys in and out of my fingers is calming for me."

"I know."

"I know you do."

"And now that's been taken from you." So many things had been taken from this girl.

Dottie dropped her chin to her chest and fell silent for a moment. Then she stepped forward to wrap her arms around Julianna. "Well, better the keys than you."

■ ■ ■ ■

Felicity loved Saturdays. Or at least she used to. After her husband had died, she'd found herself at a loss. If it hadn't been for Tommy . . .

Her son loved the local science center, so she brought him here every chance she got when weather permitted.

"Hey, Mom, look! He landed on it!"

She looked up. Tommy held a stick that had been dipped in sugar water. A beautiful orange-and-black monarch had settled on the end of it. Tommy's eyes were wide and his lips stretched into a smile that rivaled the sun. "It's a boy! He has a lighter color and two spots on his wings. Just like in the pictures we looked at."

She lifted her phone and caught the precious moment with the camera. "That's amazing."

"He likes me."

"Of course he does."

"Well, he likes the sugar water." His wry tone and wrinkled nose reminded her so much of his father that her heart cramped and warmed all at the same time. "Can I take him home?" Tommy asked.

She laughed. "No, he needs to stay here with his family."

Tommy's smile faded. "What if he doesn't have a daddy? I could be his daddy."

And just like that, the air left her lungs and a pang of grief cut so sharp, she was actually surprised she wasn't bleeding on the outside. Felicity spoke around the tightness in her throat. "But if he has a mom, then she would be very sad if he went missing."

Tommy's brows furrowed and his lips puckered like he did when he was thinking hard about something. "You mean like you would be sad if I went away?"

"Exactly."

"Okay." His eyes met hers. "Will I ever have another daddy?"

Oh, the hard questions he asked and the pain they brought. "I would like to think so," she said. "One day maybe I'll marry again." Her lips trembled at the thought, but she was a realist too. She'd always miss her first love, but she was only twenty-eight years old. She'd meet someone. Eventually.

"Will he like me as much as my real daddy?"

"I wouldn't marry him if he didn't."

"That's a relief."

The monarch flew away, and she motioned for Tommy to come to her. When he stepped near enough, she bent down to his level. "What brought this conversation on?"

"Lilly's mom is getting married next week and she doesn't like him."

"Why not?"

"Because he's not her daddy. But her daddy's not dead like mine. He just lives in another house."

"That's a different situation. But I promise I'd never marry anyone you didn't like." She paused. "As long as you're not just saying you don't like him because . . ."

"Because why?"

"Because you just don't want me to marry someone who isn't your real father."

"I know my daddy's not coming back. He's in heaven with Jesus. But until I can see him again, I'd like to have a daddy here."

Felicity's throat clogged and she had to clear it a few times before she could speak. "Okay. I'll keep that in mind."

"Thanks, Mom. Hey, there's another monarch. I wonder if that one's a girl!" He ran off and Felicity swallowed the tears and prayed. For her future, for Tommy's, and for the ability to forgive.

"I forgive him, Lord. In my head, I've made the choice to forgive. Please let my heart feel it too." She pulled in a deep breath and followed her son. "And thank you for the promise of a future. Help me walk into it with expectations and joy."

Tommy laughed when a butterfly landed on his arm, and Felicity smiled. Grief was a part of life, but she could pray that joy would come in the morning.

CHAPTER
FOURTEEN

Julianna's friends had brought enough groceries to feed an army and fixed a lunch that left Clay stuffed. Before he'd eaten a bite, he'd run to the nearest home improvement store and purchased all new hardware for Julianna's exterior doors. He'd even managed to match the ones on the interior. They were installed, and she and Dottie had new keys in their possession.

Once that was done, his stomach reminded him he was starving and he'd dug in without caring that later this evening, he'd have another good meal with his family to celebrate Reese's birthday. While Julianna and the others chatted, he'd been busy texting other officer buddies, arranging security for Reese's party. Now, he stifled a groan and refused to give in to the urge to rub his stomach. He'd have to add an extra day to his workout routine this week, but it was worth it.

Watching Julianna interact with her friends was a remarkable experience. Since he'd met her, he'd never seen her truly relaxed, but with the women, it was like she morphed into someone else. Someone who had a sparkle in her eyes and a smile on her lips.

However, as much as she enjoyed herself and the visit, Clay could tell she was still alert, with her guard up. Every so often, she'd check the windows, then the door. When she stood to gather plates, he grabbed two and followed her into the kitchen.

She tossed the paper plates into the trash and turned. He handed her the ones he'd snagged.

"Thanks. I could have gotten them," she said. Those landed in the can as well.

"I don't mind. Besides, I wanted to talk to you a minute alone."

"Okay." She frowned and stiffened like she was bracing herself for whatever was coming.

"There's no easy way to say this, but I'm pretty sure Dottie's being bullied at school."

Julianna froze. "What?"

"I've been thinking about it, going over in my mind the incident with the other student, and it's the only thing that makes sense." He told her about the occurrence with Mary Ann and Dottie outside his office. "I don't think that's the first time something's happened."

"I see."

"And I talked to Dottie."

"She admitted she was being bullied?"

He rubbed his chin and nodded. "Sort of, but she asked me to let her handle it."

"I'll talk to her."

"No, don't," he said. "Not yet, please." He smiled. "She said she'd handle it and she did. Beautifully. She put the other girl in her place without being a bully in return." His smile faded. "For the moment anyway." A pause. "I'm fine with letting students handle their problems as long as any bullying stops or I don't see anything that alarms me."

"Alarms you like what?"

"Suicidal tendencies, gonna-shoot-up-the-school tendencies, that kind of thing. I don't see that at all with Dottie, of course, but still wanted you to be in the loop."

Julianna frowned at him. "All right. Thanks for the heads-up." She paused. "You're sure?"

"Yeah."

"Okay then. I'll leave it alone for now."

She trusted him. She'd listened to his advice and taken it. A feeling like none other swept over him and he wished he had a label for it. But it felt good.

And then his elation nose-dived. Once he told her everything about his role in the incident that took an innocent man's life, her trust would evaporate and she'd look at him differently.

So, yeah, maybe they could be friends, but anything more—anything that required baring his heart? He really didn't see that happening.

Pray about it.

He jerked. Where had that thought come from?

"Hey, guys," Grace said, sticking her head in the door, "y'all going to stay in the kitchen forever or come join us?"

"We're coming," Julianna said. She led the way out of the kitchen and back into the living area while Clay mulled over the fact that he was hearing voices. He'd quit praying a little over a year ago when it seemed God had closed the door on his prayers. Why would he start now?

You were willing to pray for Reese. But that was different.

"Clay?"

He blinked. Everyone was staring at him. Heat crept into his neck and he cleared his throat. "Sorry. Was thinking about something."

"Obviously." Reese shot him an amused look. "I was just asking if you were ready to go. I need to get to Mom and Dad's house to get ready for the party, and Dad wanted your help with something to do with the fireworks."

"Fireworks?" Julianna asked.

"Every year, my parents put on a big display of fireworks over the lake because I loved them as a kid." A fond smile curved her lips. "It's a little over the top, but everyone that lives on the lake looks forward to them each year, so I don't protest."

"Exactly," Clay said. He glanced at his phone and saw the text from his father. "I'm just going to say my goodbyes now so I can call my dad. Everyone, it was nice to meet you. I can't thank you enough for the food."

They echoed the goodbyes and he slipped out the door with Reese and Dottie on his heels.

Dottie grinned at him. "I'm coming too. Is that all right? I'm good at decorating."

"Of course," Reese said.

Julianna stood and followed them out the door, pulling it shut behind her. "Hang on a sec, Clay. I want to talk to you about something."

Clay nodded to his sister and Dottie. "I'll be there in a minute." He handed Reese the keys. "Get the air going if you need it."

"That's our cue, Dottie."

"Yep," Dottie said, "I caught it too."

They went to his SUV and climbed in. Clay turned to Julianna. "What's the frown for?"

"The more I think about it, the more I don't know if I should come to the party. I don't want to bring trouble with me."

He sighed. "I get what you're saying—and I appreciate the sentiment behind it—but I'm going to have tons of buddies there. Not just inside, but around the perimeter of the property. I know Reese is really wanting you to be there." He paused. "She feels a special connection with you, thanks to the whole courthouse incident. I know she'll be super disappointed if you don't come."

"But the danger . . ."

"It'll probably be the safest place in the city tonight."

She bit her lip, then nodded. "All right. I'll be there."

"Good." He hesitated, then decided to be up front. "Everything I said about security is true, but if I'm going to be transparent, I want you there because I like being around you."

She blinked. Then smiled. "I like being around you too, Clay." She opened the door and stepped inside, while Clay called himself every kind of fool possible. It was apparent that he had no self-control when it came to keeping Julianna at arm's length. She'd given him the perfect opportunity to agree that she shouldn't come to the party that night. Instead, he'd talked her into being there.

It looked like the only way he'd be able to keep his distance was by telling her his deepest secret. She'd run fast and far once she knew, so he might as well get it over with.

■ ■ ■ ■

Still not convinced this was the best idea, but feeling better about it after the guard checked her ID and waved her through the gate, Julianna pulled into the drive of the Fox home and cut the engine.

Dottie would have protection at school, and Julianna would allow the tech guys to install an alarm system on her home.

But for now, she'd try to enjoy the evening.

Clay's car was already there, along with two police cruisers sitting in plain sight. No doubt, there were more officers around, as he'd promised. Out of sight, but on guard. Good. She relaxed a fraction and climbed out of her SUV. She'd left the Bucar at home since she wasn't on the clock at the moment. Well, she was always on the clock, but they'd call her as a last resort, which meant she might be able to stay for the whole party.

She made her way to the front door, her gaze sweeping the area. The weather had cooperated and the temps hovered in the midseventies. A perfect evening for a birthday celebration.

"Jules?"

"Dottie." The girl had come around the corner of the garage.

"Come on. All the fun's in the back. We're getting ready to crank up the music and jump in the pool."

Clay's parents had three acres located on a small private lake. There were only five other houses along the perimeter of the water, and she could see the chairs on the lawn in preparation to enjoy the show.

For a moment, a pang of jealousy shot through her. What would it have been like to grow up with a family like Clay's? With parents who put on a fireworks show simply because they loved you and wanted to celebrate you?

She couldn't fathom it. She followed Dottie around to the back of the home to find a magazine-worthy backyard. "Wow."

"I know, right?"

Wrought-iron fencing surrounded the pool, and multiple lounge chairs were spread out on the concrete. Beyond the pool was a green lawn that led down to the lake. A pontoon boat tied to the massive dock rocked gently on the water, and two Jet Skis looked ready to go at any moment. "What do his parents do?" she murmured.

In the yard, there were several groups playing games. Corn hole and volleyball looked to be the two most popular.

"His dad is the CEO of a pharmaceutical company," Dottie said, "and his mom works for a nonprofit."

"Wow." It seemed to be the only word she could find.

"The pool is heated so they can use it year-round."

"Impressive." For the first time in a long time, old feelings of insecurity welled up inside. That little voice she thought she'd silenced once again whispered in her ear. *You're not good enough. You should be ashamed of your past. Once Clay learns everything about you, he won't want anything to do with you.*

"Julianna?" Clay's deep voice sent shudders rippling through her.

For a moment, she was tempted to run, but thankfully managed to hold on to her composure.

She turned and smiled. "This place is amazing."

"Yeah, it is." He laughed and shook his head. "Mom and Dad have worked hard." He shrugged. "I'm happy to see them enjoying this place."

"Absolutely."

"Dottie, come on!" Reese stood in the middle of the volleyball court and waved at Dottie.

"Coming!" Dottie backed up. "See you later, Jules. Come play if you get bored." She headed for the group of people her age and Julianna shook her head. She seriously doubted boredom would be an issue.

"Come on," Clay said. "I'll introduce you to a few people. My parents have been wanting to meet the woman who rescued Reese."

"I had a little help." She paused. "To be honest, Reese pretty much rescued herself and everyone else."

"Yeah, she's a fighter."

"How have the newspapers not hounded her to death for a story?"

"Oh, they have, but she's already promised the exclusive to a friend of ours. Once word got around about that, the reporters moved on." He took her by the hand and pulled her over to an older man working on some scrumptious-smelling food at the grill. He had his salt-and-pepper hair buzzed in a military cut, but the lines around his eyes said he smiled a lot. "Dad?"

"Yeah?" The man flipped a burger.

"I want to introduce you to someone."

That got his attention and he turned. When his gaze landed on Julianna, he grinned. "Julianna Jameson. I'd know you anywhere. I'm Patrick Fox and I'm very happy to meet you." He set down his spatula and engulfed her in a bear hug. When he let go, Julianna gulped in air and Clay grinned at her. His father patted her shoulder. "Reese has sung your praises and my son confirmed them. Welcome to the party."

"Thank you, Mr. Fox," she said, her voice husky. "I appreciate the invitation."

"It's Pat. Most of the food is inside in the kitchen. Go make yourself a feast." He piled burgers on a plate and passed it to Clay. "Take this in, will you?"

"Of course. Mom's inside?"

"Yep. Something about getting another bowl of the banana pudding out of the fridge."

Clay nodded to Julianna. "After you."

She made her way to the door Clay indicated and stepped inside a massive kitchen with an island the size of her bathroom. He set the steaming burgers on a hot plate, and she eyed everything that had been laid out. Burgers, hot dogs, chicken, chips, beans, potato salad, pasta salad, and about six different desserts. "*That is a lot of food.*"

"Mom cooked it all. Well, except the cupcakes."

"I'm surprised they wouldn't cater something like this."

"Cater?" Clay laughed. "Not Mom. Not for Reese. This is a labor of love for her."

"Yeah," Julianna said. "Your family is great."

"Clay, darling!" A woman in her midseventies peered around the open refrigerator door. "Come get this platter of cheese, will you?"

He went to do as asked, and Julianna once again had to battle the voices that told her she was out of her league. *God, I know that's not coming from you. I am who you made me to be, and as long as I'm walking the path you've set me on, I have no reason to feel inferior or "less than."* The reminder helped. A little.

■ ■ ■ ■

Clay and Julianna wound up sitting at the table next to the pool with Vince Covelli. The man questioned Julianna about the hostage situation at the courtroom, and she was gracious enough to fill him in on what she could talk about. For the most part, she managed to satisfy Vince's curiosity.

"Come on, man," Clay finally said, "let her enjoy the party. Just because you're a big bad US Marshal now, doesn't mean everyone wants to spend every minute of the day talking shop."

Julianna laughed. "I don't mind, but while we're on pause, I think I'll visit the ladies' room. Inside next to the kitchen, right?"

"Or in the pool house over there."

She rattled the ice in her cup. "I think I'll head to the kitchen and get a refill on my way out. Can I get anyone anything?"

He and Vince said they were fine, and Julianna walked toward the house. Clay let his gaze follow her. He couldn't believe how much he enjoyed her company, and it didn't take much to admit he wanted more than friendship from her. But again, insecurity plagued him. If he told her the whole story of his time in the military, would she walk away from him? He wouldn't think so but wasn't quite ready to find out. Then again, like he'd decided earlier, sooner was probably better than later. He couldn't fully enjoy getting to know her with this hanging over his head.

"She's the one you ditched me for over the Braves game, isn't she?" Vince asked.

"Uh . . ."

"I thought so. And I have to admit, I don't blame you. She's a keeper."

Clay glanced at his buddy. He and Vince had gone through twelve years of school together, then basic training, and served on the same police force before his friend had moved on to the US Marshals. He was the only one who knew every detail of Clay's time overseas. Clay knew the man prayed for him daily. Looking into his friend's dark brown eyes, he couldn't lie to him. "I think so too, but . . ." He shrugged. "I have too much baggage, man. I feel like I can't put that on her."

"She looks like a grown woman to me. She's smart too. Might want to let her be the one to make that decision." Vince's eyes went wide. "Incoming on your six."

"What?"

"Speaking of baggage, Mallory is here."

And that was all the warning he got.

"Hello, Clay."

Mallory's soft voice washed over him, and his breath caught for a brief second before he turned to see his old girlfriend walk over and take the empty seat next to him. Julianna's seat.

Clay took a swig of his tea and swallowed. "Hello, Mallory." He didn't bother to ask who invited her. She didn't need an invitation. She'd been coming and going from this house since they were teens. "How are you?"

She lifted a shoulder in an elegant shrug, then tucked strands of long dark hair behind her ear. "I'm fine."

"How's the interior decorating business going?"

"Very well. I have two of your neighbors as clients."

"In my neighborhood?" That was kind of shocking. He didn't live in the worst part of town, but he definitely didn't think his neighbors were the type of clientele Mallory would cater to.

She laughed. "No, silly. I guess I should say your parents' neighbors. I forget you don't live here anymore."

"I haven't lived here in two years." Longer, if he counted his time in the military.

"I know." She placed a hand on his and gazed intently into his eyes. "I've missed you, Clay."

Clay glanced back toward the house, wondering how long he had to sit there before he could leave without coming across as rude.

Vince cleared his throat and stood. "Think I'm going to check out the volleyball game."

Meaning he was going to sweep the property.

And leave Clay alone with Mallory.

Behind Mallory's back, Vince gave him a short salute, then left. Clay drew in a deep breath. When he looked up again, his eyes collided with Julianna's blue gaze. She gave a pointed look at Mallory's hand on his, then bit her lip and turned to walk toward the dock.

Clay removed his hand, finished his tea, and tossed the plastic cup into the recycle container ten feet to his right. He stood. "I have a friend I need to go talk to. Have a nice night, Mal."

Her smile flipped and hurt flashed in her eyes. For a brief second, he was sorry, but memories washed over him, and he gave her a short nod, turned, and went after Julianna.

He caught up with her halfway down the pier. "Hey."

"Hi."

"That was Mallory Simpson. She's an ex-girlfriend. I didn't expect to see her here."

"You don't owe me any explanation," Julianna said, her gaze somewhere in the distance. He took her arm and pulled her around so she had to look at him.

"I know I don't necessarily *owe* you one, but what if I want to *give* you one?"

She hesitated, and for a moment, he thought she might shrug him off, but he should have known better. She nodded. "Okay."

He let his hand slide down her arm to curl around her fingers. "Want to sit on the boat and watch the fireworks? They're going to start in about five minutes. I can tell you about her while we watch."

"Yeah, okay."

Not that she needed it, but he helped her onto the boat and into the double seat facing the water. "See that little island out there?"

"Yes."

"My uncle takes all the fireworks out there and sets them up. Then he gets in the little boat and uses his remote firing system to set them off."

"Sounds very professional."

"It is. And safe."

"Definitely safe. Safe is a good thing. I know you were in the Army overseas—or maybe I just assumed that, since you were a Ranger."

"I was overseas."

"And the fireworks don't trigger any PTSD stuff?"

"No. I'm fortunate in that. They don't bother me. Maybe it's because I can see where the pops are coming from." He paused. "I don't know. I can't explain it."

"Then don't. Let's just enjoy."

He sat beside her. "You know when I said I killed an innocent man?"

She looked at him. "Yes."

"I was a sniper with the 75th Ranger Regiment. We were in Afghanistan and intel came in about a terrorist cell. I had orders to take out the leader. Only the intel was . . . deliberately corrupted and I shot an innocent man."

"Deliberately corrupted?"

He nodded. "The man had witnessed one of his unit buddies beating an Afghan national trying to get information from him. When he tried to intervene, the other guy told him to get out. He refused, freed the unjustly held national, and said he was going to report his team member to a superior. That night, I got the call and the target. I did my job and walked away, only to learn the next day of a 'friendly fire' incident. There's more, but that's the gist of it."

For a moment, she didn't move. When the first burst of fireworks lit up the sky, he looked over at her, and the compassion in her gaze tightened his throat and he had to look away.

She reached over and took his hand. "I have no words, Clay. I'm so sorry."

Clay locked his jaw, refusing to break down. Instead, he released her hand and slid his arm across her shoulders. She leaned into him.

"When did that happen?" she asked.

"About a year ago."

"How did you get all of the information leading up to getting the bad intel?"

"Another member of the unit came forward and told the whole story."

"Wow. I'm sorry." She squeezed the hand he hadn't realized he'd curled into a fist on his thigh.

He forced himself to relax and enjoy the moment.

Another flare exploded overhead and rained down. Yeah, Clay decided, he could stay right here, on the boat, with Julianna snuggled beside him for the rest of his life.

CHAPTER
FIFTEEN

Clay's warmth radiated, wrapping around her like a fleece blanket on a cold night. His pain had become her pain, and she wished with all her heart she could make it go away, but just like she had to live with hers, he had to live with his. However, that didn't mean she couldn't try to comfort him—and her words seemed to do that. His stiff posture loosened and he pulled her closer.

Julianna let herself get lost in the moment, relaxing in a way she hadn't done since she was a child. She felt . . . safe. Secure. Protected.

Which was so at odds with her nature. She was the one used to doing the protecting and making sure others were safe. To be on the receiving end was incredible—and weird.

But comfortable and . . . and . . . She was out of adjectives, so she settled for wonderful. Before one thought intruded. He hadn't told her about Mallory Simpson. Or had he? "She walked away from you, didn't she? When you told her what happened?" she asked, her voice soft.

"Yeah."

"You're better off without her, then."

He looked down at her and a slow smile curved his lips. "I knew that when she left. Meeting you—and this moment right here—is just confirmation of that fact."

"She came here because she wants you back."

"Yeah, she made that pretty clear." He paused. "But I don't want her, so it doesn't really matter."

"Would you have told me about the Afghanistan incident if she hadn't shown up tonight?"

"Yes. Maybe not tonight, but yes. I'd already decided that I needed to do that sooner rather than later."

"Okay, then."

"Just like that?"

"Just like that." She paused. "Clay, I like you . . ."

"Good, I like you too. Why do I hear the silent 'but' on the end of that statement."

"Because while I like you, I also have a past I can't seem to move . . . past." Still, the echo of the gunshots rang through her mind like it was yesterday. The vision of Dennis falling to the floor . . .

"Wanna talk about it?"

"Not really."

"Then don't. Why don't we just enjoy the moment and worry about unpacking later?"

Julianna returned his smile and settled her head back against his shoulder. "That sounds really nice."

For the next twenty minutes, they watched the rest of the show. And it was a good one. But once it was over, her smile faded and memories intruded. The date she'd circled in red on her calendar was coming up fast, and she knew her brief moment of peace wouldn't last much longer. Again, she had a tiny niggling in the back of her mind, and she let herself go with it instead of pushing it away. She never liked to remember that day, of course, but had a feeling she needed to.

She sat up slowly, her mind spinning.

"Please, Dennis, drop the gun. I'll go with you. I'll do whatever you want."

"Yeah, now that I have a gun on you. Well, it's too late."

"Dennis, just let them go. It's me you want, right?"

"Not anymore. And I have to make sure you don't do this to anyone else."

"Do what!" Kane yelled from behind her. *"What did she do, Dennis? Walk away from a guy who was hitting her? Who told her she was stupid on a regular basis? What exactly did she do that she shouldn't have done?"* Her friend screamed the words at Dennis, who lifted the weapon and took aim.

At her. *"Mine forever, Julianna. Forever."*

There was a blur of motion, and the crack of gunfire filled her ears.

"Kane!" Kara's high-pitched shriek turned into a keening wail.

"No!" She rushed toward the shooter—

"Julianna?" Clay's distant voice cut into her thoughts.

"I need to go."

"Wait. What? You okay?"

She blinked. "I just thought of something that might be connected to the case and I need to go see if I'm right." The uncertainty on his face and the tight jaw said he wasn't sure if he believed her or not. She leaned over and pressed her lips to his cheek in a quick reassuring kiss. "I promise. This has nothing to do with what you told me."

His eyes cleared and he nodded. "All right, then, let's go."

"No, I need to go into the office. And I need you to watch over Dottie and Reese." She hesitated. "Can they stay here for the night?"

"Yes, of course, but this place has great security. Let me go with you."

A footstep sounded on the dock, and Julianna stepped back to see Dottie and Reese looking down at her. "Go where?" Dottie asked.

"To the office." Julianna climbed out of the boat and waited for Clay to join them. "I need to check on something."

Dottie scowled. "You can't do that from here?"

Julianna hesitated. "Possibly. I'll call Daria and see if she can help me out."

"You can use my father's office," Reese said. "He won't care, and it will give you some privacy."

Julianna nodded. "Okay. Lead the way."

Reese did, and Clay followed at a slower pace, walking with Dottie. Julianna didn't even want to know what they were talking about—or if Reese and Dottie had witnessed her impulsive kiss. Not that she regretted it. She didn't. Not one single bit.

"Right in there," Reese said.

Julianna stepped inside the plush area. "Thank you. I hope I won't be long."

"Take your time. I'm just going to go tell my friends goodbye."

She and Dottie left, and Clay raised a brow at her from the hallway. "I'm going to see what I can do to help clean up. Come find me when you're finished?"

"Sure."

Julianna didn't even know if Daria was working at this time of night. Sometimes she was, sometimes she wasn't. Julianna dialed the number and let it ring.

"This is Ahmed."

So, tonight she wasn't. "Hi, Ahmed, this is Julianna Jameson. I need some information. Can you help me out?"

"It's a busy night, but go ahead. I'll do my best."

"Can you find everything there is to find on a person by the name of Kara Williams?" She added all the information she had, including a birth date and last known home state and city.

"Should be easy enough," Ahmed said.

The keyboard clicked in the background. Mid-click, her phone buzzed with an incoming text from Hector.

Hostage situation.

The address popped up next.

"I've got to go. Can you email everything to me?"

"Absolutely. I'll send it as soon as I have it put together in a way that will make sense."

"Thanks." She hung up and rushed from the room, only to almost collide with Clay.

"What is it?" He grasped her upper arms.

"I got a call. There's a situation about fifteen minutes from here."

"Is it him?"

"I don't know." She pulled out of his hold and headed down the hall toward the front door.

"You need someone to go with you, watch your back."

"Just watch Dottie's. I'll be fine. There will be plenty of law enforcement where I'm going."

"Julianna?" Dottie stood near the door, a frown on her face. "You got a call, didn't you?"

"I did."

The teen's jaw tightened, but she nodded. "Okay. Be careful."

"Of course. I'll text you. Like always." She paused and turned back to Clay. "I appreciate the concern. I really do. But this is my job."

"I know, but—"

"I'll be careful. I'm going to get in my car and not stop until I get to the scene." She glanced at her phone. "Now I've really got to go. Hector's waiting on me." She turned to say goodbye to Dottie, only to find the girl gone. Julianna sighed. "Tell her I'll be in touch, okay?"

"I will."

She hurried out the door and climbed into her trusty Suburban. Her phone continued to blow up with information, and she pressed the gas.

Her phone rang, going straight to her Bluetooth. Clay. She sent him to voice mail. If he was going to be this high maintenance, then there was no hope of them being together.

Not that they were together at the moment.

It rang again and she jabbed it. "Clay, I'm in the middle of—"

"Is Dottie with you?"

"What? No, of course not. What are you talking about?"

"I was looking for her and someone said they saw her climb into the back of your Suburban."

"What!" Julianna's gaze shot to the rearview mirror. "Dottie! Are you in here?"

Her sister's slight form rose from the back floorboard. "Yeah, but I—"

Something slammed into the side of the vehicle and Dottie's scream mingled with Julianna's.

"Dottie!" Julianna whipped the vehicle back on the road. "Get your seat belt on!"

Another hard hit sent her skidding back onto the edge. She fought the wheel, desperate to find a way to go on the offensive. She had a big vehicle that could take a lot, but the other person was in a Hummer. A big black machine that blended with the night and came out of nowhere.

Panting, she brought the SUV back under control once more and aimed it back toward the road.

The next ram spun the wheel under her hands and sent her slamming against the seat belt. Dottie let out another scream. The Suburban hit something, went airborne, then bounced off a tree. With no way to control the vehicle, Julianna threw her arms up to protect her face just as the airbag deployed. The vehicle went into one final spin, tipped, then landed on its passenger side and came to a shuddering halt.

Julianna hung suspended, the seat belt cutting into her while she waited for the shock to wear off and the world to stop spinning. Her arms burned and she struggled to drag in a breath around the smoky interior. "Dottie!"

"Jules."

Just hearing Dottie sent relief shooting through her. "You okay?"

"Yeah. I think. You?"

Julianna scrambled to undo the seat belt and couldn't get it undone. "I think I'm stuck," she rasped.

Dottie grunted from the back seat and Julianna heard the rear door open. She had to get out of the belt. Someone had run them off the road on purpose and she needed to get free. Now. She jammed her thumb on the seat belt button, and finally, it released. She only had a fraction of a second to brace herself before she tumbled to the passenger side.

"Jules!"

Dottie's voice held a different tone. Ignoring her aches and pains, and using the console for leverage, she shoved open the driver's door. "Dottie!" She pulled her weapon from her holster, pushed off the steering wheel and out the door. Before she could catch her balance, she tumbled down the side of the SUV and hit the pavement with a thud that knocked the breath from her.

Pulling in a gasp, she looked up and froze.

A figure dressed in black, an outline illuminated only by the headlights from the Suburban, stood next to the Hummer, a knife pressed to Dottie's throat. Dottie's eyes met hers and the terror there sent a wave of fury through her.

Julianna lifted her weapon and aimed it at the person. "FBI! Put the weapon down!" She desperately tried to get a bead on the person's head, but Dottie was in the way. A human shield.

"It's time, Julianna."

The air left her lungs and Julianna stepped forward.

The person pulled Dottie backward, forcing her with the knife to stay in step. If Dottie resisted, the knife would cut. "What do you want? Why are you doing this?"

"Because it's time."

The attacker then whispered something to Dottie, whose eyes widened. The driver slid into the Hummer and over the console, and Dottie ducked into the driver's seat.

Julianna stepped forward. "No! Dottie, don't!"

But Dottie did. The engine roared and the Hummer pulled away from the curb. Julianna raced after them, then gave up. There was no way she could chase them on foot.

A car pulled next to her battered SUV, and she could see Clay behind the wheel. He opened the driver's door, and she bolted toward him. "Someone just kidnapped Dottie!"

"What!"

She threw herself into the passenger seat and slammed the door. Clay did the same on his side.

"Drive!" she yelled, her voice thick with fear.

Clay hit the gas and they sped down the back road. Julianna got on her phone and called in a description of the black Hummer.

"Which way did he go?" she asked Clay. "You pulled up just as he drove away."

"I saw taillights." He paused. "But at the stop sign, I think they went left."

"Then you do too." Clay did so, and she arranged for a chopper and a roadblock and gave the best description she had of the vehicle, her sister, and the person who took her, while her eyes scanned every vehicle that might have Dottie at the wheel. A BOLO went out to local law enforcement with the same information, and Dottie's face would be on the television as an endangered missing person. It wasn't much, but they'd work with it. They had to. The streetlamps shone bright, but distinguishing the taillights of the Hummer from the other vehicles on the road was surprisingly impossible.

"No," she whispered, "please . . . oh, God, help. Where is she? He's got a knife," she said. "Not sure about a gun."

Clay drove faster, passing cars while Julianna held out desperate hope that one of them would have Dottie driving. None did. "He could have turned off somewhere," she said, her voice low. He could have. Probably had. The terror Julianna had been pushing down surged to the surface. Her sister was gone. And it was all her fault.

■ ■ ■ ■

Clay had nearly had a coronary when he discovered Dottie missing. He'd sent Reese to find her, and when she came back with a frown on her face and shaking her head, he had a sneaking suspicion of what the teen had done. So he asked around and got confirmation. He'd called until Julianna picked up. The sound of the first thud still echoed in his head. Their screams and the subsequent crash were etched in his memory.

And now Dottie had been taken. "It's my fault," he said. "I'm sorry. I—" His fingers flexed around the wheel. He dragged in a breath and decided to just shut up. There was nothing to say.

"It's not your fault, Clay," Julianna said. "Dottie's a big girl and made the decision to stow away. I'm sure she didn't expect these consequences, but it's not your fault." She breathed in through her nose and let the air out slowly through pursed lips. "Can you take me back to the scene?"

"Yeah."

"I have to let Hector know I won't be there. Someone else can handle this. I've got to find Dottie." She glanced at her phone. "Twenty-two messages wondering where I am." She dialed her boss, and Clay fell silent while she explained the situation. "I know, Hector. Yeah. Thank you." She hung up and glanced at Clay. "He said he had another negotiator en route and to do whatever I needed to find Dottie. Two agents are on the way as well."

"Good." They rode the rest of the way in silence, and he pulled to a stop next to a police cruiser with flashing blue lights.

She climbed out with a wince and a low groan, then raked a hand over her head and surveyed the scene. Clay tried to view it through her eyes.

Several officers were near her vehicle. Others were up on the road directing traffic. "There aren't any security cameras around here," he said. "A perfect spot for an ambush. Someone's been watching you. They either followed you or Dottie out here."

She shook her head. "I still don't get it. Why go after Dottie?

If the person is after me, why take Dottie when I was right there at the wreck?"

"To get your attention is the first thing that comes to mind. Especially after that note the person left."

"Yeah. That's all I could come up with too. I was hoping you might have something different."

"Who was the first person out of the SUV after you wrecked?"

"Dottie. I was still struggling to get my belt undone. About the time I did, I heard her call my name. It still took me a minute to get out of the vehicle, and when I did, the person was standing there watching me, holding a knife to Dottie's throat." She snapped her lips together and her jaw was so rigid, Clay was surprised her teeth hadn't shattered from the pressure. "But who?" she whispered. "If someone hates me this bad, I should be able to figure that out, right?"

"You'd thought of something earlier."

"Yes." She pressed a hand to her forehead. "Ahmed, an analyst, is checking on that for me, but another thought's come to mind."

"What?"

"I've never lost a hostage, but hostage takers . . . there have been three." She bit her lip and looked away. "I try so hard to convince them to give it up, to walk away, and have managed to do that every single time, except for those three . . ."

"You think it could be someone angry about one of the hostage takers getting killed?"

"Maybe," she murmured.

Two agents dressed in FBI attire approached, and Julianna turned her frown from him to them.

"I need to be involved in finding Dottie," she said, her fists clenched at her sides. "And they're not going to let me help investigate."

"You'll help by telling them everything you can remember about what just happened."

"Of course."

"Then let's get talking. Dottie's waiting for someone to find her."

■   ■   ■   ■

Dottie's head pounded and her throat was dry. Like the time she'd had a raging fever in the fifth grade and she'd had to go home from school. Her mom had been ticked about having to leave work and pick her up. She was working as a real estate agent at that point, and her every waking hour was focused on sucking up to her rich clients. All the way from the school to the house, she ranted about the money she might potentially lose because of Dottie.

Even at the age of ten, Dottie had long since learned how to tune the woman out and had no idea what was said after that. She felt too lousy to listen. Her mother had barely stopped to let Dottie out of the car before peeling away from the curb to head to her next appointment.

Whatever. She had no idea what she'd done to make her mother hate her and had given up trying to figure it out.

She wanted to shake her head to clear the cobwebs but didn't dare move as the memories tumbled back in waves. Someone had run her and Julianna off the road, and that someone had forced Dottie into the car, telling her to drive or Julianna would die. So, Dottie had driven. Two minutes later, she'd been ordered to pull into a private driveway, and the person in the black mask had sprayed something in Dottie's face. That was the last thing she remembered.

Until now. And now she was here.

Which was . . . where?

As the drug wore off, Dottie took a physical inventory. Her wrists were red and sore where the zip tie had rubbed them, but aside from the headache, nothing else hurt. She was starving, though, and desperately thirsty.

She blinked and pulled the room into focus, thanks to the flashlight someone had left on in the far corner. The pale beam illuminated the eight-by-ten room. It smelled of . . . cleaning products? Definitely old bleach, but this place hadn't been cleaned in forever. She lay on the tile floor, noting there were less-dirty spots among the filthy. Like the room had been cleared of any possible weapon or tool? Sickness engulfed her, and she gagged, then pushed herself into a sitting position.

From her vantage point, she could see a half bath through the open door. Dottie shoved to her feet, swayed, then lurched to the toilet and lost the contents of her stomach.

When the retching passed, she dropped to the dirty, peeling linoleum floor to suck in air. "Breathe," she whispered, "just breathe." And that's all she focused on for the next few minutes. Finally, the nausea faded and she sat up, wiped the sweat from her face, and flushed the commode. Which did nothing. Great. No water. Things could get terribly unpleasant if she didn't find a way out soon.

With gritted teeth, she hauled herself out of the bathroom and shut the door. She walked back across the room while she worked to keep the panic and tears at bay. She had to think, and crying wouldn't solve anything. She'd learned that lesson well enough as a child.

"Think, Dottie." For some reason, hearing her own voice helped get her fear under control.

Okay. Someone had taken her at knifepoint. The only thing that gave her any kind of hope was the knowledge that Julianna had seen it all happen. She'd be turning over every stone and calling in every favor to find Dottie.

But would it be in time? She scanned her prison, looking for anything she could use as a weapon. The toilet tank lid had been removed. So, basically, unless she could get the toilet seat off, or remove the sink from the wall, she was out of luck for a weapon.

The door opened and a brown paper bag landed with a thud on the floor, followed by three bottles of water. "Eat." The door shut. It happened so fast, Dottie didn't have time to call out or have a spike in fear.

Her stomach rumbled, but the nausea returned at the same time. She eyed the bag and swallowed hard, the thought of eating sending her stomach into spins again. She waited until the sensation passed, weighing her options. She should probably eat to keep her strength up if she was going to have to fight her way out of this place.

She walked over and picked up the bag. Surprisingly, it was still warm and smelled good. A burger and fries from the Bad Burger Barn. She pulled the burger out and went to remove the onions, but found none on the sandwich. In fact, it was exactly like she would have ordered it.

The nausea returned. Whoever had taken her had definitely been watching her.

Had seen her order a burger at the restaurant.

Had been close enough to hear her ask for no onions.

Dottie thought she might throw up again. She curled her fingers around the food and considered tossing it across the room, but . . . she was hungry. She sniffed the burger, trying to decide if she could smell anything that shouldn't be there. Like a drug or whatever. But she knew that smell wouldn't necessarily guarantee the food wasn't drugged. Or the bottles of water.

But the wrapper didn't look disturbed, and it had the little thank-you sticker holding it together. Just like every other to-go order she'd ever placed. Dottie decided if her kidnapper wanted to kill her, he wouldn't bother feeding her.

Right?

Only one way to find out.

She bit into the burger.

CHAPTER
SIXTEEN

Hours had passed and Saturday had slipped into Sunday with no word from Dottie—or her kidnapper. However, Max called to let her know both Evelyn and Christopher had airtight alibis for the bank situation as well as the time of the crash and Dottie's kidnapping. It wasn't either of them. She'd also given Max the other three names of the hostage takers who'd died on her shift, and their family members had alibis as well. So, they'd reached a dead end. But she couldn't *have* a dead end, because that would mean Dottie could be lost to her forever. And that wasn't something she could live with.

For a moment, she considered whether to call her mother and fill her in, but the truth was, she probably wouldn't care. Oh, she'd pretend she did, and she'd rake Julianna over the coals for allowing this to happen, but in the end, she'd milk Dottie's disappearance for all it was worth, then get on with her life once that ran dry.

But still . . . didn't she owe it to her to tell her?

Unsure why she felt that way, Julianna picked up her phone and punched in her mother's number. Then hung up.

She'd give it a little more time. Maybe Dottie would be home in a few hours.

Please, God.

Fatigue pulled at her, but how could she sleep when Dottie—
"Ugh! Where are you, Dottie?"

Two agents she worked with on a regular basis, Special Agents
Calvin Taylor and Margot Dean, were in her den in case a ransom
call came in. Clay insisted on staying with her and had sacked out
on the couch to snag a couple of hours' rest. Reese was in Dottie's
room sleeping, after talking to her boss about taking a few days
off. Julianna thought that was probably a good idea. Hector had
suggested the same thing to her and she'd agreed. For the moment.
She paced from one end of the room to the other, thinking.

Her phone buzzed and she glanced at the text, heart in her
throat. Grace. Her heart dropped back into place.

I know it's late, but I also know you're not
sleeping. I'm coming with food. Will be a couple
of hours before I get there.

Julianna tapped back.

Thank you.

Telling Grace she didn't need to come was pointless. The woman
would show up regardless. Just like Julianna would do for Grace
should their roles be reversed.

On her last turn around the kitchen, she whirled to see Clay
standing in the doorway, hands shoved into the front pockets of
his jeans.

"Hey," he said. His posture said he was eaten up with guilt, in
spite of her reassurances that he wasn't to blame.

"Hey. Still nothing, huh?"

He shook his head.

"I'm not surprised," she said. "This isn't about a ransom. They
won't call for that." Maybe for something else, but not a ransom.
And Ahmed still hadn't gotten back to her about Kara Williams.
She glanced at the calendar on the refrigerator. The date loomed

one day closer. She cleared her throat and did her best to shove aside the memories—and the habits that came with them. But tuning out the world wasn't an option at the moment. "Um . . . I know that you want to do a big culmination thing on your law enforcement month. Can I help you plan it? You know, and we can talk about what you want me to do for the hostage negotiation part?"

"Aw, Julianna, no. You don't have to worry about that. Not right now."

She clasped her hands together in front of her. "What else am I going to do? I need to do *something*. Stay busy."

"Yeah, I get that. I'd be the same way." He studied her for a brief second. "Okay." He took a seat at the kitchen table. "You have a pen and paper? I'll take some notes. Hopefully, I'll have a day and time soon."

"Perfect."

She went to the drawer next to the sink and grabbed a pen and pad. When she slid the items across the table to him, he covered her hand with his. "We'll find her."

Her fingers spasmed, but she met his gaze and nodded. "Absolutely."

"Okay, then."

"Okay, then."

For the next two hours, they worked on the end-of-year program, with Julianna glancing at her phone every few seconds. She caught Clay watching her. "I can't help it."

"I know."

"Grace is almost here. She's bringing food."

"It's the wee hours of the morning and over an hour's drive back. She's a really good friend."

Julianna smiled. "Yeah. She has insomnia sometimes, so time doesn't mean a whole lot to her."

Three minutes later, a knock on her kitchen door pulled her to her feet and she let her friend in.

Grace hugged her. "Nothing?"

"No."

"Well, I've got burgers and chicken fingers, salad, fruit, a side of mac 'n' cheese, and your favorite . . . asparagus."

Julianna's throat clogged once more at the love Grace so easily bestowed, and she hiccupped a short laugh. "Gross."

"I know, but I like it. Clay probably does too. Hi, Clay."

"Hi, Grace." His deep voice rumbled through the kitchen, tinged with amusement. "I love asparagus."

Grace smiled at Clay. "Julianna hates vegetables."

"I've heard."

Grace set the bags on the counter and the fruit in the refrigerator. "I want to help."

Clay nodded to the den. "I'll give you two some space."

"It's not necessary," Julianna said.

"I don't mind. Holler if you need anything."

He left, and Grace pulled a chicken finger from the bag and handed it to Julianna. "Eat. I know you haven't."

Julianna took a bite, then placed the food on the napkin on the table.

"That's a start," Grace muttered. "Now, tell me everything you know about this person who took Dottie."

"That's the problem, I don't know who took her. I'm waiting on Ahmed to get back to me with some information I requested about someone I know." She bit her lip and pressed fingers to her forehead.

"Who?" Grace asked.

"Kara Williams."

Grace's eyes widened and her nostrils flared. "Oh. I thought she was in a psychiatric hospital."

"I did too."

"Why would you think she would be the one to come after you, then?"

"I don't, really. It's just that the anniversary of the shooting is coming up and I keep flashing back to the day . . . and after. When it was all over, she went from screaming that it was all my fault to refusing to speak to me at all." She shrugged. "I don't know. I'm probably grasping at straws."

"Maybe. Or maybe your subconscious is working and there's a reason it's nudging you."

Julianna smiled at her friend. "Hmm. That sounds like something you'd say."

"Come on, Jules, you have a lot of psychology in your background and training. There's a reason your mind went to her."

"Okay, fine. Let's say that's true. Why would my mind go there? I think about her often, of course, have always wanted to reconcile, but never once did I consider that she might be plotting to kill me."

"Your mind went there because with everything that's happened, she's simply a possibility in the midst of all the cases you've worked."

"But that's just it. That wasn't a case." She shook her head. "But I do know that Kara decided it was my fault her brother died—and I can't say it's not."

"Her brother died because a maniac took a school hostage and shot him."

Julianna slammed a fist on the table. "A maniac that I invited into our lives—" She broke off when her words threatened to become sobs. She drew in a steadying breath. "It's been fifteen years, Grace. How do I get past it? And I know I'm a rotten person because I want to, but it's like that one day has shaped my life and every decision I've ever made. Does that ever get to stop?"

Grace reached out to curl her fingers around Julianna's, and the tears shimmering in Grace's eyes made it hard to keep from crying herself. "Jules," Grace said, "until you accept that the incident wasn't your fault, that Dennis made his own decisions, you're not going to be able to put it in the past where it belongs." Grace's fingers tightened. "And if you don't get some sleep, you're not going to do Dottie any good. Will you please just go lie down? I promise if anything at all happens, I'll come get you. Or Clay will."

Sleep would be nice. Her brain was misfiring and her emotions were right on the surface. A lack of sleep would make her careless. She finally nodded. "Yeah."

"Good." Grace rose and Julianna followed her to her bedroom, where she simply fell across the bed and closed her eyes.

When Grace left, Julianna lay there, her heart heavy, her mind in chaos. She drew in a deep breath and sat up, then slid from the bed and walked to the table, where she settled into the chair and opened her laptop. She needed some answers before she could close her eyes, in spite of her fatigue. But first—

"Lord, I know you've got Dottie. You've had her since she was born. She's yours because I gave her to you when I realized I couldn't protect her." She swallowed hard. "But this is something I never imagined and I'm struggling to trust you. Please, God, protect her. If anything happens to her because of me—"

A soft knock at the door broke off the prayer and sent her heart racing. "Come in."

Clay stepped into the room and raised a brow. "Grace said you were sleeping."

"And you wanted to wake me up by checking? Have you heard something about Dottie?"

"No, sorry. I saw the light come on under your door and wanted to make sure you were okay." He paused. "Or, if not okay, then ask if I could do anything for you."

While her hope that they'd heard something withered, she managed to offer him a smile. She liked him. A lot. His thoughtfulness and kind heart drew her like a magnet. His good looks didn't hurt either, but she worked with a lot of handsome men. That didn't mean she'd consider trusting one of them with her heart. Clay might be a different story—once Dottie was home safe. "I'm all right. Just thinking about something I talked to Grace about—and the thing that occurred to me at your parents' house."

"What's that?"

It was time to tell him. Everything. He'd unloaded his deepest hurts to her. Could she not do the same? Pulling in a steadying breath, she swiped a hand over her face and organized her words. "During my senior year of high school," she finally said, "I was best friends with a girl named Kara Williams. It's a long story, but her twin brother was killed by my ex-boyfriend, Dennis Collins."

He flinched. "Oh, Julianna, how awful."

"It was. Truly so awful and hard, I didn't think I'd survive that day, or a lot of days after. Anyway, it occurred to me that maybe Kara is somehow behind all of this."

He nodded to the computer. "And you want to do some digging."

"Yeah. I know Ahmed or Daria have access to more information than I'll find on here, but it's a start."

"Don't you have anyone from high school that you can call? Someone who kept in touch with her?"

Julianna frowned and thought, mentally flipping through some of the people she'd been friends with. "I wasn't one of the popular kids in school, because I hung out with Kara and defended her against the bullies. She was different. Fragile. She was so sensitive and easily hurt that Kane and I did our best to protect her."

"Kane?"

"Her twin brother. The one Dennis killed."

"She doesn't sound like a killer to me."

With a shake of her head, Julianna tapped the touch bar on the laptop to bring it to life. "She wasn't. But when Kane died, something inside her broke. I want to see what I can find out now. If I get sleepy, I'll lie down."

"Can I stay?"

His soft question caused her throat to tighten and tears to threaten, so she simply nodded, grateful for his presence.

■ ■ ■ ■

"Melissa Green," Julianna said.

Clay blinked at her. "What?"

"There are lots of Kara Williamses on social media, so I'd rather just start with a friend. Melissa was a cheerleader and she hung out with the popular clique, but she had a kind heart. She was there and witnessed the shooting." Julianna leaned in and narrowed her eyes at the screen. "She still lives in Burbank. I'll call her."

She reached for the phone and Clay rested a hand over hers. "It's three hours earlier there."

Julianna stilled under his touch and glanced at the clock. "Which means it's midnight there." She paused. "Think that's too late to call?"

"A bit."

"Well, at least I know she'll be home."

"If she's not sleeping elsewhere."

"Gotta try." She dialed the number she'd retrieved from the FBI site and pressed the phone to her ear.

"Put it on speaker?" he asked.

She did so and set the phone on the desk next to the laptop.

"Hello?" a sleepy voice croaked.

"I'm so sorry to call in the middle of the night, but this is Julianna Jameson. I hope you remember me."

"Julianna Jameson?" Melissa sounded a lot more alert this time. "From high school?"

"Yes."

"What in the world? Do you know what time it is?"

"Yes, I'm really sorry. I wouldn't have called if it wasn't important."

"Hold on a sec." A pause, then her soft voice explaining it wasn't an emergency and to go back to sleep. Then a shuffle and the soft snick of a door closing. "Okay, I'm in the bathroom so I don't wake up the rest of my household. I have six kids and don't need them awake anytime soon."

"I'm so sorry."

"It's okay. I'll just look on the bright side and enjoy the alone time while I can."

At the tinge of humor in her voice, Clay shot Julianna a small smile and she nodded. "Thank you for not hanging up on me," she said.

"No way. I'm rabid with curiosity at why someone I haven't talked to in fifteen years would call me at midnight. What's up?"

"I don't know if you've heard, but I work for the FBI, and I need to ask you a few questions related to a case I'm investigating."

"I'd heard you were in law enforcement. And I saw the news about the hostage situation at the courthouse with Nicholas Manchester."

"Right."

"That was when I realized you were a negotiator. That was a pretty incredible thing."

"Thank you."

"But I know you didn't call to play catch-up, so what can I do for you?"

"Yes, again, I'm sorry. But have you kept up with Kara Williams at all? I know you weren't besties or anything, but you were always kind to her when others weren't."

"I liked Kara. I hate that she was treated so terribly and tried my best not to let stupid peer pressure influence me."

"You succeeded. Anyway, I thought I remembered your parents being friends with Kara's."

"Yeah, they still are. Kara's been a mess ever since . . . well, you know."

"I know."

Clay noted the subtle shift in Julianna's posture. Her spine stiffened and she linked her fingers together in front of her tight enough to whiten her knuckles.

"Last I heard," Melissa said, "Kara was in a psychiatric hospital and has been for years. She was suicidal and depressed after Kane was killed."

"What's the name of the hospital?"

"I'm not sure, but I can find out from Mom in the morning." Because she wasn't going to call or text anyone at this time of night.

Clay raised his brows at the subtle rebuke. Or maybe it was just his imagination and Melissa meant nothing more than what she actually said.

"Your mom would probably appreciate that."

"She's a pretty early riser, so it might only be a few hours."

"That would be great. Just text this number."

"Sure thing."

"Anything else you can tell me?"

"Um, no, I don't think so. Mom might have more information, but from what I understand, the Williamses don't talk about Kara. In fact, they've pretty much erased her from their lives."

Clay flinched. Wow. That was sad. Then again, if she was a killer . . .

"Oh, wait. One more question. Do you remember if Kara wrote poetry? I don't ever remember her doing that in high school, but she could have started after we lost touch."

"Um, yes. That's so weird that you would ask that, but yeah. I think she mailed her parents a poem not too long ago. It was dark and horrible, and I remember Mom saying that Kara's mother threw it away."

"So, they just ignored it?"

"Yeah. Like I said, they pretty much disowned her. I mean, she shot them in their sleep, so yeah . . . I can't really fault them for wiping their hands of her."

Julianna gasped and Clay jerked. "What?"

"Oh, you hadn't heard?"

"No. I've pretty much tried to put that entire chapter of my life out of my mind."

"I can certainly understand that. There was a whole write-up in the newspaper about it."

"Okay, thank you. And again, I'm sorry to wake you." Julianna said her goodbyes and hung up with a grimace. "Well, that was . . . enlightening."

"Yeah. Very. But there's nothing to be done for a few hours. Why don't you lie down and get some rest? It's going to be a while before she calls her mother. And by then, Ahmed might have something for you."

Julianna yawned, then shook her head. "I knew Kara had issues, but I had no idea the extent."

"I know you're going to want to read that article, but let's let Ahmed find all the info while you sleep. Dottie needs you rested and able to think."

"Hmm."

She sounded like she was humoring him, but when she stood and walked to the bed to stretch out, he kept his mouth shut. He covered her with the blanket from the end of the bed and ran a hand through her hair. He liked it loose from her usual ponytail. She stared up at him, then captured his hand in hers and kissed his palm.

In a totally cliché move, he curled his fingers around the kiss. "Sleep."

"Right."

He turned the lamp off and headed for the door.

When he glanced back, he could make out her form, thanks to the night-light glow coming from the bathroom. Her eyes were closed and her breathing already even and slow, but her fingers were curled tight around her phone.

CHAPTER
SEVENTEEN

Felicity sat at her kitchen table with her Bible open in front of her. Once again, the Lord had awakened her to read and pray long before Tommy would be up. She read the passage in Matthew for the third time. This time out loud. "Then Peter came to Jesus and asked, 'Lord, how many times shall I forgive my brother or sister who sins against me? Up to seven times?' Jesus answered, 'I tell you, not seven times, but seventy-seven times.'"

She dropped her head into her hands. "How, Lord? How do I fully forgive like you've commanded? Some days I think I'm close. Other days the anger is like a tsunami, triggered by the most innocent thing. Wyatt's death didn't take you by surprise like it did me, but knowing you could have stopped it . . . hurts. I'll be honest, it feels like a betrayal that you didn't. And yet . . . I know that's not your character. I know who you are and you love Wyatt more than Tommy and I ever could." She sniffed and swiped the tears she hadn't realized she was crying.

"Mommy? Are you okay?"

Tommy's sleepy, soft voice reached her before he did. She pulled him into her lap and rested her cheek against his head while drinking in early-morning little-boy smell. "Yes, I'm okay, sweetheart. I'm just missing Daddy and asking God some questions."

"Is he answering?"

She glanced at the open Bible and the verses she now had committed to memory, she'd read them so often. "Yes. He is."

"Good. I like it when he talks to me."

Her breath stilled in her throat. She cleared it. "What does he say to you?"

"One time I had a dream and I went up to God and asked him if my daddy was happy in heaven. God let Daddy show me himself."

The tears flowed once more and she didn't even try to stop them. "And?" she choked. "What did Daddy show you?"

"He picked me up and swung me around and said he was super happy. He also told me he'd see me when I got to heaven. But I could only come when it was my time. Not before. And then he put me down and told me to take care of you and that he loved you."

She couldn't speak. Only God could have let her son dream such a thing. What a gift. "Thank you," she whispered.

"You're welcome." She didn't bother to tell Tommy she hadn't been thanking him. He hopped down from her lap. "Are we going to church? It's Sunday."

"Yes sir, we're going for sure."

"Good." He touched her cheek. "You look happier."

"That's because I am."

■ ■ ■ ■

I wasn't exactly sure how I'd managed to pull off taking Dottie from the scene of the accident. It hadn't occurred to me that she'd be there. I'd half made up my mind to simply shoot Julianna and be done with it, but when I saw Dottie, the words echoed in my mind.

There are some things worse than death. Sometimes simply losing someone we love is enough to end all chance at happiness.

Enough to silence laughter and squelch any kind of joy. Sometimes.

I thought about those words often because they were so true. I thought about the one that I lost and remembered the searing pain as though it had happened yesterday. It was funny that those words came to mind as soon as I saw that Dottie was there in the midst of the crash. I figured she would have been at the party, and I'd tried to get in, but there'd been way too much security. So, I'd called in a hostage situation, asked for Julianna, and the rest was history.

Destiny.

Dottie had been there, and I knew then that I was supposed to take her. Take Dottie and make Julianna suffer. That was my mission. It was so simple.

Stick to the plan. If you stick to the plan, everything will work out like it's supposed to.

Well, I'd varied the plan a bit, but I'd done a good job. I'd wanted the Hummer when I saw it idling in the parking lot at the gas station. I laughed, and didn't recognize the sound for a minute. Then let the chuckle linger. Because . . . who leaves their keys in a *Hummer?* I'd have settled for a basic SUV. I had the element of surprise on my side and would have achieved the same result no matter the vehicle. But the Hummer? That had been fun. I think. It'd been so long since I could use the word *fun* that I wasn't sure I even recognized the feeling to attach to the word. Then again, I did feel something for the first time in . . . well, since what seemed like forever. I felt . . . I couldn't pinpoint the emotion.

I continued to roll the sensation around, looking for the word. It finally came to me.

Glad.

More adjectives rolled in.

Happy. No, happy was too much. More like *relieved. Purposeful.* Like I finally had a reason for being alive. I'd only experienced that emotion once or twice before, but now it was so clear. I was here to complete the plan.

Everyone has a reason for being born. Every one of us. Sometimes it takes time to discover that reason and we figure it out after an event or incident that changes our lives and gives us a new focus and purpose. Sometimes it takes someone wiser or more knowledgeable than us to point us in that direction.

I could agree with that. I picked up the phone and dialed the number I'd used during the bank situation.

Today was Sunday. There weren't many federal buildings open on Sunday. But I'd found one. I'd make it count.

CHAPTER
EIGHTEEN

Clay pushed open the door to Julianna's room. She lay on her side on top of her comforter, one fist tucked up under her cheek while the other hand still clutched her phone. She'd been sleeping for about two hours.

Her body had demanded rest and Clay was glad to see her cave to it. He walked over to her and brushed the hair from her face. She was frowning even in her sleep. "Julianna?" he said, his voice soft, not wanting to spook her. "Hey." He gave her shoulder a slight shake and she opened her eyes.

When she sat up, she was fully alert. He blinked. How in the world—?

"What is it?" she asked.

"The agents think they may have something."

Without another word, she raked a hand through her hair, rose, and hurried into the den. He followed her. Grace was still here, talking in low tones with the other agents. The three sat on the couch, their laptops open on the coffee table in front of them.

"What'd you find?" Julianna asked.

Calvin looked up. "We found traffic footage. Or rather, Ahmed did. He said to tell you he had to pass your previous request to Daria in order to switch over to do this."

"That's fine, but I thought she was off."

"She's not now."

At her grimace, Clay frowned. "What?"

"Hope she didn't have any major plans for the day."

"It's the nature of the job, Jules," Margot said. "You know that."

"I'm not feeling guilty, just a little bad for her. Where's the car?"

"Ahmed said he pulled up a map and tracked every way the Hummer could go from the scene of the crash. With your description and some common sense, he found it heading toward downtown. Then it turned off the main road and we lost it around this area here. It's a neighborhood."

He pointed to the screen and Julianna bent for a closer look with narrowed eyes.

"That's not too far from the courthouse where Manchester pulled his little stunt. I wonder if that's on purpose?" she murmured.

"We sent agents into the area to look for the vehicle," Margot said, shoving her long dark bangs behind her ear. "I mean, it's a Hummer. You wouldn't think it would be that hard to spot, but so far, we've got nothing."

"He's there," Julianna said. "Somewhere. And so is Dottie. Where does that street go? The one he turned onto just before you lost him?"

"It splinters off in about five different directions, but there's no outlet."

Hope flashed on her face and Clay knew his features reflected the same. "Then that's good," Julianna said. "We need agents on the street at the entrance. If he went in, he has to come back out, right?"

Margot nodded.

Julianna bit her lip. "What's there? Rentals? Vacant homes? It's not the best area in downtown."

Calvin grabbed his phone. "I'll get Ahmed to pull up all the rentals and houses for sale that might be empty. We may just have to see if the local officers will be willing to go door-to-door."

"They will," Clay said.

Margot got on her phone and Julianna pressed fingers to her eyes. Clay frowned. She was still exhausted, but suggesting she head back to bed wouldn't go over well. Even he knew that. He walked over to stand next to her.

Before he could offer to get her something to drink or eat, her phone rang and she snatched it up to swipe the screen. "Hector. Hi. Yeah, we're looking for her. What? Where?"

Clay listened to her side of the conversation with unapologetic interest. She hung up and looked at the three of them. "I've got to go. It's him."

Grace stepped forward. "What?"

"He's asked for me by name again."

Clay blinked. "What do you mean, 'again'?"

"He's targeting me," she said, not really answering his question. "Which made Dottie a target too—and I didn't do enough to protect her." She shook her head and her hands curled into fists. "Now he's playing with me. He's stashed my sister and then called me to a hostage situation. Well, all right, then." She marched to grab her Bucar keys off the table. "While I'm keeping him entertained, you guys figure out how to get to Dottie. At least if I've got him talking to me, he's not hurting her." She bolted out the door.

Clay stayed on her heels and Grace was right behind him. "Julianna," he said. "Hold up." He reached out to snag her bicep and she spun to face him. The sheer agony in her gaze rocked him back a step and he dropped his hand. "Julianna?"

She blinked and the look was gone. "You can't go, Clay. Please, just let me handle this. It's my job."

Clay lifted his hands in surrender, his feelings taking a jab for a brief moment. Then reason returned. She didn't mean to push him aside. She was right. This *was* her job. "Okay. But will you at least keep me updated on how you're doing?"

"Absolutely."

His angst settled. "Thank you."

"I'm going to have an agent in California go talk to Kara's parents and get back to me. I need to know what they have to say about their daughter." And then she was gone.

He turned to Grace. "I need to help."

Grace smiled and patted his shoulder. "You are. You're letting her be her."

Not exactly what he'd meant, but he'd work with it.

And find another way to help.

■ ■ ■ ■

Julianna drove with purpose, her phone resting in the clip on her dash while Hector updated her over the Bluetooth. "The post office on Dillon Street is open on Sundays with full-service hours. We managed to access the footage, and the suspect came in, shut the doors behind him, and locked them with a chain."

"Security?"

"No live guards. Just cameras."

"Is he actually still in the building?"

"That was our first question and the answer is yes. He's there."

"Why that post office?" she asked. Mostly to herself. She already knew the obvious answer.

"It's a federal building and he knew you'd most likely be the one to respond." Hector stated what she was already thinking.

But, for some reason, she thought there was more to it. "And he asked for me by name to make sure," she muttered. "What's the exit route for this guy?"

"All escape routes are being plugged as we speak."

"He'll have a plan to get out." The suspect was a he until it was a she. "When you get him, I want to talk to him," she said. "He knows where Dottie is. He can *not* get away. And for heaven's sake, please don't shoot him! I need him alive. *Dottie* needs him alive."

"I hear you, but keep in mind, the only reason I'm even allowing you on the scene is because of his request. If it'll save hostages—"

"I know, Hector. Thank you." The truth was, she shouldn't be anywhere near the scene, but if talking to the guy—or Kara—would save a life, she'd be there. In a very limited capacity, as far as the case was concerned, but maybe they could get the hostages out this time. Before Julianna had to do much of anything.

Julianna closed the distance between her and the downtown post office. When she pulled to a stop, the command post was already there and ready for her. The other negotiator was on the way, but Julianna didn't figure anyone but her would get a chance to talk to the guy. She took a moment to close her eyes and breathe a prayer for wisdom and preservation of life. *Please, Lord, don't let anyone die—not even the person causing this. I need him to tell me where Dottie is. And, in my heart, I believe all life is precious. And so do you. Please, God . . . hear my prayer.*

She climbed from her vehicle and hurried to the RV. She stepped inside and Hector passed her the phone. She settled into her seat and dialed the number he gave her.

Someone answered but didn't say anything. Julianna frowned. "Angel?"

"You remembered my name."

"Of course. You know, in all my years of negotiation, I've had only one person ever request me."

"Me."

"You." Julianna tilted her head. The voice was disguised, and Julianna listened hard, trying to distinguish if it belonged to her high school friend. "Do you know me? Have we met?"

Silence.

"Angel?"

"We've met."

"Then tell me who you are."

"Not yet. I have to fulfill my purpose first."

Purpose? That sounded ominous. "What did I do to you to make you hate me so much?" She was asking all the questions she could think of without revealing her suspicions.

A chuckle from the suspect again sparked pings of recognition. It *could* be Kara, but . . . "It'll come to you."

"What I did or who you are?"

"Once you figure out one, you'll know the other."

This was getting her nowhere. "You rammed my car last night and kidnapped my sister."

A pause. "I did."

Well, good to know they had the right person. Julianna swallowed. "Is she okay?"

"For now. But I have plans for her."

Julianna was not liking that idea. "What kind of plans?"

"Complicated plans. And yet simple. In the end she'll die and it'll be your fault."

Her fingers spasmed. She grappled against the desire to scream at the person on the other end of the line. But years of suppressing that very thing allowed her to bite off the words. Then again, she'd never been in such a personal negotiation situation before either. Hector's hand on her upper arm helped her keep her cool. "I see. I'm not sure how that works, Angel." She was relieved the tone in her voice didn't reveal her agitation. "How is it my fault if you kill Dottie?"

"Not if. When."

Again, she had to close her eyes, but a tremor shuddered through her. "Is there anything I can do to stop that? If you hate me so much, why don't I walk in there right now and you let Dottie go? I'll give you me and you can have your revenge."

Angel laughed. A deep, harsh sound that Julianna *knew* she'd never heard before. *God, how do I know this person?*

"Are you scared for Dottie?" Angel asked. "Are you worried? Is your heart pounding? Are you afraid you'll never see her again? Would you do anything at all to save her?"

"Yes. To all. You know that." So, this person had felt the same and wanted Julianna to feel it as well. Why? *Who?* It had to be Kara, but should she let on that she knew or not? "I've never lost a hostage—"

"Yes, and you pride yourself on that, don't you?"

Julianna blinked. "What?" Where had that come from?

"I'm not letting these people go, Julianna Jameson, no matter what you say."

"A SWAT team is on standby, Angel." Julianna had filed the comment for further investigation, but for now, she needed to get the hostages out. "They'll shoot you."

"I know. I also know that I'm not finished with my mission, so I won't be captured or killed today. The same doesn't go for Dottie. You might as well say goodbye to her now, because you'll never see her again."

Click.

Julianna flinched. Dottie was almost out of time. She looked at Hector. "You said there were three employees, right?"

"Yeah."

"Where are they?"

"Don't know. He's hidden them."

A cold certainty settled in her gut and she drew in a deep breath. She took off the headset and stood.

"What are you doing?"

"Going in."

"I can't let you do that."

Julianna clenched a fist. "I have to. This is what she wants."

"*She?*"

"I think so."

He frowned. "You know who it is?"

"I think it's someone from my high school days. You remember my telling you about the school shooting my senior year?"

"Yeah. You think this is someone from way back then?"

"I do, but I'm just not sure. I have Daria working on finding out all she can on her." Her phone buzzed with a text from Max.

Hummer was stolen.

"Of course it was," she muttered.

"Julianna?" Hector nudged her. "How do you know this is what she wants?"

She sighed, impatience warring with the need to explain to her boss what she was thinking. No, what she was feeling in her gut. "She's studied me. I don't know why or how long, but she has. She knows if she quits talking, I'll come in. I've done it before and she's betting that I'll do it again."

"Like you did at the courthouse?"

"Yeah." And other places.

"So, what you're saying is, you want to walk into a trap?"

Julianna steeled her spine and jutted her chin. "I'm saying I want to do whatever it takes to save my sister."

"What if this guy—woman—*person* has already killed her and is just waiting for you to walk in to kill you too?"

A valid argument. "I don't think she's killed her yet, but I think she plans to very soon." And it wouldn't be a quick death. Dottie would suffer, and somehow her kidnapper would make sure Julianna knew just how much. Nausea swarmed and she swallowed hard. "She wants me in there."

"And you're going to give her what she wants?"

"For Dottie?" She huffed a short, humorless laugh. "Yeah. I need something that will cut through the chain on the door." She walked to the supply closet and opened it, found what she needed, and shut the door. Hector placed a hand on her arm. She met his gaze. "Please don't stop me."

For a second, he didn't move, then dropped his hand. "All right. But you wear a vest and a wire. I want to hear everything that goes on in there."

She nodded and within seconds had the wire strapped to her. But she wouldn't wear an earpiece. Nothing that the hostage taker might spot. She'd stuff it in her pocket and pull it out if she needed it.

Once she was ready, she stepped out of the command post and shut the door behind her.

CHAPTER
NINETEEN

The double glass doors to the post office were just ahead. The building wasn't huge, but it had two wings. To the left was the counter that held four empty clerk stations. The wing to the right contained the self-serve keyed mailboxes. With a picture of the blueprints in her head, Julianna mentally mapped out a route.

Intel said the doors had been locked with chains. With the cutter in her right hand, she approached the door and pulled it open far enough to cut the nearest link. The chains dropped to the floor with a clank and she stepped inside. Cold air hit her. Someone had cranked the air-conditioning way down.

The eerie quiet echoed around her. She kept her hand on her weapon and glanced left, then right. "Angel?" No answer. Nothing but the hum of the air-conditioning. What if she was wrong? She was taking a mighty big risk. But what choice did she have? "Angel, you in here? I'm here like you wanted. Where are the hostages? Are they all right?"

Knowing Hector wanted answers to those questions too, she could only pray the suspect would answer. Julianna kept going toward the counter, feeling exposed, like she had a big red target on her back. "Angel? Anyone?" There was no way Kara had managed to escape, so if she was hiding, Julianna didn't want to give her any more opportunity than was necessary to get the drop on her.

A hitch in breathing snagged her attention. Behind the counter?

Backup would be right behind her. Hector might let her go in alone, but he wouldn't let her stay in alone. They both knew that. But while backup would be close, they'd stay hidden. Julianna stepped lightly, her tennis shoes quiet on the tile floor. Mentally preparing herself to find the hostages dead, she slid up to the very end of the counter and kept her back to the wall at the end window. Plexiglass hung in front of where a clerk would stand. Julianna narrowed her eyes and leaned forward. Nothing behind this one window, but she needed to see behind the counter. She slid over the granite and under the plexiglass, lowering her feet to the floor on the other side.

Now, she could see them. Three bodies laid out side by side, hands zip-tied in front. They were dead with a bullet hole in each forehead. Grief stabbed her and anger surged. She pushed it back with effort. "Angel?"

Something moved to her right, and a figure dressed in a baseball hat, hoodie, and sunglasses stepped around the last counter space cubicle to face Julianna, gun at her side.

Julianna lifted her weapon. "Stop right there."

"You came." The person seemed unfazed by the gun pointing at her . . . him? She couldn't tell. And interestingly enough, the voice still sounded like they were using some kind of changer. And yet, she couldn't see a device.

"You wanted me to." The chilling thought that she was going to have to protect this mad person from a sniper because Julianna needed her alive had her heart pounding.

"You love your sister very much, don't you?"

"I do."

"Hmm."

"Did you lose someone you loved?"

"I didn't come here to talk to you. I just wanted you to see your handiwork. You've lost hostages now."

Julianna's throat worked. "No, I didn't," she said, keeping her voice soft.

Angel grunted. "You saw them. I held them hostage and they're dead. Just like the ones in the bank."

"But not because of me or any failure on my part. You never gave me the chance to save them." She spoke the words in a gentle tone but held her ground, feeling her way around, trying to get a read on the individual.

Julianna couldn't make out the person's features at all, but she was tall and almost painfully skinny. "What good would that do? I'd just kill them anyway."

"What do you want from me?" Julianna asked, her throat tight. "What will it take for you to let Dottie go?"

"I won't."

"Then I have no reason not to stop you."

A laugh slipped from the woman. And Julianna's ears pricked. She knew that laugh, but it was different. "Sure you do. I'm the only one who knows where Dottie is, and as long as that's the case, you need me alive."

"Your voice. It's familiar, yet different."

"It'll come to you."

A red dot flashed across the person's head and panic flared. Julianna stepped sideways to block the shot. She needed her alive. In her head, she could hear Hector yelling at her.

The woman stepped back, and lifted her weapon. Blood exploded from the woman's shoulder, followed by the sound of the sniper's shot. She screeched and Julianna lunged at her. Her arm knocked against the hand with the weapon and the clatter of the gun hitting the floor registered. She closed a hand around the woman's wrist, surprised at how fragile it felt.

With her other hand, she knocked the sunglasses away. Bandages covered most of the person's face, but Julianna was most focused on the pair of familiar blue eyes. "I knew it was you."

Kara screeched again and lashed out with a fist, catching Julianna in the jaw. Stunned, Julianna froze for a moment too long, trying to clear her vision. That was all the time Kara needed. She turned and ran, hit the door at the end of the hall, and disappeared through it. SWAT and other law enforcement flowed into the building while Julianna shoved aside her shock and raced after the killer.

■ ■ ■ ■

Clay had decided to stay at Julianna's house and now paced between the den and kitchen, thinking. He knew that area of Charlotte where the car with Dottie had disappeared. Something was niggling at the base of his skull, so he returned to the den. The agents were glued to the television. National news had already picked up the story of the post office hostage situation. Choppers swirled overhead and Clay wanted to be on scene to help. To keep Julianna safe. But the best thing he could do would be to figure out what his subconscious was trying to tell him. "Any word?"

"Nothing concrete. Officers and agents are still going door-to-door, asking neighbors if they saw the Hummer enter the area around the time it did. There are a couple of vacant rentals that came clean."

"Okay, I have an idea."

Calvin pulled his attention from the television and focused on Clay. "What is it?"

"That area where they're searching for Dottie. I know it pretty well. It used to be part of my patrol beat."

The man nodded. "Okay. What are you thinking?"

"There's an apartment building. It was scheduled for demo two months ago, but then someone bought it with the intention of fixing it up. I don't think they've started on it yet, so it could be a possible place to hold Dottie. There are signs about the danger of trespassing, and there's a huge chain-link fence around the property, but . . ."

"Anyone still live there?"

"Some of the homeless ignore the warnings and manage to sneak past the fences, but no paying tenants are there, obviously." He rubbed a hand over his chin. "It would take some time to search it. And the foundation is pretty unstable. One side has started to crumble and nearby residents are unhappy that it's still standing. Lowers their property values for sure."

"Sounds like a real possibility. We can use heat-sensing equipment to see if anyone is inside."

The television distracted Clay's attention and he locked on to the sudden burst of activity that was going on at the downtown post office. The agents did the same. Clay took a step closer, and the cameras panned in and covered the front door of the post office. SWAT had breached.

Where was Julianna?

He glanced at his phone. No texts, no calls, nothing from Julianna.

His phone buzzed again. This time an alert from the police station. All officers on deck at the neighborhood where Dottie was suspected of being held. He didn't have to think twice. There was nothing he could do about helping Julianna, but he might be able to help Dottie. He checked in with his supervisor and let him know he was on the way.

■ ■ ■ ■

Dottie sat and stared at the door at the top of the short flight of stairs. As far as she could tell, that was her way out. She'd managed to break the zip tie, thanks to a maneuver she'd watched Julianna practice one afternoon with some of her weird agent friends. Now, she was very grateful they'd talked her into trying it. Unfortunately, that was as far as she'd gotten on the whole escape plan. She'd tried every other avenue of escape and only managed to come away with painful and bleeding hands.

"God, can you hear me?"

Silence echoed back at her.

She grimaced. "Well, I feel kind of stupid talking to you, but if you're real, I could use some help. Julianna says you hear everyone's prayers." Dottie swallowed. "I want to believe you're real and can help me out. But if you're real, then I feel kind of bad for only talking to you when I'm in trouble."

Something above the door caught her eye and she stood. A piece of the ceiling hung low. She hadn't noticed it before because it was in the shadows. She grabbed the flashlight and stuffed it into the waistband of her pants, then hurried to the door. There was enough doorframe exposed to get one foot on it and the other foot on the opposite wall, right next to the frame, and climb up, just like she'd done as a child.

Balancing, she closed her eyes and pushed on the ceiling tile. Debris rained down around her. She coughed, then waited for the dust to settle. She refused to bang on the door and scream like an idiot begging to be let out. Seriously. Dumbest thing ever. A waste of time and energy. Whoever had put her in here wasn't going to change their mind just because Dottie made some noise and begged.

Legs and arms burning from exertion, she scooted herself higher. Her head popped through the hole, and she grabbed the flashlight and lifted it to wave it around inside the area. Rats skittered across the beam, and she let out a scream, lost her balance, and dropped to the floor. She landed on her feet but stumbled backward and fell. Somehow, she managed not to break the flashlight, and she set it down, aiming the beam toward the ceiling to get the most possible light coverage.

"Ugh." She shivered and looked at the floor. She stomped her feet and clenched her fists. Then picked up the biggest piece of tile she could find. The edge was sharp. It would do for a weapon.

But she really wanted to get out before she had to use it.

She snagged the flashlight once more and aimed it at the floor. With the tile broken in places, the mortar had come up with the tile, exposing the underflooring. And no concrete. What? She looked at the piece of tile in her hand and then the rotting wood. "Okay, God, I'm starting to believe Julianna might be right about you. Thank you."

She dropped to her knees and went to work.

CHAPTER
TWENTY

Julianna stuffed the comms in her ear, reported her position, and pounded down the steps and into the basement of the post office. She ran down the hall and into an open area full of old postal castoffs and storage. Pausing, she listened, trying to hear over the hard thrum of her heart. She heard the swish of a door closing just ahead and bolted toward it. "FBI! Stop! Kara, stop!"

She only yelled to say she'd done so, not because she thought the woman would listen. Footsteps sounded behind her, spurring her on, knowing backup was right there with her.

Julianna raced through the door and paused. Three closed doors faced her. Gun ready, she yanked open the first. Some kind of storage room. The second opened to a bathroom. Again, she stood to the side and pulled open the third. A stairwell leading up. "Going up."

"Backup is right behind you, Jules," Hector said.

She took the steps two at a time, up and around, up another flight and around again, hearing backup behind her. When the stairwell ended, she pushed the door open and found herself on the roof.

And no suspect in sight. Officers and agents swarmed behind her, spreading out.

Julianna pointed. "Don't let her get away!"

"Julianna!"

"Hector," Julianna said into her comms, realizing the man had been trying to get her attention for several seconds. "I was right. It's Kara."

"The one you told me about."

"Yeah. Her name is Kara Williams. I went to high school with her. My ex-boyfriend shot and killed her brother during a hostage situation fifteen years ago. Daria should have some information on her. She has bandages on her face, but I'd recognize her eyes anywhere."

"Come back to the command post. We need to talk."

"On my way."

Her phone pinged with an email from Daria. She left the chase to the other agents and officers and made her way to the command post. When she stepped inside, Hector was pacing in the small area.

His head snapped up at her entrance. "Are you out of your mind?"

She winced. "No, Hector. Come on. I couldn't let him shoot her. She knows where Dottie is."

His hands worked. Fist, relax. Fist, relax. "I should suspend you." Julianna closed her eyes and nodded. "But I won't." He sighed. "I get it. Just please don't ever do anything like that again."

"I won't."

"Good." And just like that, the hand-slapping was over.

Thank you, God.

"Daria sent an email containing information about Kara." She slid into the chair in front of the monitor and logged in to bring up her email. The faster they found Kara, the faster they would find Dottie. She grabbed her phone and shot a text to Clay.

Are you still at the house?

No. Just pulling in to the place where Dottie may be held.

She stilled.

Where?

The old Castle Estate Apartments.

Those things are falling down!

I know.

Julianna pulled in a breath.

Keep me updated? Please?

Absolutely.

She set her phone aside. "Okay, Hector, I have to go. I'm sorry, but they think they know where Dottie is, and I need to be there if they find her."

"I need information on this Kara Williams."

"Daria will give you everything you need. She just sent me an email, but I'm going to call her and talk to her on my drive to the apartments." She gave him the address, forwarded him the email from Daria, and stood. "I have no idea how to find Kara, but I promise to figure it out on the way. Let me know when you have her in custody, and I'll meet you at the office when you interrogate her. You have the email. Read it and you'll know what I know."

"Go. You're no good to me like this. But stay in touch."

"Thank you," she whispered. "I will." She darted out the door before he could change his mind.

■ ■ ■ ■

Clay climbed out of his SUV and eyed the apartment building. It was four stories, held nine units and a basement for laundry. The first floor had been business offices, a gym, and a game room. The top three floors were one- and two-bedroom apartment units. The radio crackled once more. Clay joined the others, and

SWAT stood ready to move at the command. He itched to get inside and start searching, even while the thought of pulling his weapon to aim it at another person made him want to throw up. But he'd do it for Dottie. For Julianna. The only positive was that if the person Julianna was dealing with at the post office was the same person who'd taken Dottie, then it was highly likely he wouldn't have to worry about it. But he'd be prepared nevertheless.

Captain Graham motioned to him, and Clay hurried over. "Yes sir?"

"We're going to be careful about this. That place looks ready to come down at the slightest provocation. Firefighters are on standby as well as a medical team. I'd prefer not to have to use them."

Clay would be happy with that.

"Looks like the heat sensors have picked up four people inside," Graham said. He pointed to the blueprints spread across the hood of his Escape. "Here and here. These three are in a room at the end of the hallway on the first floor. None of them are moving, but they're alive. This one is on the second floor and moving a lot." His gaze met Clay's and traveled to three other officers standing next to Clay. "You four start on the first floor, find those four people. The rest of you clear the building to make sure we haven't missed someone. These machines aren't foolproof. Be careful."

"Got it." Clay took the lead and made his way to the front door. He stepped inside and grimaced when the odor of unwashed bodies and rotting trash hit him. He ignored it and held his weapon ready. "Guess we head for the heat source, clearing as we go?" he said.

"I got your back, my friend," Jay Knotts said.

"Same here," Ryan Weston said. "Lead on."

Matthew Hardy aimed himself toward the stairwell. "I'll check the one upstairs. Looks like that one's right over the other three at the end of the hall."

"Stay in touch," Clay said. He headed to the right with Jay and Ryan on his heels. They cleared the offices to the left, then checked the former fitness center. Needles and other drug paraphernalia littered the floor. Rats skittered, screeching at their intrusion, and Clay shuddered. But no Dottie.

"Oh gah," Jay said. "I can't handle those things."

Ryan snorted. "Man up, chicken."

Clay didn't bother to respond. He continued down the hall, checking the rooms.

Jay stayed right behind him. "Bathrooms on the right," the man said.

"Got it."

The door to the men's room lay across the opening, the hinges long gone. He kicked it in and walked over it.

The radio crackled and he listened to the agents clearing the other floors.

Old insulation rained down on him, and a hard piece of wood fell, knocking him in the shoulder. He grunted and went to his knees. Jay grabbed his bicep while Ryan aimed his weapon at the ceiling. "Police! Who's up there? Show yourself."

Silence.

The wood above them creaked. "Get out!" Clay said. "The ceiling's coming down!"

■ ■ ■ ■

In her car, Julianna dialed Daria's number and connected it to the Bluetooth.

"Did you get my email?" Daria said in greeting.

"Yes, but I haven't had a chance to read it yet. And now I'm on the way to another incident, so can you just fill me in?"

"Sure. Kara Williams is thirty-three years old. Her current residence is listed as Burbank, California, but after an unsuccessful suicide attempt when she was nineteen—she set herself on fire and was burned over a large percentage of her body—and a two-year recovery period, she was ordered to Fresh Start Psychiatric Hospital. She was there for six months before she was released.

The day of her release, she went home, waited for her parents to go to bed, then shot them while they slept."

Julianna closed her eyes and shook her head, the friend she remembererd and the person being described two different people. "So, it's true. But . . . Melissa made it sound like they're still alive."

"They are. Both parents survived and were able to be at her trial to testify against her."

How had she not known this?

Because she'd buried her head and tried to forget everything and everyone connected to that day. Remorse clutched at her while guilt slammed her. She'd given up on her friend too soon.

She tuned back in to Daria. ". . . jury found her guilty, but in need of continued psychiatric intervention. The parents pressed charges to the fullest extent, but it was noted that they begged the court to help her. Kara was sent to another facility, but this time it wasn't the rich-people private place. It was a state facility where she remained ever since she was sentenced. But . . ."

"But what?" Julianna asked, her mind reeling.

"She was released three weeks ago."

"I'm sorry, did you say she was released?" Melissa obviously hadn't heard the latest.

"Three weeks ago. Apparently, they deemed her stable and ready to be reintroduced into society."

"After all these years?" Julianna took a right and pressed the gas. She was almost there.

"She was the perfect patient, according to her records. She attended meetings, therapy, took her meds, everything. Seriously, she was the model patient. The doctor had no reason to keep her. And she'd served her sentence for shooting her parents."

"I know they didn't just release her and hope she made it on her own."

"Absolutely not. There's an organization that works with patients like Kara once they're released from the hospital. They get them set up in an apartment, make sure they have a job—or at least have several job interviews lined up. They check in on them weekly and they have an emergency number that's available 24/7."

"She fooled them all."

Daria sighed. "Yeah, when you look at it that way, I'd say she did."

Julianna turned left in the subdivision and made her way back toward the apartment complex. "I'm almost here. Gotta go. Thank you, Daria."

"Read the email when you get a chance. There are more details in there. Nothing pressing, but might answer any questions you have."

"Will do. Bye."

"Bye."

Julianna hung up and pressed the gas harder. "Hold on, Dottie, I'm coming."

■　■　■　■

Clay pushed to his feet and shoved Ryan out the door. Jay followed as more debris spilled down, just missing the man.

A hard thud sounded and then a grunt. Clay hurried back toward the area and looked up. Two feet covered in red tennis shoes appeared in the three-by-three hole. He recognized those shoes and holstered his weapon. "Dottie?"

The feet froze. Lifted from the hole. And then her face appeared, eyes wide, mouth gaping. "Officer Clay?" Then the eyes filled with tears. "Oh boy, am I glad to see you. Help me down!"

She disappeared, then her feet reappeared. Clay grabbed her around the waist as she lowered herself through the hole. He let her slide down his body until her feet touched the floor.

She wrapped her arms around his waist and buried her nose against his chest. "I've never been so glad to see someone in my whole life."

Her words were muffled, but he was able to make them out. He gripped her arms and stepped back to look into her face. Tears streaked her cheeks, but her chin jutted out. "Are you okay?"

"My hands hurt."

He slid his hands down her arms to her wrists and she turned her palms up. A ragged slice in her right palm bled, the liquid pooling, then running down the side to drip on the floor. Clay reached under his vest to grab the hem of his T-shirt. "Give me a knife, will you?" he asked Ryan.

His buddy dug in his vest and pulled out a Swiss Army knife, opened it to the biggest blade, then passed it to Clay. Clay cut off a large strip of the T-shirt and wrapped it around Dottie's wound. She gasped, then bit her lip.

"Sorry," he said.

"It's fine. I just want to get out of here."

He nodded. "You and me both. Let's go before Julianna gets here and storms the building looking for you."

"She's coming?"

"Nothing could stop her."

CHAPTER
TWENTY-ONE

Deep underground, in one of the tunnels I'd seen on the television, I glanced at my little setup. It wasn't a five-star hotel by any stretch, but it suited my purposes. I had a sleeping bag and a pillow, clothes hung on the rocks on the wall, a small cooler with cold cuts, a large bucket with washing water, and plenty of drinking water. It took skill to come and go without being seen, but since I traveled mostly at night, I did fine. Avoiding the police presence was a bit tricky at times, but so far, so good. If someone caught me, they'd just send me on my way. Another faceless homeless person. I had to be faceless. If anyone saw my scars, they'd remember them. But if I kept my head down, I could blend in pretty well.

Fire burned along my shoulder and I pressed the cold washcloth to it. For the first time in a very long time, I held my breath and stared at my reflection in the piece of broken mirror I'd found in a dumpster. Bandages covered my face, but Julianna had recognized me when she knocked the sunglasses away. She'd known the eyes. Kane and I had shared the same color eyes and they were striking. Memorable. I should have worn contacts. But it hadn't just been my eyes. Julianna had suspected even before she saw me. She was smarter than I gave her credit for. It was probably the timing of it all. With the fifteenth anniversary of the shooting just a few days away, she'd been thinking about it. Naturally, her mind would go to me. She knew I hated her. She'd left me to suffer the consequences of that day and had run across the country to get away from it. And from me, I was sure.

I turned away from the mirror, disgusted at my weakness, my failure. Everything had gone according to plan. Except for taking Dottie. That had been a huge mistake, but from now on, there could be no more mistakes.

Stick to the plan! If you deviate from the plan, that's when you'll get caught!

"Shut up. Shut up!"

I was tired of *the voice* that did nothing but criticize. I needed to shove it away and think. No, the voice wasn't all bad, so maybe I wouldn't completely ignore it. Regardless, one thing was certain. I needed to plan once more. And hopefully, the plan would appease the voice urging me on, pushing me to make things right.

Julianna knew who I was now, and that would complicate things. But I still had a mission to complete, and I would finish no matter what it cost me. In the end, it would cost me my life, of course, but that was okay. At least I would die knowing my life finally counted for something.

Finding our purpose in life is important. Sometimes it seems like some people are born knowing what they're supposed to do. Other people have to work at figuring it out. Or sometimes, an incident shapes our lives and sends us seeking that. And sometimes, our purpose changes depending on circumstances.

The words echoed in my mind. I'd thought about my purpose for a long time and there just didn't seem to be one. Everything had been so hopeless after Kane died. And then my parents had been so angry with me because they'd lost their shining star. I hated them. I'd tried once to kill them. Maybe I'd finish the mission here and return to take care of them once and for all.

I can't remember exactly when it became clear that my purpose

was to seek justice for Kane, but now that I knew what I was supposed to do, I would take great pleasure in doing it.

The wound would heal. I was fortunate to still be alive. Shot by
a sniper and all I got was a flesh wound. I laughed. I was starting
to think I was immortal. Three times I'd cheated death, and had
even managed to get out of the post office without capture. I'd
planned to be out before Julianna entered, but she'd moved faster
than I'd anticipated. However, her sudden entry had a positive side
to it. It had been entertaining to see her reaction to the three dead
hostages. She prided herself on never losing a hostage. My total
was six now. I frowned, remembering her statement that I hadn't
given her the option to save them, so technically, she'd still never
lost a hostage. Well, she would.

I wasn't sure how I'd managed everything so far, but I had. The
spirits were with me. Nothing bad could happen to me until I'd
finished the mission. I felt like some kind of warrior.

Another chuckle escaped me and I bandaged the wound as
best I could while I planned the next step in the mission. One that
would give Julianna the opportunity to negotiate for the lives of
my hostages.

I tried to decide how long I'd let her beg for their lives before I
killed them. And her.

■ ■ ■ ■

Julianna tucked her phone into her front pocket and headed
for the nearest officer. She flashed her badge. "Where are they?
Did they find anyone?"

"No word yet."

Julianna stood watching the officers and other law enforcement
combing the area.

The hair on the back of her neck spiked and she placed a hand
on her weapon. She turned to scan the scene behind her while staying in the shadow of one of the SUVs for protection from anyone
across the street. Opposite the apartment building was an old park

Crossfire

with run-down playground equipment, a few scattered trees, and a fence that had long since rotted to the point of collapse.

But she saw nothing that should cause her nerves to be on high alert. Then again, why wouldn't they be? She was a target. Someone wanted her to suffer, then die. Yeah, she would be feeling antsy regardless of whether someone was out there watching. But there was no way Angel—or Kara—would get away from all the law enforcement officers after her. Julianna had nothing to be worried about except finding Dottie.

But she couldn't help scanning the area once more before turning her attention back to the building. She walked over to one of the firemen holding the thermal-imaging device. "Is she in there?"

"Someone is," he said. "Not sure if it's her or not. The heat sensor picked up four bodies—er, people. They're warm so they're alive."

"Warm is good," Julianna said, a relief like nothing she'd ever experienced before flowing through her.

"Yeah."

But was she hurt? And if so, how bad?

Julianna shoved her hands in her pockets and shot another glance at the park behind them. The feeling of being watched simply wouldn't go away.

Her phone buzzed and she lifted it to her ear. "Julianna here."

"Hey, this is Agent Grant Peabody. I interviewed Kara Williams's parents."

"Yeah, thanks. What did they have to say?"

"Basically, that she was a lost cause. Said she tried to kill them in their sleep." He cleared his throat. "I remember that case. I was a detective with the department at that time and actually went to the scene."

"No way."

"Yeah. That's why I snagged your request when it came in. I did CPR on the wife, Mrs. Williams, and kept her alive until EMS arrived. She sends me cakes and other things on my birthday every

LYNETTE EASON

year. Anyway, she and her husband haven't had any contact at all with Kara since she tried to murder them."

"Can't say I blame them, I guess," Julianna murmured.

"Right? I remember Kara. She shot her parents, then went and crawled in her bed and went to sleep, not realizing her father's wounds were superficial. She shot them both three times. Her dad's bullets were mostly through and through. He said he played dead, hoping she'd stop shooting. When she walked out of the room, he crawled to a phone and dialed 911. Warned them his daughter was armed. When we got there, we found her in the bed. She didn't resist, gave us the weapon, and told us she did it. I ran to the parents' room, and that's where I found her mom and started CPR."

Julianna closed her eyes and forced herself to believe his account. "I'm beyond dumbfounded. I simply have no words."

"I'm sorry. And I'm sorry her parents aren't more help, but they haven't had contact with her since she was sentenced and committed to the psychiatric hospital."

"Thank you, Grant. I appreciate you taking the time to help me out."

"No problem. Let me know if I can do anything else for you."

"Kara's been released and is out for justice. Her brand of justice, anyway. Can you make sure the parents are protected in case she decides to come after them?"

"Absolutely."

"Thank you."

She hung up and pressed a hand to her head. Then lowered her attention to her phone and texted Hector the update.

Just as she hit Send, the officer's radio gave a burst of static. "I've got her," the familiar voice said. "She's fine. Hungry and thirsty, but insists she's fine. We're on the way out. Have an ambulance ready for transport."

Julianna snagged the radio, her heart thudding. At the officer's frown, she shot him a pleading look. "It's my sister."

215

His frown cleared and he nodded. She pressed the button. "Dottie?"

"Jules?"

The sound of her sister's voice nearly sent her to her knees. She must have wobbled, because the officer's hand went under her elbow. "Yeah, hey. I'm here. I'm standing right outside."

"Officer Clay found me."

"I know." Her throat constricted for a brief moment. Then she cleared it. "And I'm forever grateful for that."

She handed the radio back to the officer. "Thank you."

"Yeah. Always happy for a win like this."

It was definitely a win. She waited as three other men were led out of the building and bundled into the rear of three different cruisers. They'd be questioned, of course, but Julianna wasn't holding out hope that they'd have a lot of answers. She had a feeling they spent a lot of their days in a drugged stupor, oblivious to anything going on around them. Then again, she'd had leads come from stranger people and places.

Finally, Dottie and Clay appeared with three other officers behind them. Dottie ran to Julianna and grabbed her around the waist. "I'm so sorry. I was so stupid. I didn't mean for—"

"Shh." Julianna leaned back and placed a finger on her sister's chapped lips. "Stop. It's over and you're okay. Let's get you to the hospital and let them check you out."

"I don't need or want a hospital." She held out her hands. Someone had wrapped a piece of T-shirt around one hand, and it was soaked through with blood. "I have a few bruises and my hands hurt from digging through a floor with broken tile, but I'm fine. A lot more fine than I'd be if Clay hadn't gotten here when he did."

Julianna gripped her sister's wrist. "This needs medical attention."

Dottie grimaced. "Yeah, maybe so, but I still don't want to go."

Julianna met Clay's gaze over Dottie's shoulder. "Thank you," she whispered.

He nodded and Julianna gave her sister another hug. "Just let them check you out. For my peace of mind."

A heavy sigh slipped from Dottie, but she nodded. "Fine, but I'm not riding in an ambulance."

"I'll take you," Julianna said. She looked at Clay. "You want to follow?"

"Right behind you."

She turned to the officer who'd let her use his radio. "Could we get an escort?"

He nodded. "I can request that." He lifted the radio to his lips, and while he worked on that, Julianna went back to Clay and Dottie.

Once again, she had that little niggling sensation that they were being watched, and once again, she looked into the overgrown park area.

"Something bothering you?" Clay asked.

"Yeah. I keep feeling like someone's watching me."

"Then maybe we should find out."

CHAPTER
TWENTY-TWO

I stood behind the tree, pressing a hand to my throbbing shoulder, watching all of my hard work circle the drain. I had really messed up. No wonder the voice was so critical. I shouldn't have taken Dottie.

Taking Dottie wasn't the plan. You have to have patience. Fulfilling the mission is all that matters. You messed up. Don't do it again.

I pressed my hands to my ears. *I know I messed up. Stupid, stupid, stupid. I'm stupid.*

But it doesn't matter now. Everything will still work out.

Yes, it would. But I'd made things a little harder with my impulsive move. I should have just stuck to the plan of following them and keeping an eye on them.

They'd be more cautious and careful now. Honestly, I didn't really care. All I cared about was the fact that Julianna had had some really bad moments when I'd taken Dottie. That was good. It motivated me, encouraged me. I'd let her enjoy her relief that she'd gotten her sister back.

She wouldn't have her long.

I frowned. They were walking this way. Julianna and the cop

she liked to hang around with. Why? Had I done something to tip them off that I was here? I backed up, stumbled over an exposed root, and went down hard, jarring my wounded shoulder. A pained cry escaped my lips, and I rolled to my feet, spotted them running, and took off to the place where I'd stashed my car.

"Kara! Stop!"

So, she really did remember me. Well, I remembered her too. Every single thing about her. But I couldn't get caught yet. Desperation drove me.

If you get caught, it's all over.

Stupid voice. Like I didn't know that. I hurried faster, ignoring the pain in my shoulder, fighting the tears and the sudden doubts that surged.

You can do this. Don't let the doubts win. You're stronger than you think. That's why you've been chosen for this mission. You can do it, but you have to stick to the plan.

"I will. I promise. Just tell me how to get away."

. . . .

Julianna had made sure Dottie had protection, with the promise that she'd be right back, then darted toward the old park. "Kara!" She'd called that name twice now.

Clay ran after her, crossing the street right behind her, his gaze scanning the area and wondering who she'd seen—or felt.

Personally, he was grateful for the vest, but it wouldn't do much for a shot to the head.

"Kara! Stop!" She hit the broken concrete path and dodged tree limbs and other debris in her hurry to catch up to whoever she had spied watching the scene.

Seconds later, the roar of an engine in the distance seemed to light a fire under Julianna and she ran faster. She burst through the tree line with Clay fighting to keep up with her. When he caught her, she was bent double, hands on her knees, breathing hard. "BLS 555," she said.

"Got it. Who were we chasing?"

"I think she's the one who kidnapped Dottie and is the hostage taker."

"What?"

"I'll explain in a bit." She dialed and lifted the phone to her ear. When she spoke, she reported the plate, the vehicle description, and the direction it went. "The suspect is Kara Williams. She's wearing bandages on her face, presumably to cover scars from a fire about fourteen years ago. She has blue eyes and I'm not sure of the color of her hair. It used to be a dark brown but was covered today, so I can't say. Thanks." When she hung up, she raked a hand over her messy ponytail. "They'd better catch her this time."

"Let's get Dottie taken care of. Hopefully, by the time she's done at the hospital, this Kara person will be in custody."

"Yeah."

"And you can tell me why she's out to kill you."

"Yes. I know why she's out to kill me." She shoved her phone into her pocket. "She was in a different vehicle. That wasn't the stolen Hummer. Did they ever find it?"

"It was parked in a garage. Someone called in to report they'd come out and found their car gone and the Hummer in its place."

"What is up with people leaving their keys in their vehicles?"

He shrugged. "When it's shut up in a garage, you expect it to be safe."

"I guess so."

Thirty minutes later, Clay stood outside Dottie's room with Julianna, finishing up the conversation she'd started earlier, and he filled her in on everything that had gone down at the apartment building.

When he finished, she checked on Dottie, then stepped back outside the room, leaving the door cracked in case her sister needed her. "Her hands are in rough shape. They're cleaning them and giving her something for pain, as some of the cuts are pretty deep. One is especially savage and needed a few stitches."

"That was an incredibly brave thing she did. She dug through the floor with a piece of tile." He shook his head, still not sure he believed it. Then again, desperation could make people do things they'd never have thought possible.

"I know. They want her to speak to the psychiatrist here, and then the police want to get her statement. Right now, she's on the phone with your sister. They plan to release her in a couple of hours." Julianna walked over to lean against the wall, then slid to the floor.

Clay did the same and reached for her hand. He rolled his head to look at her. "You going to be okay?"

"As long as Dottie's okay, I'm okay."

She pressed fingers to her eyes and Clay squeezed the ones he held. "She's okay."

"For now."

"How did the suspect get away from them at the post office? Law enforcement was all over that building."

"No idea. She went up on the roof and then down the side on the fire escape, and we thought she was going back into the post office, but she just . . . disappeared." She frowned. "It was like she had the thing mapped out ahead of time. Everything was planned right down to the last detail. I don't know much, and all Hector knows is that she got away. But they've got another chance at her at the park. They've got the chopper searching as well."

"So . . . she? You were right?"

Julianna bit her lip. "Yes."

"Tell me about her again. This time with all the details and why she hates you."

Julianna groaned and stared at the ceiling. She went quiet and Clay wondered if she planned to tell him or not. Instead of pushing, he simply waited.

Finally, she took a deep breath and let it out slowly. "I told you my senior year of high school, there was a school shooting."

"Right."

"Kara hates me because the shooter was my ex-boyfriend. He came after me and wound up killing Kane, her brother." She turned her gaze to meet his.

"And you think Kara is the one behind everything."

"I know she is. I saw her in the post office when I knocked off her sunglasses."

"But . . . why? After all this time?"

"I'm not sure, but from what Daria told me, she's been hospitalized for most of the past fifteen years. She was recently released—like three weeks ago—so maybe it's simply she's been planning this for that long and finally had the opportunity to act on her desire for revenge." She hesitated. "I don't know."

Sounded logical. "Why did he shoot Kane?"

"Dennis wasn't trying to shoot Kane, he was trying to shoot me. And Kane threw himself in front of the bullet. And then Dennis was going to shoot Kara and a sniper—" Tears filled her eyes but didn't fall. They hovered on her lashes, and she sniffed, closed her eyes for a brief second before opening them once more. The tears were gone. "After it was all over, Kara had an emotional breakdown. I tried to see her. I called, went by her home, everything. She refused to see me."

"She blamed you because her brother took a bullet for you."

"Yes, but it was more than that." She huffed a laugh, but Clay didn't hear any humor in it. "After that whole incident with my step-grandfather, I'd vowed never to lose my cool again. Never lose my temper and to guard my words like a fanatic. I studied everything there was to know about the power of words, and one day I read about a hostage negotiator who talked a killer into giving up his hostages. That story changed me. I became fascinated with the idea that I could use my words for good, and I set a goal to become a hostage negotiator. So, I started studying and planning."

He narrowed his eyes. "But?"

"But when Dennis came to school that morning, he had his father's Glock. He started asking people where I was. Word got

LYNETTE EASON

back to me that he was looking for me, and deep down I knew that it wasn't going to end well."

"He found you."

She nodded. "I was in the science lab, working on a project with Kara. There were three other students in there at the time. I remember Kara and I were talking about graduation and college plans when Dennis slammed into the room, waving his gun. He fired his first shot at the ceiling, and everyone either dropped or scattered like ants, while all I could do was stand there and stare at him."

"Julianna—"

"No, just let me finish."

"Yeah, okay. Sorry."

"Kane must have heard Dennis was looking for me, because all of a sudden, he was in the room, yelling at Dennis to leave us alone. Dennis fired at him but missed. He yelled at the three of us to back up against the wall." She swiped a hand over her eyes as if clearing away unshed tears. "All I could picture was a firing squad. I started talking to him, pulling on everything I'd learned about hostage negotiation. And he seemed to be listening to me. Then the real hostage negotiator showed up and started talking. He told me to be quiet." She bit her lip. "But I knew Dennis was listening and I was confident I could get him to put the gun down."

"But?"

"But"—she shrugged—"I was wrong. And it cost one of my best friends his life."

■ ■ ■ ■

Memories from that day rolled over her in waves. She could no more stop them than she could push back the tide. "I asked Dennis what he wanted from me and he said it was too late. I said it wasn't. He waved the gun and said if he couldn't have me, no one would."

And then she'd gotten him killed.

"Answer the phone! Make it stop ringing!"

Julianna grabbed the cell phone and snatched it to her ear. "Hello? He won't talk to you. He's told you over and over. You need to stop calling." She kept her voice even. Smooth and low. It took every ounce of her self-control.

"Get him to the window. We have a sniper ready to end this."

She hung up.

"Why'd you break up with him?" Clay asked.

"He was abusive. The crazy thing is, I couldn't see it. Kane did, though, and told me to break up with him, but all I could see was someone who wanted to be with me. Someone who said he loved me. Even when he hit me, he always apologized after."

"Aw, Julianna . . ."

"I know. It's so stupid," she whispered. "I look back and see how *stupid* I was."

"Not stupid. Never stupid. You wouldn't say any other person in that situation was stupid, so don't do it to yourself."

She stared at him, stopped by his words, his passionate defense of her. She nodded, hesitant at first, then in agreement. "You're right, I wouldn't."

"Thank you. I know."

She shot him a quick smile. "Anyway, one night, he was going out with his friends and told me I had to stay home. I told him that if he was going out with the guys, I was going to do something with the girls or Kane. He grabbed me and shoved me up against the wall and told me if I did anything other than what he said, I'd be sorry. So . . . I stayed home." She shook her head, remembering her actions. "It was so out of character for me. I'd always been headstrong and independent, until after I got out of juvie—I was only there six months—I figured I'd be sent to a foster home or something, but my mom petitioned the court and asked them to let me come home—"

"Wait, why would she do that?"

"Free babysitting services." Julianna grimaced. "She and my stepfather had split up at that point, and it was definitely *killing her vibe* on the dating scene when she couldn't go out because she had no money for a sitter." She waved a hand. "Whatever. I didn't care. I just wanted to be home and with Dottie."

"Was it better with your stepdad out of the picture?"

"Yes. For the most part." She sighed. "Anyway, back to Dennis and his weird hold on me. I couldn't seem to make a decision with him. I let him walk all over me, order me around, hit me. But that night he was out with his friends, I was watching one of those true crime movies, and the more I watched it, the more my eyes were opened. It was like I was seeing my life play out on the screen. The guy behaved just like Dennis, and I was . . . horrified. When the abuser wound up killing his girlfriend, I knew that's where I was headed. I had to get out. So, I called Kane and asked him to come over. Kara came with him and we talked about it. They were with me when I told Dennis I was done and he was to leave me alone."

A tear slipped down her cheek before she could stop it. Clay wiped it away, his eyes narrow and filled with pain. For her.

"He left without a word, but then started stalking me. Everywhere I turned, he was there. I went to his parents—well, his mom and stepdad—and begged them to talk to him. They did, but Dennis must have told them some lies, because the next time I saw them, they told me to stay away from Dennis, that they were going to get a restraining order if I didn't leave *him* alone. Which prompted me to get one first. That night, he was standing outside my bedroom window, and I very calmly told him that I was going to the cops and getting that restraining order. The next day he came to the school with the gun."

"What a horrible experience. I'm so sorry."

"I am too."

"What did his parents have to say after their son killed someone?"

"His dad wasn't around, so I'm not sure what he had to say, but his mother and her new husband were in shock, of course. His mom just kept saying she didn't understand it. She came over to talk to me once, but I was a wreck and not sure I made much sense."

He winced. "Somehow, that doesn't surprise me."

The door to the room opened and Dottie stood there, still in her gown. "Why are you sitting on the floor?"

Julianna laughed. "I'm tired and the floor was convenient." And it was a good place to watch the hallway.

"There's a chair in my room." Her gaze swung to Clay. "And a bench."

Clay rose and Julianna chuckled. He held out a hand and Julianna placed hers in it and let him haul her to her feet. As she gave the area one more scan, she could see Max and Lydia heading their way. They were going to take Dottie's statement. Clay nudged her, signaling he'd seen them too.

She and Clay followed Dottie back into the room and Dottie slid beneath the sheet and pulled the blanket from the foot of the bed to wrap around herself.

Julianna went to her side, knowing she didn't have much time to talk to Dottie before Max and Lydia walked in, but she had to know if Dottie was up to talking about the experience. "Tell me how you are and don't say fine."

Her sister's gaze found hers. "I heard what you were telling Clay."

"Oh." Regret cut sharp and Julianna looked away. Then back. "I was going to tell you."

"I know."

"It was just the timing. I don't like to think about it or talk about it, but three days from now, it will be fifteen years." She paused. "I need to be able to move past it."

Dottie nodded. "Did you ever talk to anyone? Like a shrink?"

"Yes. I saw a therapist for several years. And I talked to Grace, of course, but she was in school, too, working on her degree. But talking to her as a friend helped. It's just . . . every year around this time, I guess my subconscious kicks in and I don't deal with it very well. And every year on the anniversary, for the past fifteen years, I've canceled the day, stayed in bed, and shut out the world."

Dottie swallowed and dropped her gaze to the sheets. "It's weird, but knowing you went through that helps." She gave a light shrug.

Julianna sat on the bed and clasped her sister's hand. "Hey, Dot? What did the person who snatched you say to you that made you get in the car?"

"That there was someone watching with a rifle, and if I didn't cooperate, you were dead."

"Oh."

"I didn't know whether it was true or not, but I wasn't taking any chances."

"Yeah." She squeezed her sister's hand. "I love you, kid."

"I know." She frowned. "She said one more thing that I just remembered, right before she sprayed me."

"What?"

"She muttered something like she needed this to all end because she hadn't signed up to be a tunnel rat."

"Tunnel rat?"

"Yeah."

"What's a tunnel rat?"

"No idea. Ask Google."

There was a knock on the door. Clay opened it and stepped back to admit Max and Lydia. "They're here to get your statement."

Julianna made the introductions and Dottie nodded. "I'm ready."

"I'll be out here, putting my own statement together," Clay said. "Let me know when you're done."

"I want some chocolate," Dottie said. "I can't do this without chocolate."

Clay smiled. "I'll get you some."

"Pizza too."

This time he laughed. "Sure."

Dottie finally let him slip out the door, then looked at Julianna. "I have to tell all that all over again, don't I?"

"Yeah. Sorry."

"Well, at least it's short, seeing as how I was unconscious for most of it."

Julianna straightened her shoulders and prepared herself to listen as a sister.

But the agent in her would be listening as well.

CHAPTER
TWENTY-THREE

Clay noted the security on Dottie's floor. Officers at the stairwells, near the elevators, and at every other entrance. Good. He didn't think the hostage taker—Kara—would dare make a move with all the law enforcement presence, but that didn't mean he'd be letting his guard down.

He made his way to the gift shop, where he purchased three chocolate bars. Armed with the candy, his next stop was the cafeteria. He could only hope they had pizza.

On his way there, he passed the information desk and saw a figure dressed in jeans and a flowered top, and bandages covering most of her face. Why she captured his attention for more than a passing glance in a hospital, he couldn't say at first, but she did. She said something to the person behind the desk and headed for the elevator. As Clay detoured and fell into step behind her, Julianna's words echoed in his head. *She's wearing bandages on her face, presumably to cover scars from a fire.*

If this wasn't Kara Williams, he would apologize profusely. If it was . . .

He pressed the earpiece into his ear, got on his radio, and requested backup. If it was Kara, she'd have a weapon of some sort. "Suspect is near the East Wing elevators. She spoke to the person at the information desk." But even if she requested Dottie's room number, the woman at the desk wouldn't have it, for security purposes. So, what was her plan? Search each floor? He stayed with her, keeping an eye out for hospital security. The woman stopped in front of the elevators, hesitated, then walked past them and into the hallway. She picked up the pace and headed for the stairwell. Clay followed. Fortunately, there were enough people around that he could try to blend in. Although his uniform made him stand out in a crowd.

The woman never looked back. Instead, she pushed through the heavy metal door and disappeared into the stairwell. Clay hurried after her, dodging people and reaching the door just before it clicked closed. He slipped through and let it shut with a clang. He could hear her on the stairs. On silent feet, he started up.

"Security is en route," a voice said over the comms. "Location?"

He couldn't speak or he'd alert the woman. But when the door on the next floor opened, then closed, he moved faster. "Second floor, East Wing."

"Closing in."

"Consider the suspect armed. I haven't seen a weapon, but I know her history."

"10-4."

Clay pushed through the door and entered the second-floor hallway. The suspect was just ahead, walking slowly, her head swiveling from side to side. "Don't stop her," he said into his comms. "I don't know that she won't start shooting. The person she's looking for isn't on this floor. Let her get into the stairwell and we'll trap her there."

"Copy that."

Clay continued to keep his eyes on her. As long as he could see her hands, he was okay with not confronting her. Yet.

Like he'd guessed, when she didn't see what she was looking for, she headed back to the stairs. "Come in from the third floor. I'm coming from the second."

"Copy."

As soon as she was in the stairwell, Clay followed her. He allowed her to get halfway up. "Kara Williams? Is that you?"

The footsteps froze.

Then resumed. Faster and more urgent. "Kara." He drew his weapon, heart racing at the thought of using it. But he would to protect others. "I'm a police officer, and I need you to stop right now."

She stopped. He climbed, carefully putting one foot in front of the other. When he rounded the rail and looked up, she aimed her gun and fired.

He jerked backward, the bullet whipping past his face to embed itself in the wall. He stumbled down the steps, lost his balance, and grasped for the railing. His fingers finally wrapped around it, and he slid to a stop.

"Put the gun down! Put it down!" echoed down the stairwell from above him.

Clay scrambled back up the steps and, seeing Kara's attention on the officers yelling at her, dove at her knees and tackled her.

She went down with his arms wrapped around her legs. Her head cracked against the step and the gun bounced from her grip. The nearest officer grabbed it from her reach and Clay yanked her hands behind her back. He snagged the cuffs from his belt and secured her wrists with them.

When he looked up, three officers held their weapons on her, but her eyes were closed and blood flowed from the wound on her forehead. A low moan escaped her.

He looked up. "She needs medical attention."

"On it," another officer said. He hurried out the door and returned with a nurse in tow.

When they got the woman onto a gurney, Clay left them and headed for the elevator, wanting to be the one to tell Julianna that she and Dottie were safe.

■ ■ ■ ■

Dottie had fallen asleep after giving her statement, and Julianna leaned back in her chair to stare at the ceiling. She had listened to Dottie's story, and with each word, her fists curled tighter. Max and Lydia had been gone for about thirty minutes, and still, Julianna couldn't tear her thoughts away from Dottie's description of her efforts to dig through the floor. She was so proud of Dottie—she'd been super brave, and Julianna had told her so.

"I didn't feel brave, but I *was* mad." Her breath had hitched and her voice wobbled.

"Mad is good sometimes. You used it. Channeled it into being productive and you *got away*."

"Yeah, well . . . I guess."

Julianna leaned forward to take her sister's bandaged hands in hers. "It's okay, hon. You've overcome so much in your short life. You'll overcome this too."

"I suppose we'll find out." She shook her head. "Once I got through the plywood, I was able to pull it up and make a hole big enough to drop through. I couldn't believe it when I saw Officer Clay down there."

"And he couldn't believe it was you," Julianna had said.

Now, Dottie slept, her deep breathing aided by the pain meds.

A knock on the door pulled her attention from her sister, and Julianna walked to the door. "Clay?"

"We got her," he said. The smile on his face conveyed his deep satisfaction at being able to say that.

"What?"

"Kara Williams. She's in custody."

A feeling of relief, like nothing she'd ever experienced before, swept through her. "How?"

"I heard you mention the bandages on her face. I was heading for the cafeteria to get Dottie her pizza when I saw this woman standing at the information desk. Being in a hospital, the bandages wouldn't draw much attention from anyone else, but after

232

your description of the person in the post office . . . and the fact that it was a female . . ." He shrugged. "That stood out to me. Also add in the fact that Dottie was here in the hospital, it seemed likely that the person might come looking for her—or you, knowing you'd be with her. Anyway, I decided to go with my gut and followed her while calling for backup. Long story short, security showed up along with your agent friends who were still in the hospital."

"Max and Lydia."

"Right."

Julianna turned to Dottie, who'd awakened during the exchange, and smiled. "They got her. We're out of danger now. It's all over."

Her sister's eyes widened. "Seriously?"

"Seriously."

"Thank God."

"Yes," Julianna whispered. "Thank him."

Dottie bit her lip. "I prayed to him."

"You did?"

"Didn't figure it could hurt."

"No, it definitely couldn't hurt."

Dottie turned her gaze to Clay. "And then you showed up."

"I'm glad I was there."

"Me too. But we can talk about the God stuff later. I'm ready to get out of here. Somebody please find the papers I need to sign to make that happen."

Julianna gave her a nod. "I'll go see what I can do while you get dressed."

"Oh, wait," Clay said. He reached into his pocket, pulled out three chocolate bars, and waved them at Dottie. "Sorry I didn't get the pizza. I got interrupted before I had the chance to see if they even had any. Maybe we can grab some on the way out of here."

Her eyes lit up and she held out a hand. "Gimme, gimme, please. It will tide me over until we can get the pizza."

Laughter spilled from all three of them and Julianna's vision blurred. She blinked until she could see clearly again. It was over. They'd survived. Nothing to cry about now. Not even happy tears. "Be back in a few."

Clay followed her out of the room. "I still have a report to write," he said, letting the door shut behind him, "but I wanted you and Dottie to hear the news from me."

"Thank you, Clay, for everything. If you hadn't been there . . ." He pulled her to him and Julianna let him, savoring the moment, knowing it would end all too soon. When he stepped back, she ran a hand over her ponytail. "Okay," she said, taking a deep breath. "Before we leave, I need to speak to Kara. I'll find out where they're taking her and arrange to talk to her."

"One thing," he said. "I didn't mention it, but when I tackled Kara, she fell and hit her head against the edge of the step. It didn't knock her out, but it bled a lot and she's being treated for the wound."

"Where?"

"The other end of the ER. Max and Lydia went with her."

"Thank you."

Clay rested a hand on her shoulder. "Do you want to head there and I'll see if I can spring Dottie? You know it's going to be at least an hour before she goes anywhere."

"Yeah." Julianna nodded. "I need to talk to Kara. Something's niggling at me."

He raised a brow. "What?"

"Just . . . this was all planned out. Daria said she'd been released from the hospital three weeks ago. Is that really enough time to plan this?"

"She was probably planning it before she was released."

"True." Julianna frowned. "But . . ."

"What?"

Julianna shook her head. "Nothing, I guess. I'm going to go see if I can talk to Kara." She left Dottie in Clay's capable care and made her way to the far side of the ER.

She flashed her badge and found the room. Three uniformed officers and Max stood outside. "Hi."

"Hey, how was Dottie after we left?"

"She's all right. She'll have some PTSD moments, no doubt, but we'll make sure she has the right help to get her through them." He nodded and Julianna glanced at the room. "I want to talk to her."

"She's asked for you. I was getting ready to call you when you walked up."

"So, her head injury isn't serious?"

"Naw, it bled a lot and she'll have a headache, but no concussion. She's fine. Physically."

Mentally was the question. "All right."

Julianna reached for the knob and Max stopped her. "Are you okay to do this? She's your friend, right?"

"She's no friend of mine." Julianna heard the frosty tone in her words, but this woman, her former bestie, had tried to kill her and Dottie. Yeah, she'd overstepped the bounds of friendship with that one.

Max let her go, and she took a moment to say a prayer for wisdom, then stepped inside.

When the door snicked shut behind her, the woman cuffed to the bed opened her eyes. "You came."

The deep, robotic voice was so different than the light soprano she remembered. From the fire, no doubt.

"Hello, Kara." The bandages had been removed from her face, and she sported a new bright white one on the top of her head where she'd hit the edge of the step when Clay had tackled her. Julianna took in the scarred face, the evidence of her desperate act, and couldn't see any remnant of her high school friend. Except for the eyes. She'd know those eyes anywhere. And even those were different. Hard and cold. And filled with hate.

"Why?" Julianna asked.

"You killed Kane."

Julianna closed her eyes and bit back unhelpful words while she pulled on all of her professional training. Never had she faced a situation like this, and she was floundering.

Compartmentalize.

She opened her eyes. "Dennis killed Kane."

Equally scarred hands, although bound, clutched the sheets she could reach. "Because of you! It was all *you*! If you had just done what he wanted you to do, then none of this would have happened."

Julianna narrowed her eyes. Kara was ill. She had years of psychiatric problems behind her. Would arguing or explaining or reasoning have any effect on her? "Why did you shoot your parents?"

The woman flinched. "Because they put me in that awful place."

The "awful" place that most people couldn't even dream of affording. The place with the outstanding reviews and highly ranked success rate. "They wanted to help you."

"No, they didn't. They wanted to get rid of me." She pulled at her restraints, then let her hands fall back to the bed. "They wanted Kane. It was always about Kane. After he died, I ceased to matter. All they could do was blame *me* that he was dead. Me!"

"Why you? It wasn't your fault."

"I know that! But I had to be at school early to help with the stupid project because *you* couldn't meet after school." Her glare could have lasered holes in Julianna's head. "And Kane had to drive me because we had to share a car."

"You had to share a car because you'd wrecked yours coming home from a party you weren't supposed to be at."

"I'd finally gotten asked to one of the most popular social events of the year and my parents weren't going to let me go." Her tone was flat, almost disconnected from the emotion in her eyes. "There was no way I wasn't going."

"They asked you there to be their entertainment for the night. So they could bully you and get you drunk. They put you behind that wheel and told you to drive home. You knew they weren't your friends. You knew they just wanted to torment you. Why would you do that? Kane and I told you—"

"Because no one else saw me."

Julianna blinked. "What?"

"I was invisible to everyone, including my family. Those friends may have been awful, but at least they saw me."

"I saw you. Kane saw you. Melissa Green saw you. What about us? What about the people who loved you? Why weren't we enough?"

Her words must have struck a chord somewhere in the depths of Kara's mind, and she blinked. Then stared and blinked again. "I . . . I don't know."

And Julianna couldn't tell her, either.

Once again Kara's scarred face twisted. "But it was your fault. It was all your fault. If you hadn't made us be there early, Kane wouldn't have had to drive me and he would still be alive."

"I had to get Dottie, Kara," she whispered. "You know that."

"You were so eager to please everyone, and then when Dennis wanted you to do something, you just . . . didn't. And he killed Kane because of it."

"*Please Dennis?* He *hit* me, Kara. He punched me in the face that last time—"

"And then you pushed Dennis," she said, never acknowledging that Julianna had spoken. "You pushed him in front of the window—"

"Stop it."

"And the sniper shot him! You killed Kane and you killed Dennis too!"

"He was going to shoot you!" Julianna flinched. She hadn't raised her voice in so long, she'd forgotten what it felt like. Sounded like. She cleared her throat. "He was going to kill us all, Kara. He shot Kane and turned the gun on you—"

I'll save the best for last. He'd looked her in the eye and said those words.

"I couldn't let him kill you too," she finally ended on a whisper.

"You should have let him! Kane was my brother and you stole him from me even before Dennis shot him. He always wanted to hang out with you. Do you know why?"

"No." Yes, she did. Kane had been crazy in love with her, and Julianna hadn't felt the same, so she'd treated him like the brother she'd never had.

"You took him from me, then you let him get shot. He was dead and I didn't want to live anymore. So you ruined my life too!" She clamped her lips together and glared at Julianna through a sheen of tears.

Julianna steeled herself. She still wanted answers. "Kara, what's a tunnel rat?"

The woman stilled. "What?"

"A tunnel rat. Dottie said you muttered something about not being a tunnel rat."

"Someone who lives underground in a tunnel because they have no place else to go or live! And it's all your fault! All your fault! Ahhhh! It's not my fault. Stop saying it's my fault. It's not! It's not my fault!" She shook her head over and over, and a nurse rushed in with a syringe. "I don't want drugs! Stop giving me drugs! I need Dr. P, please, please. I need Dr. P. I have a mission. I have to finish the mission. It's not finished! Stop!" The nurse pushed the needle into the IV port and within seconds, Kara's screams fell to whimpers, then finally to no sound at all. She breathed deep, rolled her head to the side, and was still.

Julianna backed out of the room and shut the door. Then released the breath she hadn't realized she was holding. She closed her eyes for a brief moment, trying to get herself together, then glanced at Max. "I think they need to call her psychiatrist."

"I agree. I'll make sure they do. Whoever she was seeing will be in her records. I'll mention it to the psychiatrist on call and see if he knows who it is."

"It'll be someone in Burbank, California, I'm sure, but maybe she can do a teleconference call or something."

"Of course."

"Thanks."

"Jules?"

She looked up to find Dottie standing next to Clay and cleared her throat. She shot a tight smile to Max and Lydia and walked over to join her sister and Clay. "I'm ready to go home."

Dottie linked her arm with Julianna's. "I'd race you, but I'd rather just walk with you."

"Where's your wheelchair?"

"I let them roll me out, then I walked back in to find you."

"Sneaky."

"When the need is there."

"I love you, Dot."

"I know. I love you too."

CHAPTER
TWENTY-FOUR

When Clay pulled in front of Julianna's house, Reese's car was parked in the drive. Julianna braked to a stop behind him. As soon as he climbed out and shut the door, Reese appeared on the front porch. "Oh, I'm so glad you're here!" She raced down the steps and Clay opened his arms . . .

. . . only to drop them when she bypassed him and grabbed Dottie in a breath-stealing hug. "I was so scared for you!"

"Officer Clay saved me," Dottie managed to choke out before pulling back from his sister's clutches.

"You saved yourself, my friend," Clay said.

"Whatever. I don't want to think about it anymore. I want a hot bath, another one of those chocolate bars, the whole box of pizza, and my desk. I have my last chemistry test tomorrow before the final exam and I'm not missing it."

"Dottie." Julianna gaped, climbing out of the Bucar in time to hear Dottie's words. "Seriously?"

"Absolutely. I'm not giving Mary Ann McKinney the satisfaction of missing that test. She doesn't get to win just because I had a bad day." She headed for the steps with Reese right beside her.

Julianna started to follow and Clay caught her hand. "Are you all right?"

"Not really. But I will be."

He waved his phone at her. "I have a date for the final program at the school if you can still do it."

"I'll have to run it by the higher-ups, but I don't think it'll be a problem. When should I be there?"

"The only time available is Wednesday."

She froze. "That's three days from now."

"I know. I also know it's the fifteenth anniversary of the shooting, so if it would be too traumatic to—"

"No. I'll make it work."

"But you don't have—"

"Clay, hush. I'll make it work." She lifted her chin. "Dottie just said something that's echoing in my brain. It's like a light bulb just went on."

"What's that?"

"'She doesn't get to win just because I had a bad day.' It's time I stop giving that day power over my life. It was a day. A horrible, tragic day. But that's all it was. It happened and I need to move on. God is bigger than the events of that day, and I'm not honoring him by allowing it to still have so much impact on me." Her eyes widened. "In fact," she said, "and I can't believe this hasn't occurred to me before this very moment."

"What?"

"By giving that day so much power, it's almost like I'm honoring Dennis. I'm letting him win because I 'had a bad day.' Granted, it was a really bad day, but . . . ." She shook her head. "I don't want him to win. And while I haven't let him ruin my life completely, he still has way too much influence over my thoughts and actions." She met his gaze. "And that's going to stop. Right now."

Her words smacked him right in the face. Was he doing the same with his own past? His own incident? Letting those who'd set him up to kill one of his own have too much power over his thoughts and actions?

"I'll always remember Kane," she said. "He was a great friend, and he would be shattered at what's happened to Kara. But I want to honor his memory and live life to the fullest. Like he did. Not honor the person who killed him."

"I didn't know him, but I bet he'd be proud."

She shot him a small smile. "He would be." Then her smile flipped into a thoughtful frown.

"What is it?" he asked.

"I want to do some research."

"On?"

"Kara. I want to know everything about her and what happened from that day forward." She shook her head. "I'm pretty sure she was living in the tunnels. They'll search them and find out."

"What?"

"She told Dottie she was a tunnel rat." She waved her phone at him. "I googled it and tunnel rats were used in Vietnam. They used to hide in tunnels and mount surprise attacks. They'd hide the air vents under bushes. They started out simple at first but turned into a massive, complex maze of tunnels in the 1960s."

"Wow. And you think she was living underground?"

"I do. I know it sounds weird, but I just want to know about her. I . . . I want to know about her time in the psychiatric hospital. I want to know what happened to her to turn her into . . . who she became."

"And if you could have done something to save her?"

Now, she just looked sad. "No. I couldn't have done anything. Any more than I could have saved Kane from Dennis's bullet. It's hard to admit, but I'm coming to realize it's true." She paused. "But I *did* save *her*," she said, her voice low. "That day."

"What do you mean?"

She swallowed and looked away. "I've worked so hard to push the details of that day away and I just can't . . . let them go."

"Tell me," he said, gripping her fingers.

"I'm afraid to."

"Why?"

"Because I dream about it. And if I talk about it, the dreams intensify. They turn into nightmares."

"How often do you talk about it?"

She huffed a soft laugh. "Um . . . like never?"

"Then tell me and you can call me, and I'll come over and hold you if you have a nightmare." He pulled her closer.

"Oh, Clay." She drew in a deep breath, and the agony on her face almost made him take back his request. But he had a feeling she needed to tell him. She nodded. "Before Dennis killed Kane, when the phone rang, Dennis ordered me to pick up. He refused to talk to them. I know now, he had no intention of talking anything out. He was there to say his piece and kill all three of us, but at the time, I thought . . ."

A shudder rippled through him and his hands flexed on her biceps. "Julianna . . ."

"Shh. Let me say it. When the phone rang, I picked it up. The man said to get Dennis to the window, that there was a sniper who would end everything. I . . . hesitated. I thought I could talk him down. He lifted the gun and Kane jumped in between me and the bullet. Kara was screaming, Dennis lifted the gun one more time and said while looking at me, 'I'll save the best for last.'"

"Ah, Jules . . ."

"He aimed it at her. I ran forward and shoved him in front of the window and the sniper pulled the trigger. Dennis was hit in the head and died instantly."

"Oh, Julianna, I'm so sorry." He wiped the tears from her cheeks and pulled her against him. He pressed his lips to the top of her head. "I'm so sorry."

"So, you see, Clay, it's not that I can't signal for someone to take the shot, I really just haven't had to. I've been able to talk down most situations." She sighed. "Because I know if I hesitate, like I did with Kane, then someone could die. I just have to figure out how to forgive myself for hesitating that day and letting Kane get killed."

"You were a kid."

"I know."

"There's nothing to forgive."

As soon as the words left his lips, he knew he had some serious thinking to do if he was ever going to get past his own trauma. And accepting that he'd been a pawn in something he had no control over was the first step in moving on. He met her gaze. "Just so you know, you've taught me a lot since we've met."

"What do you mean?"

"I mean, you've made me think about a lot of things. You've allowed me to . . . hope again."

"Hope is good."

"Hope is very good." He clasped her hand and together, they walked to the front porch and into the house.

She led him into the kitchen, released his hand, and grabbed two waters from the refrigerator. "What have you found yourself hoping for?"

"Several things." He took a seat in the nearest chair. "That I can be forgiven, for one."

"Of course you can."

"In my head I know that, but you know as well as I do, it's harder to convince the heart."

"True." She frowned. "Why is it we can give other people more grace than we'll give ourselves?"

"I don't have an answer for that one."

"What's another thing?"

He looked at her. Really looked at her and wondered how much more he should bare of his heart.

"Clay?"

"I want to spend more time with you."

Her eyes widened and a small smile curved her lips. "I'd like that." Her phone rang and Julianna glanced at the screen. Then frowned. "Sorry, I have to take this."

Clay nodded, noting the sudden tension in her face. Whoever it was, she was worried it wasn't good news.

■ ■ ■ ■

"Hey, Max, what's up?"

"I'm calling from the hospital, Jules. Kara Williams is dead."

Julianna sank into the chair next to Clay. "What? How?"

"We're not sure, but it looks like an accidental overdose of meds. The hospital is looking into it, of course, but that's what they're saying at the moment."

"I don't believe this," she muttered.

"Yeah. Lydia and I are here until we get some answers, but the families of the hostages she killed will finally have some closure."

"Maybe."

"We did find something interesting, though."

"What?"

"There was an old map in her pocket of the underground tunnels. Apparently, she was hiding out in one of them downtown under the courthouse. Agents went to investigate and found she'd been living there for a while. And get this . . ."

"What?"

"The dirt from that tunnel matched the sample from Reese Fox's townhome."

That didn't surprise her. Julianna already knew Kara was the one who'd tried to break into Reese's home, and the evidence would have been used at her trial. Unfortunately, there wouldn't be a need for one now. "I thought the city had locked those tunnels down."

"They did. Sort of. I mean, no one was patrolling them very heavily. They had them blocked off with barricades, but she managed to bypass them and set up camp."

"No wonder she could come and go so easily."

"And guess where one of the tunnels led to?"

No guessing required. "The post office."

"Got it in one. We finally figured out how she slipped away from us. There are two ways up to the roof. She took one, worked her way over to the other entrance, and reentered the building on the side with stairs leading all the way down to the basement. In the basement—that was thoroughly searched, by the way—there's an old manhole covered up by the new building. She simply slipped inside it and waited for the all clear."

"Unbelievable." Julianna paused. "And now she's dead. From an accidental overdose."

Clay's brows rose at that statement.

"You're not buying it?" Max asked.

"Are you?"

"I don't have a reason not to. Why aren't you?"

"I don't know. I mean, it's possible, of course."

"But . . ."

"Yes."

"Okay, well, you think about it and let me know why we might need to consider this as a murder rather than an accident."

"It just seems awfully convenient."

"Who would want her dead? Any ideas?"

"No," Julianna said, her voice low. "None."

"I'll pass your thoughts on to Lydia and see what she thinks. I'll keep you updated."

"Please do."

She hung up and looked at Clay. "Kara's dead."

"I got that from your end of the conversation. And all I can say is . . . wow."

She blew out a low breath. "Wow. Yeah."

"You don't think it was an accident."

She groaned. "I don't know. I can't even figure out what I'm feeling at the moment." Kara was dead, and her grief was tangible. But it wasn't for the present-day Kara. She grieved for the friend she'd lost fifteen years ago. Julianna cleared her throat. "All right, what if we switch gears?"

"Okay. What do you have in mind?"

"How about we fix some food and veg on the couch in front of an old movie?"

"I like that plan very much."

His gaze was soft and concerned, and her pulse hummed a little faster than it should have.

But ten minutes later, with salads piled with ham, turkey, bacon, cheese, and boiled eggs, they sat on the sofa and Julianna turned on the television.

The news played and Kara's face flashed on the screen.

". . . Williams. She was from Burbank, California, and had spent a number of years in and out of psychiatric facilities. One source reports that she was the sister of Kane Williams, who was the victim of a school shooting almost fifteen years ago. Authorities say it's too early to speculate on the motive behind the killings—or why she traveled across the country to conduct her deadly killing spree. This is Channel Seven News, Kate Allison reporting. We'll have more as the story unfolds."

Julianna stared at the screen, then clicked on the streaming channel app. "Do you mind if we find something funny?"

"Funny sounds perfect."

She could hear the faint sounds of Dottie and Reese talking, their voices coming from Dottie's room upstairs. Once more, she thanked God for his protection and deliverance of Dottie from Kara. Then settled her head against Clay's shoulder and focused on the movie.

The classic black and white was humorous and interesting, but soon, she found her eyes closing. She and Clay had a lot to talk about, but for now, she'd just enjoy his company, share some laughter, and try to keep her eyes open so she could soak in every moment.

■ ■ ■ ■

Felicity found herself fascinated with the story of Kara Williams. Each update brought more information. Apparently, she'd been obsessed with revenge, but no one could figure out the connection of her victims to the death of her brother. The shooter who'd killed him fifteen years ago, Dennis Collins, had died from a sniper bullet—after he'd killed Kane Williams—ending the stand-off. But the media speculated that there was definitely a connection. They didn't know what it was, but they'd report it as soon as they knew.

"What you watching, Mama?"

She hit the remote and turned the television off to find her son standing in the doorway, dressed in shorts, a T-shirt, and his tennis shoes. "Just the news."

"Why do you look sad?"

"Sometimes there are sad things on the news."

"Oh." He frowned at her. "Then let's do something that makes us happy."

She caught him in a hug. "Let me guess. You want me to push you on the swing."

He giggled and her heart warmed. "Well, that would make me happy. Will it make you happy?"

"If you're happy, then I'm happy." She set him on his feet, and he raced out the back door at full speed, heading for the swing set in their neighbor's yard.

Giles Hampton had moved in four days ago and put up the swing set. Tommy had watched, not bothering to hide his longing. She'd come inside to get them drinks, and when she returned, she found her son and their new neighbor chatting at the fence. Not sure she was thrilled with the idea of him being so friendly with a stranger, she walked over to Tommy and placed a hand on his shoulder. "Hi." She met the man's light blue eyes. "I'm Felicity Banks. This is my son, Tommy."

"Hi. I'm Giles Hampton."

"You got kids, Mr. Hampton?" Tommy bounced on his toes trying to see behind the man.

He smiled. "No, but I have two nieces and a nephew about your age. I plan for them to visit a lot."

Tommy clapped, his eyes wide with pleasure. "That's phenomenal!"

Giles laughed. "That's a big word for you, kid."

"I like words."

"Well, Tommy, you can swing on that swing any time your mom says it's okay. How's that sound?"

"Spectacular!" He glanced up at her. "Doesn't it, Mom?"

"Absolutely."

"Come on over and give it a test run if you like."

Felicity had smiled. "Why not?"

Now, she held Tommy's hand and led him to the neighbor's backyard fence. It still felt weird going onto his property, but he'd been so kind and she didn't get any icky vibes from him. Once she closed the gate behind her, Tommy raced to the swing and took a seat. "Push me, Mom!" She did, and for the next five minutes, he was content to swing. Then he hopped down and ran over to the kid-sized rock wall and started climbing. Then sliding. Then starting all over.

The back door opened and Giles stepped out onto the porch.

"I hope it's okay we're here," she said. "I took you at your word."

"It's perfect." He leaned against the wood column and crossed his arms. "Is Tommy your only one?"

"He is."

"And his father?"

She flicked a glance at him. "He's dead."

Giles winced. "I'm sorry. None of my business. Just to let you know, I'm very good at inserting my foot in my mouth, so if we're going to be around each other much, I'd like to ask in advance for your forgiveness."

And just like that, he'd put her at ease. "Wyatt was my best friend, but he was killed in Afghanistan a little over a year ago. What about you?"

"Divorced, no kids." He glanced at her from beneath his long, dark lashes. "My wife left me for my best friend."

She gaped. "I'm so sorry."

He shrugged. "It was two years ago. Seems like I should be past it by now."

"Is there a timeline for getting past something like that?"

A laugh slipped from him. "No, I don't guess there is."

"Then give yourself some grace. Some things take time."

Like forgiveness.

Lord, I'm trying. Her mind wandered back to Kara Williams. A woman so broken and bitter that she'd killed people in her quest for revenge. *God, I definitely don't want to become bitter or allow my soul to become so black I can't find my way back to you. Give me forgiveness. Give me peace. Give me closure in whatever way you see fit.*

CHAPTER
TWENTY-FIVE

THREE DAYS LATER

Clay pulled into the school parking lot, parked, and texted Julianna his location.

Julianna
Be in shortly.

We're set up and ready to roll whenever we get the green light.

Everything for the program had been set up in the gym. Each branch of law enforcement would offer a short behind-the-scenes look at each job. How a drug bust went down, how an undercover detective worked, how the Secret Service tracked counterfeit currency, an abridged version of how the NTSB investigated a plane crash. A US Marshal would talk about tracking a fugitive and more. Julianna and another agent would demonstrate how a conversation with a hostage taker might go. Clay was actually surprised at how smooth everything had come together.

In a short time, the first batch of students would file in and take their seats in the bleachers, where they would have a bird's-eye view of the setup. Then they would be released, and the second group would enter. He'd had to schedule two sessions, as the interest in watching was high.

Clay made his way to the gym, where Dottie met him with wide eyes. "This is going to be amazing. I'm actually going to get to see Jules in action."

He laughed. "I'll admit I'm looking forward to it too."

Dottie darted off to join a group of girls in the bleachers, and Clay noted Mary Ann McKinney watching her with narrowed eyes and a pinched mouth. He'd been so wrapped up in everything else, he hadn't had a chance to check on her like he wanted to. He walked over to her. "Hi, Mary Ann."

Her lip curled. "Why do you bother to speak to me?"

"Because I'm worried about you. How are you doing?"

Surprise flashed before she covered it with another smirk. "I'm just fine, thanks."

"You're eighteen, right?"

Her smirk slipped into a frown. "Yes. Why?"

Her age meant her parents couldn't be held responsible for kicking their kid out. "Just wondering. My offer to help still stands."

"I'll pass."

She turned her back on him, heading for the exit, and Clay rubbed a hand down his cheek. *God, I know we've not been on speaking terms lately—which is my fault, not yours—but if you could take it upon yourself to keep an eye on that girl, I'd appreciate it. She's got a lot of anger stuffed down deep, and I'm afraid it's going to come bubbling up one day to explode all over anyone in her vicinity.* He paused. *Show me how to help her.*

He stopped. He'd prayed. He'd actually prayed. And done so almost without thinking about it. It felt good. He glanced at his watch and noted they had a little time before the program started. He made his way to the SRO office, where he found Julianna, Andre, and Curly at the table in the center of the room. Andre looked up and grinned. "Hey, Ms. FBI said she'd let me interview her for my final project."

Curly shook his head. "I can't believe you're actually interested in joining the FBI."

Andre jabbed a thumb in Julianna's direction. "Dude, they got agents that look like her? I'm all in."

Julianna sputtered on a laugh and Clay stifled a groan. "Get out of here, you two."

The teens left and Clay met her gaze with a smile. "I gotta say, I can't blame Andre. You do make the FBI look good."

This time her laughter rang through the office. She stood and kissed him on the cheek. "You're cute, Officer Fox."

He glanced at the clock. "I wish we had more time to discuss my cuteness, but it's time to get this show on the road."

Julianna smirked. "Don't let Dottie hear you use that phrase. You'll be officially old in her book."

Clay nodded to the door. "How about 'Showtime.'"

"Yeah, I don't think that's much better."

■ ■ ■ ■

Dottie's pulse hammered in her chest. She was super excited to be able to see Julianna in action. Even if it was just a brief snippet of the big picture. She'd take what she could get.

She sat next to two girls she hung out with when she wasn't with Reese or being kidnapped by crazy people. Jennifer and Li Jing. They'd taken her under their wings almost as soon as she stepped foot inside the school. It hadn't hurt that she was giving Mary Ann McKinney a run for her money for valedictorian. They couldn't stand her. What would they say if they knew Dottie felt kind of sorry for her, now that she knew more about the girl's home life?

Li Jing nudged her. "You know, you're the coolest person in the school right now, right?"

Dottie frowned. "Why?" Although, she thought she'd noticed people being more friendly.

"Duh," Jennifer said. "You got kidnapped by a psychopath and survived. And your sister is a hero."

"Why does that make me cool? I'm the same person I was before all that happened." It was stupid, but she got it.

Principal Callahan walked out onto the court. Everyone hushed and turned their attention to the man. "Good morning, students," he boomed into the mic. "I want to welcome you to this exciting event arranged by one of our SROs, Clay Fox. Clay's got a few words to say, then he'll introduce our special guests. Clay?"

Clay took the microphone and stood tall in front of the crowd. "Thank you for being here today. I'm honored to be a part of this program and think you'll have a new respect for law enforcement once we're finished here. Feel free to hang around and speak to those who're involved in this simulation. Keep in mind, this is a small-scale demonstration, but it will give you a good idea of how different agencies work. With that, I'm going to introduce Charlie Hall, who's going to talk about the process of setting up a drug bust."

For the next thirty minutes, various law enforcement officers spoke and did short demonstrations related to their field. Dottie enjoyed it but was anxious for Julianna to take the stage.

When her sister finally stepped into view, Dottie's heart soared with pride. She could only hope to be as amazing as her.

"Thank you for having us here," Julianna said. "We do a lot of these demonstrations and are grateful for people like you who support us. So, what you're going to watch is a demonstration of how a conversation might go in a hostage situation. You ready?" A round of applause filled the gym and Julianna smiled. "All right. Here we go."

A nudge to her left pulled her attention from the scene and she frowned at Jennifer. "What?"

"The big guy wants you."

"What?" She turned and saw Principal Callahan motioning to her. She really didn't want to miss out on the program, so she pretended not to see him and turned back to the action.

Julianna sat in a chair to the left that had been marked Command Center. She had a headset on, her radio, and a phone. A laptop was open in front of her. Two others sat with her. The hostage taker had been positioned behind a makeshift wall. Julianna dialed the phone and the hostage taker picked up the phone. "What?"

"This is Julianna, what's your name?"

The suspect hung up and Dottie winced.

Julianna called back. The phone rang and he picked up. "I don't want to talk."

"All right," Julianna said, "would you be willing to listen?"

They went back and forth for a few minutes, with Julianna's soothing tone something Dottie had heard on a few occasions when her sister had helped her calm down from various issues. She'd remember that in the future.

Another nudge from Jennifer, and she glanced back once more to see Callahan waving at her with narrowed eyes and a "you'd better get over here now" expression.

"Ugh. I'll be right back." She stood and made her way out of the bleachers to stand in front of the man. "What is it? I mean, what can I do for you, sir? I really don't want to miss this."

"I'm so sorry, Dottie, but someone in the office said they need to speak with you immediately concerning your kidnapping."

"Who?"

"A psychiatrist who works for the FBI."

"And it can't wait? The person who kidnapped me is dead. How is me missing this going to help things?"

He shook his head. "I don't know, but she was very insistent that she only had a few moments in between clients and I needed to get you into the office."

It had to be Grace. Concern mixed with irritation and she nodded. "Fine."

Dottie threw a look back over her shoulder, and for a brief second her gaze connected with Julianna's. Her sister rose and Dottie waved her off, then shot her a thumbs-up.

Julianna settled back into her seat, her brows furrowed, but she never lost a beat in her dialogue with the fake suspect.

The route to Principal Callahan's office was a circuitous one. They took a right turn out of the gym and a long walk down the hallway, up the stairs, and down another long hallway with a row of classrooms, ending at the office area. Dottie followed the man into his office and they found it empty.

He stopped and frowned. "Seriously? Where'd she go?"

"That's what I'd like to know." Dottie followed him around to the front of the office, where two administrative assistants sat at the counter.

"Jess," Principal Callahan said, "did you or Boyd see where the psychiatrist went?"

Jess looked up from her computer and shook her head. "No, sorry. Last I saw, she was in the chair outside your office where you left her."

"Same here," Boyd said.

"Okay, thanks." Callahan shook his head. "I'm sorry, Dottie. Go on back to the program." He glanced at the clock on the wall. "It should have about five more minutes, then a Q&A. If it helps, you saw most of it."

"It doesn't help."

"If she reappears, I'll just tell her she has to wait."

With a groan, Dottie stomped out of the office and made her way back down the hall. She passed friends who'd opted out of the demonstration.

"What's the matter, Dottie, are you lost? Wandering the halls looking for trouble?"

Dottie closed her eyes at the snide voice. She was very, very tired of Mary Ann McKinney. Like she seriously didn't have the patience to deal with the girl. "Go away, Mary Ann." Mary Ann had upped her game ever since Dottie had returned to school the day after being rescued only to ace the AP Chem test.

"Everyone loves you now that you've escaped from a killer."

Mary Ann stepped in front of her, eyes narrowed and nostrils flared. "It's unbelievable that you would get kidnapped and manage to get rescued within twenty-four hours. Just shows you how my luck is going these days."

"So, you'd rather I be killed?"

Mary Ann flinched. "No, of course not. I'm a mean girl, I admit it, but no, I wouldn't wish you dead. Just . . . absent."

Wow.

"Dottie Jameson?"

Dottie turned and saw a woman in her midfifties hurrying toward her. The woman was dressed in a professional pantsuit and had her salt-and-pepper hair slicked back in a severe bun. Her makeup was flawless and she exuded authority. "Yes, ma'am?"

"Could I speak to you a moment?"

"Are you the shrink who snuck out of the office?"

"Snuck out?"

"You're not wearing a visitor badge."

"Oh. Oops. Sorry." A smile slipped across her red-tinted lips. "I got tired of waiting and decided to come find you on my own."

"You're not supposed to do that, you know."

She lifted a shoulder in a small shrug. "Well, I didn't figure it would hurt anything. Can we find a room to have a chat?"

"Um, my sister is here doing a special demonstration in the gym and I'd really like to finish it." Although, at this point, why bother?

"Oh, I see. Well, I promise this won't take long and you can get back to it. Okay?"

Ugh. Seriously? "It'll be over by then, but fine." The faster she gave the woman what she wanted, the faster she could get back to the demonstration. She could always ask to attend the second one. "You look familiar. Have we met before?"

"No, I don't think so."

Dottie felt sure she'd seen her somewhere but honestly didn't really care. "Do you want to go back to the office?"

"You're a reporter, aren't you?" Mary Ann asked.

Dottie had forgotten the girl was there.

The woman smiled again, a condescending look that immediately set Mary Ann's nerves on edge, if her curled lip was anything to go by. Dottie bit the inside of her cheek to keep from smiling. This could be interesting.

"Let's see if we can find an empty classroom," the woman said.

Just go in a classroom and make themselves at home? Sounded weird, but whatever.

The woman walked to the nearest room and knocked, then pushed the door open. "Oops, sorry." She backed out and went to the next one. Then the next. Mary Ann trailed behind them, clearly convinced that Dottie was about to get the spotlight once again.

But by the fourth room, Dottie had just about had it. "Look, I don't think—"

"This room is perfect." The woman opened the door. "After you."

Dottie stepped inside and noted the others who'd looked up at the interruption.

"I'm coming too." Mary Ann pushed inside and Dottie rolled her eyes.

The teacher opened his mouth to speak, but Dottie beat him to it. "I'm sorry, Mr. Holliday. We were looking for an empty room." She turned. "This room isn't—"

The woman pulled her hand out of her pocket, and Dottie found herself face-to-face with a gun once again while Mary Ann let out a high-pitched scream.

"—empty."

CHAPTER
TWENTY-SIX

Julianna caught Clay's eye while one of the other agents answered a question from a student. He walked over. "You okay?"

"Where did Dottie go? The principal came and got her and she looked super irritated."

"I'm not sure. Want me to find out?"

"That's all right. I'm almost done here and the next demonstration isn't for another fifteen minutes or so. I'll go find her in a few minutes."

He nodded and stepped back to wait.

She turned to the next student, paused, and excused herself. A small niggling at the base of her neck set her nerves on edge. She walked over to Clay. "I'm feeling the need to check on her. She missed the last half and I know how excited she was to see this."

"Yeah. I've been thinking the same thing. Come on."

They walked out of the gym, crossed the courtyard, and entered the office area. "Hey, Boyd," Clay said, "where's Callahan?"

"It's Principal Callahan. When are you going to get it right?"

"He told me I could call him Callahan. Said it made him feel like he was one of the guys."

Boyd rolled his eyes and Julianna wondered at the history there, but didn't have time to ask. Boyd waved a hand toward the hallway that ran along the side of the offices. "In his office, I think."

"Buzz us in?"

"Lose your card?"

"Dude . . ."

The phone rang and Boyd grabbed it with one hand and hit the button for Clay and Julianna to push through the door, giving them access to the back part of the administration offices. "This way," Clay said.

"What's his problem?"

"His brother is a cop and apparently the guy gives him a hard time."

"So he transfers his agitation to you. Nice."

"Isn't it?"

Julianna followed him down the hall and found the principal at his desk.

The man looked up. "What's up? Everything go okay with the demo?"

"Everything went great," Julianna said. "Thank you for allowing us to do it."

Callahan smiled. "Of course. What can I do for you?"

"I saw you come get Dottie Jameson from the program," Clay said. "Everything okay?"

The principal's smile dipped into a frown. "I think so. A woman came in and said she needed to speak to Dottie, that she'd been asked to do a psych eval on Dottie after her kidnapping."

"Asked by who?" Julianna stepped forward, her worry meter ticking into the concerned zone.

"She didn't say."

"She give her name?" It couldn't be Grace, could it?

"Um . . . yeah. And she had her badge from whoever she was with. I'm sure she signed in." He stood and led the way back to the front and found the guest book on the counter. "There." He pointed. "Gwen Peterson."

So. Not Grace. "All right. Where'd she go?"

"When Dottie and I walked in from the gym," Callahan said, "the woman was gone. I sent Dottie back to the program about ten minutes ago and assumed she made it back."

"She didn't," Clay said.

"I don't like this," Julianna murmured. "She would have come back. She was too excited about it to just skip it."

Callahan frowned. "But she's out of danger, right? I mean, you caught the person who kidnapped her."

Julianna nodded. "We did, but something just isn't sitting right with me about this." That little niggling was full-blown banging now. "We caught her and she died from an overdose a short time later. And now some strange woman claiming to be a psychiatrist is here to talk to Dottie?"

"It's too much," Clay said.

"Way too much."

"I'll call her to the office," Callahan said. The principal went to the front desk and picked up the mic. "Dottie Jameson to the front office, please. Dottie Jameson, please report to the front office."

She shot off a text to Daria, Ahmed, and Hector.

> I need information about a woman named
> Gwen Peterson and I need it yesterday.

She looked at the two men. "I'm going to walk the halls and peek in classrooms. See if I can spot her." Clay nodded, and she slipped out of the office, her hand going to the radio on her shoulder. "SWAT, check in."

Responses came in rapid-fire. Most were in the cafeteria grabbing snacks and drinks that the school had provided. "Fabio, you there?" His real name was Frank, but due to his GQ good looks, he'd been saddled with the nickname. But he was the best sniper she'd ever worked with.

"I'm here."

"Meet me in the hallway outside the cafeteria? Something's going on."

"What?"

"I'm not sure." She checked each classroom as she passed, thinking this would have been the route Dottie would have taken back to the gym. Maybe she'd gotten stopped by a teacher or another student had needed something. "Have the others on standby."

"What's got your Spidey senses tingling?"

"I'll let you know when I do. Stand by."

"Copy that."

Her phone buzzed and Julianna glanced at the text from Daria.

Gwen Peterson is a psychiatrist from Burbank
California. She's married to a guy named Bob
Larson.

Julianna gasped. "Bob Larson!"

The woman who'd come to speak to Dottie was Gwendolyn *Larson?*

Hold on.

Sickness churned in her belly. This was not good. In fact, this was beyond bad.

One more thing. Dr. Gwen Peterson was also
Kara Williams's doctor for the past three years
at the state facility.

Julianna sent Clay the information, ending with "Gwen is Dennis's mother!" Everything was making sense now. She looked up and saw Dottie standing in the hallway. "Dottie!"

Their eyes locked and Dottie yelled, "Run!"

Dottie stumbled back like she'd been jerked, and Julianna raced to the open door, where she skidded to a stop at the sight of an older woman holding a gun aimed at Dottie's temple.

"Hello, Julianna. I figured you'd show up at some point. Put your hands up and get in here."

Julianna lifted her hands to shoulder height and walked into the room. Her phone was buzzing left and right, but she didn't dare take it from her belt clip. Had anyone seen the two-second incident? The hall had been empty when she'd noticed Dottie in the doorway, so she didn't think there'd been any witnesses. Great. Just great.

"Put your gun and phone on the floor and move back," the woman demanded. "Gently. No funny moves or Dottie dies immediately."

Julianna did so, then drew in a ragged breath. "Hello, Mrs. Larson. It's been a long time."

"Fifteen years, to be exact." She maneuvered her way around to Julianna's gun and snagged it without taking her eyes from Julianna's.

"What do you want from me?" Julianna asked.

"I want you dead, but first I want you to suffer. Greatly."

Julianna swallowed and glanced around the room. Seven students and their teacher huddled together behind a large table that did absolutely nothing to protect them against any bullets that might fly their way.

A blond-headed girl pressed palms against her eyes and sobbed. "Get me out of here. Please get me out of here. I can't do this!" Her voice rose hysterically with her pleas.

"Shut up, Mary Ann," Dottie said.

Mary Ann. Dottie's bully?

"Yes, Mary Ann, do shut up." Gwen shook her head. "They're making spineless kids these days."

Julianna wanted her attention away from the kids. "And exactly how do you plan to make me suffer?"

"By finishing what that simple-minded Kara couldn't do."

"You played her," Julianna said, her voice low and breathy. "You were her psychiatrist for three years and you groomed her for this day, didn't you? Only she got caught and you had to kill her because you couldn't trust her not to mention your name."

The woman's nostrils flared and her eyes widened. "You're smart. It was very easy to change the dosage in her chart. All I had to do was flash a badge and simply wait for someone to leave their computer open. It actually took longer than I expected, but patience won out."

Dottie hadn't moved for the entire exchange, other than her order for Mary Ann to shut up, and neither had Mrs. Larson's weapon. Julianna *had* to get the gun away from Dottie. "Tell me what you want me to do."

"I want you to cover the window on the door—there's paper and tape on the table—and then tell the truth about what happened between you and my son. You're going to clear Dennis Collins's name and it's going to be the last thing you ever do."

■ ■ ■ ■

Clay couldn't figure out why Julianna wouldn't answer her phone. "Come on, come on. Pick up." Had she found Dottie?

The door to the office opened and one of Julianna's buddies from SWAT walked in. His eyes met Clay's. "Hey, I'm Frank. Have you seen Jules?"

"She left to go look for Dottie and now she's not answering her phone."

The big man's gaze swept between him and the principal. "She thought something was hinky and told me to meet her in the hall by the cafeteria. She hasn't shown up."

"Something's hinky, all right," Clay muttered. Dottie had never responded to the call to come to the office. He nodded to Frank. "How about we start searching this school from top to bottom? Can you and your team help?"

"That's what we do."

Clay turned to Callahan. "Bennett and Zilberstein are running crowd control with the students in the gym. We know Dottie's not in there." He rubbed his chin. "I think we should dismiss the students and get them away from the campus."

"What?"

"I have a gut feeling about this. Something's not right at this school. I don't want to do an official lockdown. Let's get out as many students as we can while we assess the situation."

The principal stared at him for a brief moment. Then gave a slow nod. "All right."

"If I'm crying wolf, I'll take responsibility for it, but . . ."

"I trust you, Clay. If you're wrong, we'll err on the side of safety."

"Thank you. Don't announce it over the PA system. We need to go classroom to classroom." He glanced at Frank. "There are enough of us that we can do it fairly quickly."

"What about the students who don't drive?"

Clay pressed fingers to the bridge of his nose, thinking fast. "Tell them to go across the street to that empty parking lot where they're building the convenience store. There's enough room for them, with shade under the canopies since the gas pumps aren't in yet. Teachers can supervise. Tell the bus drivers to stay away."

Callahan nodded. "Let's get this done."

Clay hurried out into the hallway and headed for the first classroom on A Wing. He pulled the teacher into the hallway. "Have you seen Dottie Jameson?"

"No. Why?"

"We've got a situation and we need to evacuate the school. Tell your class to get their things and head to the empty parking lot across the street."

The teacher narrowed his eyes. "Is this part of the demonstration, because—"

"It's not. Now, can you do it?"

Fear flashed for a brief moment, then he nodded and turned to the students. "All right, people, we've got a situation. Change of plans for class."

Clay moved to the next room, then the next. Teens filed out, backpacks slung over their shoulders, expressions confused but not fearful.

His heart thumped a little faster than normal. "Where are you, Julianna?"

CHAPTER
TWENTY-SEVEN

Julianna sat at the desk, paper and pen in front of her. Her gun was tucked into Gwen's waistband and her phone had been shoved into the woman's front pocket, but she still had her radio. The earpiece was tucked into the front of her vest. There was no way she could get to it without Gwen seeing her. And Gwen still held her weapon aimed at Dottie.

For the past five minutes, no one had spoken while Julianna wrote. She stopped and cleared her throat. "Can I ask you a question?"

"What?"

"That day is so fuzzy for me. I . . . can't remember everything that happened."

Her eyes narrowed. "What do you mean, you can't remember? You can't remember killing my son? Because Kara remembered it in detail."

"It was a very traumatic day for everyone involved," Julianna said, not bothering to defend herself. There would be no changing Gwen's mind. "What did Kara tell you?"

For a moment, Gwen simply stared at her, then shoved Dottie toward the other students. "Get over there."

Dottie obeyed with a brief glance at Julianna, and Julianna breathed a fraction easier when Gwen turned the weapon away from Dottie's head and aimed it at her. Dottie started to protest and Julianna shook her head with a sharp frown. Her sister settled with a scowl but kept her mouth shut.

"Kara said you used to talk to her about being a hostage negotiator," Gwen said. "That you wanted to make a difference and save people."

"I did. We all used to talk about our dreams and hopes for the future." A future Dennis had drastically changed for them all.

"She also said you told her that if you ever lost a hostage, you didn't know how you'd live with yourself."

Julianna blinked. "Yes," she said, her voice low, "I remember that conversation. It was a couple of weeks before Dennis shot Kane." The woman's eyes flashed and the gun wavered. Julianna had just broken a cardinal rule of negotiation. Don't poke the bear.

Gwen lifted the gun and one of the students in the corner shrieked.

"No more cracks like that or I end this now," Gwen said.

Why was she even hesitating? "You do realize this school is full of law enforcement right now?"

"Of course." She tapped her lips with a manicured finger. "Now, where were we?"

Okay then. She wasn't worried about law enforcement. That was a huge red flag. "You were telling me what Kara said about that day?"

"Ah, yes. Kara was so fragile. She talked and talked about how it never should have happened, that you provoked Dennis to act, and as a result, her brother died. She could find no reason to keep going. I helped her see that she had a purpose."

"Brainwashed her?" Julianna dared.

"Whatever works, right? She wanted to die. I convinced her that if she wanted to die, she should at least leave a legacy, make her life mean something, and take Dennis and Kane's killer with her."

"Meaning me."

"Exactly."

Rage bubbled. The woman had abused every oath she'd taken as a physician and used her position of power to carry out her own twisted plans. Julianna shot a glance at Dottie and the others. They were scared, but calm and listening. And no doubt praying she had a plan to get them out of there. "How am I Kane's killer? I guess I can get how you would think I played a part in Dennis's death, but Kane's? Dennis pulled the trigger."

"If you had simply been the kind of girlfriend my son needed instead of rejecting him, then stalking him, he wouldn't have felt threatened and decided he needed to take a gun to school for protection. And if he hadn't taken the gun to school, he wouldn't have been able to shoot Kane. Come on, Julianna," she scoffed, "it's all very logical."

For the first time in a very long time, Julianna found herself almost speechless. In any other conversation, she would have written the person off as unstable and walked away. And it wasn't like she'd never heard this kind of speech before, but always it had been about someone else. Having it so personal was hard to deal with. But she would. She flicked a glance at Dottie and the others. *They* were why she would. Now all she could do was keep the woman talking until someone figured out what was going on and sent help. She cleared her throat. "That's what Kara told you? Did she know Dennis was bringing the gun to school that day?"

"He's my brother, not yours."

Julianna had always suspected that Kara was a little jealous of her relationship with Kane, but she'd never come right out and said so. If she'd been Kane's girlfriend, Kara might have been able to deal with that a little better, but because he treated her like a sister, had Kara felt . . . displaced?

"She knew he had a gun that day, didn't she?" Julianna's heart broke into more pieces. One of her best friends had known her ex wanted to kill her and had done . . . nothing? "Then why blame me?" she asked. "Why not blame the person who knew Dennis had a gun?" Julianna's head pounded, and she reminded herself she wasn't dealing with a person who was on a normal mental plane. "Dennis was abusive, Gwen. He hit me."

"All men hit their women at some point, but that doesn't mean we kick them to the curb."

Wow. Okay then. Julianna nodded as though thinking about what Gwen was saying. Part of her felt sorry for all the pain the woman had suffered, but she couldn't let her sympathy get in the way of keeping the others safe. Change of subject. "Gwen, why did you have Kara kill those innocent people? What did they ever do to you?"

She narrowed her eyes. "Nothing. I just knew that the more people who died on this quest for justice, the more you'd suffer."

Most of the sympathy faded. "Is that where stealing my soul comes in?" she asked, clamping down on her desire to bait the woman. She had trained hard to negotiate with people like Gwen. She'd just never had such a personal connection before. *Easy, Jules. Go easy.* "You decide to kill hostages that I can't rescue and damage me for life—or at least before you decide to kill me?" Another broken rule. Don't mention killing.

A sharp gasp came from one of the students in the corner, and Mary Ann whimpered. "No," she said. "No, I don't want to die! Please! I don't want to die!"

"Shut up!" Gwen's shout echoed around the room, and Mary Ann closed her eyes and ducked her head. Dottie reached over and grasped the girl's hand. Gwen turned her gaze back on Julianna. A smile curved her lips. "You're very smart."

"You wrote the poems, didn't you?"

Gwen raised a brow. "What makes you say that?"

"I'm not sure. Instinct? You sent the one to her parents as well, didn't you? It was all a setup. You planned to let Kara take the fall and just walk away when it was all over."

"Like I said, you're very smart."

"Just so you know, my soul already belongs to Someone else. You can't steal it, because it's not mine anymore."

A frown flickered and confusion flashed briefly. "Shut up. You're trying to mess with me. Are you finished with the letter?"

Julianna gripped the pen. "Yes."

"Then throw the pen over there. Don't get any bright ideas about stabbing me with it."

Frustration clawed at her, because that's exactly what Julianna had been thinking.

The woman made sure the gun was aimed at Dottie. "Now."

Julianna tossed the pen toward the trash can. It landed on the floor next to it. Gwen then turned her weapon on one of the cowering students sitting against the wall closest to the door. The teen whimpered.

"Leave," she said. "You're not needed here."

The girl didn't waste a second. She unlocked the dead bolt and raced out into the hall.

Gwen turned her gaze to Julianna once more. "You didn't save that one. I did."

"I'm good with that."

"Hmm. I'm sure you are."

"The question is . . . why?" Gwen wasn't behaving like a textbook hostage taker. But then, nothing about this situation was something Julianna would call normal.

"I don't need her."

She aimed the gun at another girl and Julianna tensed. "Gwen—"

"You can go too," the woman said without acknowledging that Julianna spoke.

The student swallowed hard, eyes wide. Then she stood and hesitated, her gaze locking on Julianna's.

Julianna jerked her head toward the door. "Go."

"No!" Gwen's screech echoed through the room and the teen froze. "You stay now! *I'm* the one who's in charge here. *I'm* the one who chooses who leaves or stays. Not her! She made her choices already and those choices killed my son! So sit or I'll shoot you!"

The teen choked on a sob and dropped to the floor.

"I'll go!" Mary Ann made as though she were going to run and Dottie yanked her back down.

"Stop it," Dottie hissed. "You want to get shot?"

Gwen looked at Mary Ann and smirked. "I don't like you. You have to stay." She pointed to a boy in a dark hoodie with blond dreadlocks. "Get out of here."

He did and Gwen backed to the door and locked it once more without taking her gun off the room. Then she kicked the throw rug over to the door and made sure the crack was covered. Meaning SWAT wouldn't be able to get eyes in the room.

Julianna's fingers curled into fists. She simply had no opportunity to act. Being trapped behind the desk, she couldn't even tackle the woman without risking the weapon going off.

"Now, we have the right number left," Gwen muttered.

The right number? What did the number have to do with anything? There were nine of them in the room. The teacher, five students, and Dottie, Julianna, and Gwen. What significance could that number play in this twisted plan?

Six people were already dead. Why would nine more . . .

Julianna sucked in a deep breath as she got it.

Nine more would make fifteen.

Fifteen years to the day that Dennis Collins died.

Which meant Gwen had changed her original plan and had no intention of walking out of the room alive.

This hostage situation had just turned into an assassination slash suicide mission.

■ ■ ■ ■

Clay was in the hallway when the first student ran out of the classroom to his right. "She's got a gun!"

She threw herself at him and he caught her by the biceps. "Who's got a gun, Bailey?"

"The woman who came into my classroom. We've been in there for about twenty-five minutes. She let me go."

"And me." Clay spotted Carson Fleming hurrying toward them. His pale face made his freckles stand out. "She's evil, man. You gotta stop her."

"Planning on it." He called in the location of the hostage taker and SWAT moved in. He called Julianna's phone and it rang three times before it went to voice mail. Great.

He motioned for the two students to join him in one of the empty classrooms. "Tell me everything you know. First, how many people are in there."

"Um . . . nine, including the FBI lady."

FBI lady. His heart dropped. "Julianna?"

"Yes. And her sister Dottie's in there too."

Clay grabbed a dry erase marker from the board. "Can one of you draw me the layout and diagram where everyone is?"

"I can." Bailey Sims took the marker from his hand and went to the board. "Art's kind of my thing."

Her strokes were bold and sure, and Clay remembered some of her paintings hung in the library. He'd caught a break. He had an artist who would give him an excellent visual. He pushed his comms into his ear and heard the chatter and realized SWAT was using the same channel they'd had for the demo. A channel that allowed Clay to hear everything going on. He prayed Julianna could hear as well.

"Did the woman take her radio?" he asked Carson.

The teen frowned. "I don't think so. Just the gun and her phone."

Was it possible the woman hadn't thought about the radio?

He pressed the button. "Jules, can you hear me?"

No answer. And he couldn't hear her unless she found a way to turn her mic on and leave it on. "Okay, other officers may want to talk to you, but I'll pass on the information and show them the drawing." He shook his head at the detailed rendering. "Bailey, you're a rock star."

She flushed. "Thanks."

Clay walked her to the door, made sure the coast was clear, and directed her and Carson to the nearest SWAT member, who would get them out of the building and across the street. Clay stepped into the hall and noted SWAT had the other classroom isolated. He checked in with Callahan. "You got a head count?"

"All students are accounted for and safely out of the building, except . . ."

"Yeah." Except for the ones in the room with their teacher. And a possible killer.

Hector Rodriguez turned the corner, spotted Clay, and approached him. "I'm working this situation from out here," Hector said. "Julianna will be working in there. Anything you can tell me?"

Clay pointed to the board behind him. "That's the setup and where everyone was located ten minutes ago. Julianna's at the desk."

Rodriguez let out a whistle. "Impressive. That's like 3D, isn't it?"

"Yeah. I added the measurements of the room to Bailey's drawing."

"Perfect."

"The HT is the mother of Julianna's ex-boyfriend," Clay said. "The one who was killed in a school shooting fifteen years ago. Her name is Gwen Peterson. Her son, Dennis Collins, was the only child from her first marriage."

"Got it. Any communication with Julianna?"

"No."

Hector frowned. "That's not like her."

"I'm sure she'll find a way to get in touch as soon as she can."

"Right. I'm not wanting to wait that long. There's no window for a sniper to get a shot, and she's got something blocking the crack at the door, so we can't even get eyes in there."

Clay shuddered. "So, what now?"

"I'm afraid this one's up to Julianna. We'll give her some time, but if she can't talk this person down pretty fast, we'll have to go in."

"There are kids in there, man."

"I know." Hector ran a hand over his face. "Trust me, I know."

CHAPTER
TWENTY-EIGHT

Julianna narrowed her eyes and studied the room. Gwen had chosen well. No windows on the exterior of the building. There was literally no way a sniper could help her. It was going to be up to Julianna to deal with this, to get them out alive, and the thought chilled her. *Lord, please, help me.*

It was all the prayer she had time for. "Did you have Kara pattern the hostage situations after the Manchester courtroom incident?"

Gwen pressed her lips together, cruel eyes glinting. "I wondered if you'd put that together. I did. I thought it would make you spin your wheels a bit."

Well, it had definitely done that.

"How did you get Dottie's keys?" she asked, praying she could keep the woman talking.

"It's amazing the places you can go when you look like you belong."

Dottie drew in a breath, pulling a quick glance from Julianna. Her sister was studying the woman like she was a bug under a microscope. "I remember you now," she said. "You were at the café when I was studying with a friend." Her eyes went to Julianna, then back to the woman. "It was the night I was going to spend the night with Reese and we stopped at the café." She narrowed her eyes. "You followed us, didn't you?"

"You're as smart as your sister, I see."

"You knelt down to tie your shoe and then Mary Ann came in—" She glanced at the girl, who didn't acknowledge that she was even listening to the exchange.

Gwen turned slightly toward Dottie even though she kept the gun on Julianna. As soon as her attention flicked to Dottie, Julianna leaned forward and snagged a piece of tape from the dispenser, then rested her chin on the back of her hand while her thumb pressed the tape on the button of her radio. Someone would be listening. She needed to give them something to hear.

"I was getting ready to release Kara," Gwen said, sweeping her gaze back to Julianna, who pasted a rapt expression on her face, praying the woman didn't guess what she was doing. "I had to see this area for myself. And you," she said to Dottie. "I had to see you. As for the keys, you left your backpack—conveniently—on the floor. You weren't paying a bit of attention to it. I simply pretended to tie my shoe, unhooked the keys while you and Mary Ann went at it, made the impression, and put them back. The fact that you were quite distracted by that girl made things a lot easier than I anticipated." She snickered, obviously proud of herself. "You really should be more careful."

"You even spoke to me." Dottie's gaze roamed the woman's face. "You wore your hair down and had on glasses, but I can see you clearly now."

"Congratulations."

"And then you gave Kara a key to our house." She shook her head, her eyes bouncing back and forth between Gwen and Julianna. "Unbelievable." She swallowed hard. "She could have killed her that night."

"But she didn't," Julianna said. The thought gave her the shudders too, but right now, she wanted Gwen's attention off Dottie and back on her. "How do you see this playing out, Gwen? We've been in here a while. I've written my statement." She pushed the letter toward the edge of the desk. "SWAT has the place surrounded. There's no walking out of here. Tell me what we have to do to end this peacefully. Please." She'd need to do something soon or Hector would send in the team.

Julianna was quite certain Gwen had no intention of letting anyone walk out alive, so why hadn't the woman just started shooting?

The answer came as quickly as the question formed. Because Gwen was enjoying every moment of this. She was deliberately dragging the whole thing out. But when she decided she was done, they would *all* be done. Not knowing when that moment might come had Julianna's nerves quivering.

Her gaze landed on one of the students who'd been very quiet up to now. No doubt trying to blend in with the floor in order not to be noticed. She looked from one hostage to the next, and noticed movement from Dottie. She was pushing a yardstick across the tile. Her gaze met Julianna's, then darted back to the piece of aluminum.

Trip her, Dottie mouthed.

Julianna's pulse kicked up a notch. Could it work?

She nodded and Dottie waited. Julianna held her breath and rose to walk around the side of the desk. She propped a hip against it.

"What are you doing?" Gwen waved the weapon at her. "I didn't tell you to stand up. Sit down." She took two steps toward her and Dottie swung the heavy stick, smacking the woman in the shins.

She screeched and Julianna lunged, her fingers wrapping around the wrist of the hand that held the gun. "Breach!"

Something slammed into the door and it burst inward, but Julianna was too preoccupied with grabbing for the weapon. Gwen still hadn't let go of it. A blur of motion whipped past her and then Gwen was on the floor, screams echoing, head bleeding. But disarmed. Julianna kicked the gun out of reach.

Dottie stood over Gwen, holding a globe with a brass base as a potential weapon. She met Julianna's eyes. "*Now* it should be over."

Clay pushed his way inside and Julianna locked her gaze on his. He nodded and she offered him a small smile of sheer relief.

As a SWAT member turned Gwen onto her back, Julianna saw the woman pull her leg up and snag a weapon from an ankle holster. "Gun!"

Everyone rolled, the nearest SWAT member diving to the side. The loud crack sounded and the bullet hit the man. He hollered. Gwen turned the gun on Julianna, and for a brief moment, their eyes met. Hatred spilled from the woman's gaze.

More pops echoed around the room and Julianna flinched, waiting for the pain to kick in. Instead, Gwen's eyes fluttered, then closed. The weapon fell from her fingers and blood spread across her chest. Julianna lifted her gaze to meet Clay's. He had his weapon out and aimed at the woman on the floor. He and the two SWAT members had fired at the same time. She ran to him.

"She was going to kill you," he said.

"I knew you had my back."

He lifted a hand to touch her cheek. "Always."

■ ■ ■ ■

Clay stared at the dead woman on the floor and tried to find some kind of emotion other than relief that she was no longer a danger to anyone. Maybe that would come later.

He let SWAT deal with her while he went to the students huddled together and crying. "Come on," he said, "let's get y'all out of here."

The teacher stood and, with shaking hands, helped the teens toward the door. "Don't look at her," he said. "Don't look." But Mary Ann stayed put, her arms wrapped around her knees, forehead pressed to her right forearm. The teacher looked back at Mary Ann, then at the others. "Mary Ann, it's okay. Come on."

Dottie stopped and stared at the deceased Gwen Peterson for a moment, then turned back to the girl who'd been nothing but a bully to her. "Mary Ann," Dottie said. "You're safe. Get up and come on." Mary Ann refused to move, her hunched-over form quivering and shivering. Dottie walked over to the frozen girl and nudged her shoulder. "Get up, Mary Ann. It's over."

"She . . . she was going to kill us."

"But she didn't." Dottie held out a hand and Julianna waited. She flicked a glance at Clay and he gave a slight shake of his head. This was between Dottie and Mary Ann.

Mary Ann looked up at Dottie, black mascara streaking her cheeks. Then she held out a shaking hand and placed it in Dottie's. "Why are you being nice to me?" she whispered.

"Really?" Dottie rolled her eyes and hauled the girl to her feet. "Come on. Unfortunately, we're probably somehow weirdly bonded for life after this, so we should probably talk."

She turned the girl toward the door. Julianna hurried after them and caught her just outside the room. "Dottie?"

"I'll be all right, Jules. I just need to process." She still had an arm around Mary Ann's shoulders—a sign of forgiveness and compassion that rocked Clay back on his heels. If Dottie could do that, he was going to have some things to process for himself.

"Okay, I definitely understand that." Julianna's eyes collided with his, then jumped back to her sister's. She swallowed hard and shook her head. "I have no words for this one."

A faint smile tugged at Dottie's lips. "That's a first."

"I know, right?"

Dottie let an officer lead her and Mary Ann away from the scene, and Clay walked to Julianna. "You okay?"

"Like Dottie, I'm going to need to process, but yes. Yeah. I'm okay." She glanced at the woman on the floor, then back at Clay. "Are you?"

"I'm okay. For the first time in a long time, I'm actually okay. I hate that I had to pull my gun, but I couldn't let her shoot you."

"And I'm very grateful for that."

He pulled her into a hug and she rested her cheek against his chest. "Can I come over tonight and hang out with you?" he asked.

She looked up. "You think we'll be done with all the paperwork by then?"

He grimaced. "You have a point. We can always try." His hand slid down to grasp hers. "I have something I need to do."

"What's that?"

"Ask someone for their forgiveness. Will you go with me when we're all done with this stuff?"

"Absolutely."

CHAPTER
TWENTY-NINE

Clay pulled the rental car to a stop in front of the small white house with black shutters. He rubbed his sweaty palms on his jeans and took a deep breath.

Julianna reached over and clasped his hand. "You've got this."

"What if—"

"She agreed to see you."

He nodded. "Yeah."

"I'm going to wait here, okay?"

He closed his eyes and swallowed. "I don't know if I can do this, Julianna. I killed her husband."

"No. You didn't kill anyone. The men who set him up did. Just like I didn't kill Dennis or Kane. I'm really starting to understand that their deaths aren't on me. And this one isn't on you."

"I know. In my head, I know that. But what if she doesn't know the full story? What if she hates me as much as Gwen and Kara hated you?"

"What if she doesn't? What if she extends a hand of forgiveness like Dottie did for Mary Ann?"

That one still blew him away. "Why did she do that again?"

"Because she didn't want to harbor anger and bitterness that might turn her into someone like Gwen or Kara."

"Right. That's what she said."

The front door opened and a young woman stepped out onto the porch. She wore jeans with holes in the knees and an oversized football jersey that had probably belonged to her husband. She was barefoot and her dark hair was pulled in a ponytail. She tilted her head and offered a hesitant wave.

"Go," Julianna said, "she's going to think you're a psycho or something, just sitting here."

He chuckled and opened the door and walked toward the woman on the porch. "Mrs. Banks?"

"Mr. Fox?"

"Call me Clay." He shoved his hands in his pockets and met her gaze.

"And you can call me Felicity. Would you like to come in?"

"Sure. If you don't mind."

"I don't. What about your friend?"

He cleared his throat. "She said she didn't want to intrude on the conversation."

"She won't. Tell her to come in. She can entertain Tommy while you and I talk about Wyatt. Otherwise, we'll be constantly inter-rupted."

"Gotcha." He turned and waved at Julianna to join them.

She stepped out of the car and walked up the steps. "Hi. I'm Julianna Jameson."

Felicity's eyes widened. "What? You're the negotiator." Before Julianna could respond, Felicity laughed and turned to lead them inside. "Oh my, the Lord sure does have a sense of humor, doesn't he?"

"Sorry?" Clay asked.

Julianna raised a brow at her. "What do you mean?"

She motioned to the table. "Have a seat. We'll talk as long as we can before Tommy comes downstairs to see what's going on."

Clay drew in a ragged breath and let his gaze run over the kitchen. He spied the Bible verses taped to the refrigerator and drew strength from the fact that she had turned to God in the face of tragedy. But how would she react once he told her his part in it? "Mrs. Banks, I don't know how to tell you this, but . . ." *Oh God, help me.* "I don't know how much you know about Wyatt's role in the military, but—"

"I know more than I'm supposed to. Let's leave it at that."

Someone had told her. Probably someone in Wyatt's unit.

"I see. Okay. Well, I was a sniper in the 75th Ranger Regiment. I was deployed the same time Wyatt was."

Felicity's gaze never wavered.

"I . . . I got some bad intel—"

"And you were the friendly fire," she said, her voice low.

Under the table, Julianna's hand slid over his and he grasped it like a lifeline. "I've been trying to work up the courage to come see you since it happened and I've been . . . a coward." He choked out the last word. "I'm so, so sorry. I can't even—"

She held up a hand and tears tracked her cheeks. Clay stopped talking and braced himself for whatever she had to say.

"I know what happened," she said. "One of Wyatt's unit members broke protocol to tell me. He and Wyatt were best friends, and he couldn't stand to see me suffering and not knowing the truth. I know how the government works. And I knew the story they told me was a lie." She shrugged. "I mean, I understand why they had to lie, but when it came to Wyatt—"

"Yeah."

"Anyway . . ." She leaned forward and grasped the one hand he had on the table. "Stop blaming yourself. I don't blame you. You were doing your job. A job I'm sure you love and are good at. And Wyatt wouldn't blame you."

"I'm out," he said even as he let her words wash over him. She didn't blame him. He almost couldn't react, so great was the balm to his spirit.

She blinked. "Oh."

"Once I learned the truth about the incident, I couldn't . . ." He shook his head. "I wasn't sure I could even pick up a weapon after that day. A few months later I did, because I went into law enforcement, but—" He pulled his hand from Julianna's and ran it over his head. "But that day has haunted me, and I knew I wouldn't ever find peace if I didn't talk to you. I'm so sorry I didn't come sooner."

More tears slipped from her eyes. "Well, God's timing is perfect in every way. If you had come sooner, I'm not sure I could have given you what I can offer you today. But the truth is, with time and a lot of prayer—a *lot* of prayer—I'm able to say that I know God is still good even when I can't always see it. I know you've been grieving too. In a very different way than I have, of course, but Wyatt wouldn't have wanted you to let this keep you from living your life to the fullest. He would forgive you." She swiped her cheeks. "And I can do no less."

Clay's throat tightened and he held back his sobs by sheer force of will. "Thank you," he managed to croak. Julianna's hand snagged his again and squeezed. "Thank you."

"Mommy? Who are you talking to?"

Felicity grabbed Tommy and pulled him onto her lap. "New friends."

"Cool!" He glanced at Clay. "Are you a good swing pusher?"

Clay cleared his throat. "Only if there's a little boy in the seat."

Tommy's blue eyes lit up and he turned to his mother. "Can he?"

"Only if he has time."

Clay let his gaze roam over the little boy who looked so much like his father. He glanced at Julianna and noticed her swiping tears from her own eyes. "I think I have some time."

Julianna nodded and sniffed. "All the time in the world."

■ ■ ■ ■

ONE WEEK LATER

Julianna grabbed her buzzing phone, noting Clay was on the way. They'd spent every spare moment they could find together over the last seven days, and the future looked brighter with each passing hour.

The fact that they were still talking to each other after going car shopping for her said a lot about the strength of the relationship they were building. She grinned at the thought. Her Suburban had been totaled by the insurance company, and now she had a nice, shiny new Chevy Traverse sitting in her driveway. Well, it was new to her, but with low mileage and new tires, she'd take it.

She and Clay still had their baggage and scars from their pasts, but they were healing. Together.

She stuffed her phone in her pocket, then planted her hands on her hips and looked around. She'd spent the last two hours cleaning and making sure everything was perfect for the evening.

Snacks? Plenty.

Drinks? All kinds.

Comfy pillows? Yep.

Footsteps on the stairs pulled her attention from the room, and she walked over to find Dottie, Reese, and Mary Ann heading out to the Bad Burger Barn, deciding to leave the adults to their evening in.

"You guys good?" Julianna asked.

Dottie hugged her. "We're good. Andre's joining us."

"Andre from school? The Andre who turned his nose up at my suggestion he think about going into law enforcement?"

"Yes, that one." Dottie laughed. "He's come around after the whole thing at the school. He said he wanted to be in there in the middle of the action, kicking some bad-guy butt."

"I'm sure he did."

Dottie sobered. "He knows it's not all fun and games. I think he seriously wants to be someone who can make a difference, like you and Officer Clay and the others have done."

Julianna's emotions went haywire again. She cleared her throat. "Thanks. That means a lot."

"Good. Now, it's time for us to get out of here. See you in a few hours."

"Have fun."

Mary Ann looked up at Julianna through her ridiculously long lashes. "Thank you, Julianna. For everything."

"You're welcome, hon." The girls left and Julianna shut the door behind them, started to twist the dead bolt, and stopped. No one was trying to kill her, and Clay was coming over. She walked into the kitchen, shaking her head at all the changes that had happened in her life over the past few weeks. She still couldn't believe she'd allowed Dottie to convince her to let Mary Ann move in, but she'd agreed on a trial basis. So far, so good.

Ten minutes after they left, her doorbell rang. "Come on in!"

Seconds later, Clay joined her in the kitchen, came up behind her, and wrapped his arms around her waist. He kissed the side of her neck and shivers danced along her arms. She turned. "Hey."

"Hey." His gray eyes glinted at her and she saw . . . something there.

She frowned at him. "What is it?"

He narrowed his eyes. "What?"

"Don't what me." She poked him in the chest. "What are you hiding?"

He laughed. "Why would you ask that?"

"Because you are. I can tell. I read people for a living, remember?"

"True."

"Well?"

"It's a surprise."

"Clayyyy, tell me."

"Not a chance. They'd kill me." She winced and he held up a hand. "Sorry, bad choice of words. Let's get comfortable."

"They?" Mystified, she followed him into her den and settled on the couch.

He grabbed a handful of chips and picked up the remote. Once he had it on the channel he wanted, he leaned back and sighed. Then caught her watching. He froze. "What?"

She grinned. "It does my heart good to see you're so comfortable here."

He laughed and fed her a chip. "Only because you allow me to be."

"Well, as long as we have that straight."

The doorbell rang and she popped up. "I knew you had something up your sleeve. Who did you invite?"

The front door opened and a man she'd seen before, but couldn't place, appeared. She looked at Clay, who hurried over to man-hug the guy.

"Jules, you remember one of my best buds, Vince Covelli. He was at Reese's party. Vince and I've been friends since our early school days. He just took a job with the US Marshals."

Intrigued, Julianna nodded. "Nice to see you again, Vince. Congrats on the job."

"Thanks. Good to see you too." He handed her a bag.

"What's this?"

"Socks."

"Socks?"

"So we don't break the television."

"Of course." What?

Knuckles rapped on the door and it swung open. Penny appeared, then Grace, then Raina. Julianna let out a very un-Julianna-like squeal and raced to give them all hugs.

Even Holt, Penny's soon-to-be husband, who brought up the rear.

"What are y'all doing here? I can't believe you're here!"

Grace chuckled. "Clay said we needed to be here for a momentous event."

Julianna froze. He *wouldn't*. She looked around and relaxed.

No, he wouldn't. She laughed. "Okay." She turned and looked at Clay. The wicked grin on his face delighted and worried her all at the same time. "What are you doing?"

He introduced Vince to everyone, then picked up the remote. "Grab your snacks and drinks, y'all. Julianna, pass out the socks, will you? It's baseball time."

Penny let out a whoop and Holt seized the bowl of wings. They took the love seat, and Raina and Grace settled in the two recliners. Raina yawned. "I'm all for baseball, but I gotta be honest, I'm beat. If I fall asleep, you better just let me sleep."

Julianna laughed. "There's a blanket in the basket next to you."

Holt, Clay, and Penny groaned. Grace rolled her eyes but grinned. Once everyone was seated with their snack and drink of choice—and an assortment of rolled socks—Clay aimed the remote at the television.

Raina hefted one of the socks in her hand. "I hope these are clean."

Vince laughed. "They are. I know how to work a washing machine. Besides, those don't get worn. They get thrown."

"Whew. That's a relief."

Clay clapped his hands. "Attention. May I have your attention, ladies and gents?" All eyes turned to him. "I'd just like to say I'm proud that all of y'all could be here for Julianna's introduction to why big screens were made for sports."

"Hear! Hear!" Vince said.

Holt toasted them all with his can and took a swig of his soda. "And there's the pitch!"

Julianna let her gaze roam the room. Her heart swelled. God was good. Living in a fallen world meant there would be the bad times, but he was still good. And she'd trust in that no matter what while she soaked in every minute of the good times.

The batter swung and connected with the ball. Holt and the others stood and cheered. Even Raina, who hadn't fallen asleep, joined in. In fact, she looked wide awake.

"Home run!" Clay pumped a fist in the air. "Now that's the way to start the game!"

The room fell quiet when the next pitch flew over home plate. Then the next and the next. "Strike three! You're out!" The ump jerked his fist over his shoulder.

Groans filled the den. And the socks flew, bouncing harmlessly off her screen.

"Hey," Grace said, "this is fun!" She threw another balled sock.

The next hit landed in center field and more cheering ensued from both the television and her den.

When things calmed down, Julianna leaned forward. "So, we're pulling for the dudes with the red-and-white shirts on?"

The room went silent once more. All eyes turned to her. The only sound was the television and the roar of the crowd as the player slid into home plate.

"Oh, Julianna, Julianna. Come here." Clay tucked her next to him. "Now, the guy that hit the ball is the batter. The guy that pitched the ball is the pitcher. The guy behind home plate is the catcher. All of the bases have players." He pointed. "First, second, and third. The goal of the game is to—"

Her giggle cut him off. Then she laughed. So did Penny, then Grace, then Raina. Laughter turned to full-blown guffaws, and Clay, Vince, and Holt simply looked at them.

Clay finally narrowed his eyes. "I just got played, didn't I?"

That set them off again and Julianna finally caught her breath. "Speaking of being played, I played shortstop in high school," she said.

His jaw dropped. "You're unbelievable. All this time you let me think you didn't know anything about sports."

"I didn't say I didn't know anything. If you'll recall, I just said I didn't get what the big deal was about watching people and yelling at the television."

More laughter, then Clay caught her to him and kissed her. "You got me."

"I did."

"Good. Then you can just keep me."

She grinned. "I think I'll do just that."

The cheering that filled the room had nothing to do with the game on the screen.

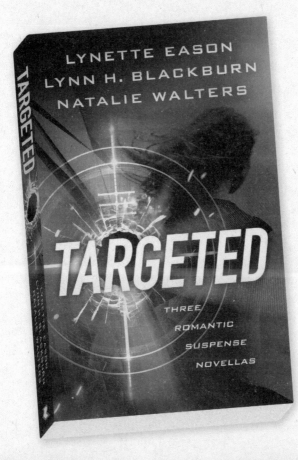

CHAPTER
ONE

Daria Nevsky slammed the door of her Ford F-150 truck and tucked her jacket under her chin to ward off the chill of the November wind. She headed toward the front steps of her Virginia townhome, thinking how nice it would be to park in a garage. But she loved this home located in a quiet neighborhood that backed up to the park where children played, dogs chased Frisbees, and couples picnicked on warm spring days.

She started up the steps and her phone rang. She stopped midstep to swipe the screen and turn to lean against the railing. "Marsha?"

"Daria, honey, I hope I haven't caught you at a bad time." Marsha McBride managed Daria's home in South Carolina. The one she'd abandoned seven years ago after the death of her mob boss father and adoption by FBI agents Linc and Allie St. John.

"Not at all." She ducked her head against the wind, but enjoyed being outside at the same time. "What's going on?"

"Someone broke into my house."

Daria straightened. "What? Are you okay?"

"Yes, I'm fine, but the lock on the door is broken and I don't feel comfortable staying there."

"All right. Why don't you stay at my father's—" She took a deep breath. "*My* house?"

"No, that place scares me, too. I'll clean it, but I don't want to sleep there." She let out a self-conscious laugh. Daria didn't blame her. She didn't care for the house, either. But it was hers. She just avoided dealing with it.

"What did they take?" Daria asked.

"Nothing that I could tell. I guess I came home and scared him off. I just wanted to let you know that I'll be staying with my sister until I feel comfortable going home—and I'm not sure I'm up to cleaning this week. Do you mind if I put it off until next week? I know I sound like a wimp, but I keep thinking, what if I'd been home?"

"Of course, I don't mind. And you're not a wimp. Anyone would be shaken to come home to that."

"Thank you, Daria. Enjoy your vacation and time with your family."

Yes, vacation—with the family who was already there and waiting for her in the sunny Caribbean. "I will. I'll check on you when I get back." She hung up and shivered. The temperatures were dropping and the wind cut through her coat. She was done with being outside. Her flight left at six o'clock the next morning and she still had some packing to do.

She dug the keys from her pocket and aimed it for the dead bolt. And froze.

The door was open a fraction. A slight crack that she might not have noticed if she didn't always shut and lock her door—and arm the alarm system.

Chills skittered up her arms and she took a step back. So, someone had either *been* in her home—or was still there? But why hadn't her alarm gone off?

She spun to leave, only to jerk to a halt with a gasp.

A man wearing a ski mask and a hoodie stood at the base of her porch steps.

"Who are you? What do you want?" She edged toward the railing.

"You. Your father sent me."

Daria froze. "My father's dead."

Eleven rows of brick steps now separated her from trouble. He started up, lessening the distance, and she caught sight of the knife in his left hand. "But he's not gone."

Daria drew in a deep breath, trying to control her hammering pulse and *think*.

He lunged.

She whirled, gripped the rail and hauled herself over. His fingers grazed her right foot. She hit the ground hard, the seven-foot jump jarring her to the bone. She stumbled, gained her balance, and headed for the side of the building.

Think!

Her feet pounded the street while searching for an escape.

"Hey! What's going on?"

Mr. Jackson. The sweet neighbor who always looked out for her had just opened his door for his evening walk.

"Get back inside and call the cops!" A quick glance over her shoulder showed the man in the ski mask gaining on her. She cut across the street to a neighbor's front yard, hoping to go around and into the back.

"Hey! You! Stop! Leave her alone!" Mr. Jackson's shouts bounced off the man chasing her.

Her foot skid over an exposed root and she landed with a breath-stealing thud.

Move! Her body wouldn't cooperate.

The knife flashed. She kicked out and connected with his knee.

"Ah!" His pained cry gave her but a second of satisfaction before he caught her ankle in a tight grip. Daria lashed out once more with her right hand, felt the burn of the blade on her side even as she slammed her fist into his jaw.

He jerked back and she lurched to her feet, ignoring the pain arcing through her hand and just below her ribs. She kicked again.

Her booted foot landed against his rib cage with a harsh crack. He screeched and rolled to his knees, his left hand clutching his side while his right hand reached for her. She grabbed it and twisted then jammed her heel in his face. His roar reverberated in her ears and he dropped to the ground once more, leaving her clutching his glove. A tattoo peered up at her from the back of his hand. Daria noted it, then covered her own bleeding wound with her right hand and ran.

■ ■ ■ ■

"Paging Dr. Donahue. Please report to the ER STAT."

Ryker rolled over with a groan and sat up. The lounge was shockingly quiet and a glance at the clock said he'd managed to snag an incredible two hours of uninterrupted sleep. He'd lost track of how long he'd been at the hospital. Too long. He should have left before he'd collapsed on the bed, but he'd been too tired to risk driving home.

"Paging Dr. Donahue. Please report to the ER STAT."

Ryker stood, went to the sink and ran cold water over his face, brushed his teeth in record time, grabbed his ever-present iPad, then hurried out the door. He rubbed a hand down his cheek and knew he needed to shave, but that would have to happen later.

He walked into the ER and Maggie, his nurse, pointed. "Door number four. Stab wound. She refused any pain meds." Maggie tapped her tablet. "Sent you the chart."

"Thanks."

He pulled it up on the device and scanned it. Daria Nevsky— why did that name sound familiar?—twenty-four years old, laceration to her right side under the rib cage. He knocked then stepped inside the room.

"Daria Nevsky?"

"Yeah." She blinked up at him, face pale, jaw tight, nostrils flared. This was a woman in intense pain and yet she didn't want meds. Her gaze flicked to the door, then back to him.

"What happened? Who did that to you?"

"There was an intruder at my house. I fought him off, but he took a chunk of flesh out of my side before I could get away from him. I stole his car and drove as long and as far as I—where am I?"

"Mission Hospital."

She frowned. "What state?"

"Asheville, North Carolina." Her light accent struck a chord with him. He narrowed his gaze. An intruder had done this to her? "Where did you drive from?"

"Virginia."

"That's quite a drive." At least eight hours.

"No kidding."

"You drove all night?"

"Pretty much."

"Did you call the police?"

She winced. "I didn't, but I yelled at my neighbor to. He probably did, so I'm sure they have a record of his account. I should probably let him know that I'm okay, but I had other priorities at the time—like getting away."

"Away from the intruder."

She shot him a harsh frown. "Yes. Why do you say it like that?"

"Was he someone you knew?"

"No."

"Hold on a second." He backed out of the room. "Maggie?"

"Yes?"

"We need the cops. Can you get an officer in here so we can file a report?"

"Sure."

"It happened in Virginia at my home." She reeled off an address.

"They'll let Virginia authorities know," Ryker said.

"Yep. And the guy's car should be in the parking lot here." She told him where she parked and he noted it.

"You stole his car?"

"I did."

"Gutsy." He gestured to her side. "All right if I take a look?" He pulled on gloves and snagged the rolling seat with his foot to park it next to the bed.

"Sure, why not?" She lifted the hem of her bloodied shirt to reveal a bandage.

"Did you do this?"

"A triage nurse."

"OK, I'm just going to peel it off and see what we have."

She nodded and he went to work. The wound wasn't pretty, and when he went to probe the depth, she flinched and let out a pained hiss. He stopped and sighed. "I really need to give you some meds so I can better assess this without causing more pain."

"Just stitch it up and give me some antibiotics."

Ryker frowned. "That's not how this works."

"Look, that guy came after me for a reason. I can't risk being drugged up and unconscious in case he finds me."

"Eight hours away?"

Her gaze, while pain-filled, was also rock steady. "Yes."

"Okay, well, seems to me, you came this direction for a reason. Don't you have some friends nearby who can sit with you? Watch out for you?"

"I do, but I don't really want to bother them."

"Then it sounds like you need some new friends. Why don't you tell me the truth? Was it a boyfriend, husband, or fiancé who did this?"

She shot him a scowl. "No, it wasn't. I don't have any of the above, so just do your job and let me worry about the rest."

"Wow, rude much?"

She groaned. "I'm sorry. I'm not usually. I'm just . . ."

"Scared and in pain?"

After a slight hesitation, she nodded. "Both are accurate. Add confused in there and you have a pretty good picture of my mental state." She sighed.

Her admission touched him. "Thanks for being honest."

"I'll be honest about one more thing. I could call my family, but they're on vacation. And I don't just mean a simple trip up the interstate. They've been saving and planning this trip for two solid years. I refuse to be the one who brings it all to a screeching halt. And . . . there are other factors in play as well."

He studied her for a moment. "All right, here's what we're going to do. I'll give you a little something to take the edge off, then I'm going to numb, clean, and stitch the wound." He held up a hand to stop her protests. "I won't give you anything that will knock you out, you'll be awake the entire time. And, I'll get the security officer to stay within sight of your room. How's that sound?"

She studied him like she was trying to figure out whether or not she could trust him. Then nodded. "Like a plan I can live with. Thank you."

CHAPTER
TWO

Daria floated in and out of awareness. Each time she nodded off, she worked hard to stay awake. And for the most part, she could. But, after she spoke with the officer and saw Ryker had stayed true to his word about the man staying within sight of her door, she allowed herself to relax a fraction. The events of the evening played through her mind—especially the part about her father sending the guy to attack her. Her father had been dead for seven years and she wasn't even worried that he'd somehow managed to fake his death. No, this was something else. The security officer opened the door. "Ma'am?"

Daria rolled her head to meet his gaze. "Yes?"

"Two officers are here to take your statement."

"Sure." She raised the bed into a sitting position, doing her best not to use her abdominal muscles. It hurt, but wasn't unbearable.

The officers entered, a man and a woman, and stood by the door. The woman took the lead. "I'm Officer Bailes and this is Officer Tate." Bailes took out a notepad and flipped it open. "You're Daria Nevksy?"

"I am." She left off the FBI Special Agent part. Word might

get back to someone in the Bureau and she wasn't ready for that to happen yet.

"Can you tell us what happened?"

Daria rubbed her forehead and debated about how much to tell them. She still needed to process and think things through for herself.

"*My father's dead.*"

"*But he's not gone.*"

She needed to know what the man meant by that. "The door was cracked when I got home. I think he'd been inside and had just come out." And hadn't left. He'd been waiting for her.

"You didn't go in?"

"No. I try to be smarter than that."

A slight smile curved the female cop's lips and she met Daria's gaze. "Good for you. What else?"

"He attacked, I jumped over the rail to run, he grabbed me, managed to slice me. I fought back, got away and ran. I didn't get a look at him because he had a mask on. He also had gloves on. And boots."

"Well, that was a very concise summary."

Gloves. She still had one of them which she needed to have run for DNA. "Wait." She snatched a tissue from the box on the end table and used the paper to pull the glove out of her pocket. "I grabbed his hand to shove him off of me and this came off." She passed it to the cop who took it carefully. "This came off in the fight. There might be some prints on there somewhere—other than mine."

He glanced at his partner. "We'll send this off and contact Virginia PD. They'll go by and check on your home for you. You got a cell number?"

She gave it to him then patted her hip and grimaced. "But I think my phone fell out of my pocket in the struggle."

"If it's still out there and they find the phone, they'll keep it for you."

"Check with my neighbor as well. He saw the guy and yelled at him." She gave them Mr. Jackson's information.

Officer Bailes wrote on her little pad and Officer Tate stepped forward. "You said he had a mask on. What about how he smelled, words he said, his height, weight? Anything?"

"He was tall. Probably a couple of inches over six feet. I don't remember any particular smells." She didn't say anything about his words and hoped they wouldn't press. She didn't want to lie, but she also didn't want to explain the connection the attack had to her father. Not until she did some digging and figured that part out herself.

Thankfully, they finally left. Seconds after they were gone, Ryker stepped inside. "Everything okay?"

His handsome features, filled with concern, touched a place deep inside her. A place she'd walled off a long time ago. "I think so." She looked away, not wanting him to see her thoughts should they be sneaking into her eyes. "But I think it's time I get out of here."

"I think you should stay the night."

Her gaze snapped back to his. "What? Why?"

■ ■ ■ ■

"Because . . . because . . . someone stabbed you. We need to make sure you don't get an infection or have any other issues."

"Like?"

"Internal bleeding." He studied her, noting her calm façade. He had no idea why he felt like she was hiding something. But—

"I'll take my antibiotics and make sure I keep an eye on it," she said.

"What if he's waiting for you to go home?"

She was a patient. What she did was her business. Why was he arguing about this? Because he was drawn to her expressive blue eyes and soft Russian accent? Why was she so familiar to him?

"I have a gun and I'm not afraid to use it," she said.

"I assume you have a weapons permit."

She quirked a smile. "Of course I do."

"Well, I still don't think you should go home, but I guess that's your choice."

"I appreciate that. And you can rest easy. I don't plan to go home any time soon." She shifted and winced, her hand going to her wound. "And, I think I will do my best to stay very still for the moment, though."

"Probably wise. If you pull those stitches out, I'll have to sew you back up."

She let out a low groan and closed her eyes.

Ryker studied her. "Since I can't talk you into some other pain meds, I've got to go check on some other patients, but I'll stop in before I leave." He wasn't obligated to, of course, but there was something about her . . . "Your name is really familiar to me and I can't figure out why."

She opened one eye. "It's not exactly a common name."

"It's Russian, isn't it?"

"It is."

"Hmm . . . it'll come to me." He turned to leave.

"Hey, Dr. Donahue?"

He stopped. "Ryker."

"Ryker." She sighed and rubbed her eyes. "Like I said, I'm not going home. I was on my way to Columbia, South Carolina, but stopped here because I felt like I was going to pass out. I used to live on the outskirts of Columbia and I thought I might find some . . . answers if I . . ." She bit her lip and looked away. "Never mind."

"Answers to what?"

"To why someone attacked me."

"You were attacked in Virginia. Why are the answers in Columbia?"

"I . . . don't know that they are, but I figured it couldn't hurt to go looking and find out for sure one way or another."

He smiled. "Well, I hope you get your answers soon, Daria Nevsky." He patted her hand. "Rest. I'll be back shortly."

Her eyes closed and he left her room, still pondering her name. He'd heard it before. It was distinct enough to send his memory bank spinning. But he had work to do so he did his best to let the nagging at his subconscious go in order to focus on his other patients.

And yet, he found himself walking past Daria's room as much as possible over the next couple of hours. Twice, he had to force himself to read the same information three times before he processed it. Being so distracted wasn't doing him—or his patients— any good. In fact, it could be dangerous. He sighed. He'd check in with Daria one more time to make sure she was sleeping as he'd recommended and then maybe his attention span would improve.

He walked back down the hall, working on his reasons for looking in on her should she be awake. When he rounded the corner, he noticed a man entering the room.

Ryker frowned. She'd said she didn't have anyone to call or anyone who might come visit. So, who had the security officer just let in her room?

Acknowledgments

As usual, I have many people to thank for helping me put this book together.

First and foremost, I thank Jesus for allowing me to tell stories that I pray draw people to him.

Second, I thank the many professionals who are willing to answer my unlimited questions.

FBI Special Agent Retired Dru Wells, who always sends me into information overload giddiness. I have no way to say thank you enough, Dru.

FBI Special Agent Retired Wayne Smith, my thanks goes out to you as well. You are always so willing to answer questions and give me those little tidbits that make the story richer and more authentic.

And I simply MUST give a shout-out to my friend Dr. Jan Kneeland. This thanks should have been in every single book I've written. Thank you, Jan, for letting me text you and ask you questions like, "What meds can I use to make a person look like they're unconscious but, in fact, can hear everything going on around them?" At first I think I scared you. Now I find it hilarious that you don't even blink! And you even say things like, "We should go visit the Body Farm in Tennessee!" Um . . . we'll have to talk about that. Thank you, thank you for the info, but most of all for the love and laughs. God knew I needed you in my life. ☺

Thank you to my brainstorming buddy, DiAnn Mills. My sister friend, I love you dearly and am honored to share a birthday with you. Thank you for all the fabulous brainstorming and hours of laughter and fun.

There aren't enough thank-yous in the world for my team at Revell. You all are amazing and knock it out of the park every time.

Thank you to Barb, who makes my books shine. Since I don't ever want to do this without you, you can never retire. Or die. You are the very, very best editor and I'm so grateful for you.

Thank you to my amazing agent and friend, Tamela Hancock Murray of the Steve Laube Agency. I can't believe we've been together for fifteen years. Thank you for your wonderful guidance on my career and all your love and support. You're the real deal and I love you dearly.

Lynette Eason is the bestselling author of the Danger Never Sleeps, Blue Justice, Women of Justice, Deadly Reunions, Hidden Identity, and Elite Guardians series. She is the winner of three ACFW Carol Awards, the Selah Award, and the Inspirational Reader's Choice Award, among others. She is a graduate of the University of South Carolina and has a master's degree in education from Converse College. Eason lives in South Carolina with her husband and two children. Learn more at www.lynetteeason.com.

It will take all they have to catch a killer—
BEFORE THE KILLER CATCHES ONE OF THEM.

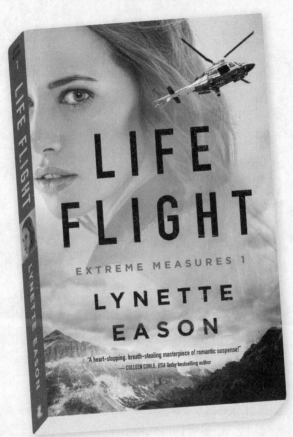

EMS helicopter pilot Penny Carlton is used to high-stress situations, but being forced to land on a mountain in a raging storm with a critical patient—and a serial killer on the loose—tests her skills and her nerve to the limit. She survives with FBI Special Agent Holt Satterfield's help. But she's not out of the woods yet.

INTENSITY. SKILL. TENACITY.

The bodyguards of
Elite Guardians Agency have it all.

Also from Lynette Eason:
The WOMEN OF JUSTICE Series

If you love Lynette Eason,
TRY ONE OF THESE
GREAT BOOKS.

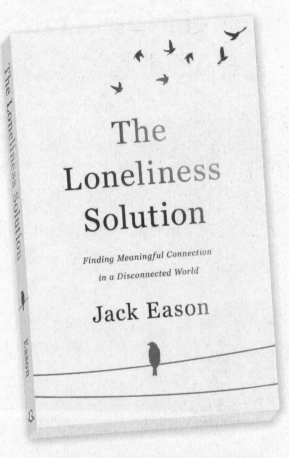